Praise for

Vulnerable

Here's what some readers have to say about the first book in the
McIntyre Security Bodyguard Series...

"I can't even begin to explain how much I loved this book! The
plot, your writing style, the dialogue and OMG those vivid
descriptions of the characters and the setting were so AMAZING!"
– Dominique

"I just couldn't put it down. The first few pages took my breath
away. I realized I had stumbled upon someone truly gifted at
writing. " – Amanda

"*Vulnerable* is an entertaining, readable erotic romance with a
touch of thriller adding to the tension. Fans of the *Fifty Shades*
series will enjoy the story of wildly rich and amazingly sexy Shane
and his newfound love, the young, innocent Beth, who needs his
protection." – Sheila

"I freaking love it! I NEED book 2 now!!!" – Laura

"Shane is my kind of hero. I loved this book. I am anxiously
waiting for the next books in this series." – Tracy

Praise for
Fearless

Here's what some readers have to say about the
second book in the McIntyre Security Bodyguard Series...

"Fearless is officially my favourite book of the year. I adore April
Wilson's writing and this book is the perfect continuation to the
McIntyre Security Bodyguard Series."
– Alice Laybourne, Lunalandbooks

"I highly recommend for a read that will provide nail biting
suspense along with window fogging steam and
sigh worthy romance."
– Catherine Bibby of Rochelle's Reviews

Books by April Wilson

McIntyre Security Bodyguard Series:

Vulnerable, Book 1
Fearless, Book 2
Broken, Book 3
Coming in 2017, books 4 and 5

Broken

McIntyre Security Bodyguard Series
Book 3

april wilson

This novel is a work of fiction. All places and locations mentioned in it are used fictitiously. The names of characters and places are figments of the author's imagination. Any resemblance to real people or real places is purely a coincidence.

Wilson Publishing
P.O. Box 292913
Dayton, OH 45429
www.aprilwilsonwrites.com

Visit www.aprilwilsonwrites.com to sign up for the author's e-mail newsletter to be notified about upcoming releases.

ISBN-13: 978-1540415127
ISBN-10: 1540415120

Published in the United States of America
First Printing November 2016

Dedications

To my darling daughter, Chloe.

To my sister and BFF, Lori.

And to all the wonderful people around the world
who read my books. Thank you for making
my dreams come true!

Acknowledgements

Books aren't written in a vacuum. Authors are often greatly indebted to the support and kindness of friends and associates. I'm no different. Here are some of the people I'd like to thank.

First and foremost, I want to thank my darling daughter, Chloe, for her unending patience as she puts up with Mom's crazy work schedule. I'd like to thank my sister, Lori Holmes; she's not just my alpha reader, she's my best friend. I'm so grateful for the friendship and support of Christy Peters Rouzie – author extraordinaire; I look forward to our daily e-mail chats! I'd be lost without you, Christy! You're the best writing buddy a girl could ever have. Thank you to Becky Morean, another fabulous author, co-worker, and friend, for sharing your insight and expertise with me. Thank you to Carolyn Egerszegi for sharing your invaluable time as a reader and as an adviser.

I'd like to give a huge shout-out to my wonderful beta readers: Lynn Amann, Becca Davis, Carolyn Egerszegi, Keely Knutton, Tiffany Mann, Becky Morean, and Lynsey M. Stewart. I'm very grateful to you all for sharing your valuable time, insight and feedback with me. Every one of you helped make *Broken* a better book!

Thank you to Hannah Webner and her mother, Marsha Quillen Webner, for their kind support. Hannah is the *gorgeous* model on the front cover of *Broken*. She really made this cover come alive, with her beauty and her poise. She's the perfect physical embodiment of Lia, and I can't imagine a better model for this book cover. Thank you, Hannah!

A giant thank-you to the extraordinary photographer Elizabeth Callahan-Stekli, of Callahan Photography in Centerville, Ohio, for shooting such a fantastic image for the cover of my book. Elizabeth is an amazing photographer! She worked with me every step of the way, totally getting what I wanted in a front cover image. My cover doesn't begin to do justice to the quality of Elizabeth's work. Elizabeth's photography is unsurpassed! Check it out for yourself by visiting her amazing portfolio on Facebook.

$\mathcal{O}$ 1

One of the perks of working in the security business is that I get paid to shoot guns and kick ass on a regular basis. I couldn't ask for a better job, and today's no exception. Later this morning, after I drop off my charge at her day job, I'll be heading to the company's private shooting range for my weekly mandatory practice. And later this afternoon, I'm scheduled to test the physical combat skills of two new recruits back at the office. We don't mess around at McIntyre Security – we keep our skills sharp. Plus, it's a lot of fun.

I've made it my mission in life to keep my skills sharp because, as the youngest of seven kids – the youngest *girl*, no less – I'm constantly being tested. Not so much by my two big sisters, but by my four hot-headed brothers, who are all pains in my ass. One of them – the eldest – also happens to be my boss, and he's got to be the biggest pain of them all.

My alarm clock goes off *again*, and I hit the snooze button for the umpteenth time. I'd really like to throw the damn thing across the room. I'm lying here trying to convince myself I don't have a hangover for the third day in a row, but I'm not making much progress. It's my own damn fault. I shouldn't have had those last three beers last night. I should have stopped way before that.

I've dallied so long in bed that I've only got thirty minutes to shower, dress and get upstairs to the penthouse apartment to pick up Beth and take her to work. Normally I don't cut it quite this close, but I knew this morning was going to be rough. I've been struggling more than usual lately, and that pisses me off. I don't want that asshat Logan Wintermeyer to have this much effect on my life six years after he fucked me over – literally. Damn it! After seeing him at my brother's birthday party a couple weeks ago, I've been reliving that nightmare like it's some perverted loop stuck in my head.

Every time I close my eyes, I see that damn video, like it's burned into my memory. I've tried to put it behind me, but I can't. I keep reliving the humiliation, the gut-wrenching sense of betrayal. I can see myself clear as day, losing my virginity to someone who turned out to be an asshole. Someone I thought I loved – someone I thought loved me too. I was so young and naive – *so stupid*! I deserve what happened. I deserved to be made into a viral laughingstock.

Feeling sick to my stomach, I haul my sorry ass out of bed with twenty-seven minutes to spare and stumble into the bathroom. My head's pounding and my mouth feels like it's stuffed with cotton.

That's what I get for drinking too much last night. For the third night in a row, I came home after work and drank way too much – alone – in a futile attempt to forget about that damn video. It didn't work.

After I use the restroom, I strip off my T-shirt and underwear and step numbly into the shower. The water's scalding hot, but I don't mind. Even six years later, I'm still trying to wash away the sick memories of that night.

Closing my eyes, I lean into the spray, letting the hot water soak into my bones and muscles. I try to still my racing thoughts, telling myself it's in the past. What that bastard did to me doesn't define me. It doesn't make me less of a person. *He* was the asshole. But I've never had much luck. The memory eats away at my soul. Seeing myself like that, seeing the raw emotion on my face, knowing how he humiliated me afterward – it eats at me! He used that video against me, out of spite... God! I could kill him! I want to smash my fists into his face until my knuckles crack and bleed. And more than anything, I hate being unable to do a damn thing about it. I had my day in court, and I lost.

I slam my fist into the tile wall and choke back a cry as a jolt of pain streaks up my arm. I hate this! I hate feeling like this! After letting out one throat-ripping scream of frustration, I grab the shampoo bottle and take my anger out on my hair. But scrubbing my scalp until it hurts only makes my headache worse.

When I climb out of the shower and comb through my wet hair, I realize how long it's grown. I can't decide whether to cut it or just let it grow.

I guess I just don't care enough either way to make a decision.

* * *

When the private elevator deposits me in the foyer of my brother's penthouse apartment a few minutes later – at eight on the dot – I'm hit instantly with the aroma of freshly brewed coffee. That improves my entire morning. I need caffeine like I need air to breathe. I'd make it myself in my own apartment two floors down, but why bother when I know I can get a cup of the good stuff up here? My brother's roomie and right-hand man, Cooper, grinds his own freaking beans. Not me. I'm too impatient.

As I walk into the spacious kitchen, I'm faced with a whole lot of PDA. Beth's seated on a barstool at the breakfast counter, and my brother Shane is standing in front of her, right between her knees, leaning into her for some serious lip action. His hands cradle her face, and his lips are molded to hers as he practically inhales her.

They've had a rough few weeks. It wasn't that long ago that Shane shot and killed Howard Kline, the man who'd abducted Beth when she was just a child. After getting out of prison, Kline – the bastard – had decided to come after Beth to exact revenge for his two decades spent in prison. After her abduction, Beth lived under a cloud of fear and anxiety. Even though Kline hadn't had time to do much physical damage to Beth, the emotional damage was immeasurable.

Twenty years into his sentence, Kline was let out early for so-called good behavior. And that's how my brother met the love of his life – when her brother, Tyler Jamison, hired McIntyre Security to protect Beth. As they say, the rest is history. My brother took one look at Beth and he was a goner. She had him wrapped around her little finger in no time.

Beth seems to be recovering pretty well from the showdown with Howard Kline. He came after her with the intention of killing her, but Shane was waiting for him, and he ended it once and for all, with a bullet to the guy's brain.

They've been through a lot. And I'm happy for them. I really am. Beth has an engagement ring on her finger now and she's deep in wedding planning mode. But still, it's way too early in the morning for me to deal with all this lovey-dovey crap, especially on an empty stomach. "Hey, Princess. Do you guys mind? Take it to your bedroom, will ya?"

Beth jumps, looking flushed and guilty as hell as she pulls back from Shane. "Oh! Hi, Lia!" she says breathlessly as she peers around Shane, trying to look innocent. Her smile falters a little, though, when she sees me. Yeah, I know I look like crap this morning. I have dark circles under my eyes. That's what drinking too much and getting just three hours of sleep will do to a person.

My brother glances back at me, annoyance written all over his face. "Yes, I mind. This is our home, Lia. If I want to kiss Beth, I will." He looks stern, but he doesn't fool me.

"You call that *kissing*? It looked to me like you were trying to swallow her whole."

He gives me a long suffering look. "My, aren't you funny this morning."

Naturally I ignore him and take a seat beside Beth at the breakfast counter.

They're both dressed for work, Shane in his white shirt and charcoal gray suit and tie – honestly I don't think he owns any other color suit – and Beth in a pale yellow, sleeveless fitted dress, her long blond hair drawn up into a carefree ponytail. As always, she looks effortlessly gorgeous. And so girly. Now that my blond hair's growing out, she and I look like we could almost pass for sisters. Actually, since she's marrying my brother, I guess we really will be sisters.

I'm surprised Shane's still here. He's an early riser, like before-the-crack-of-dawn-early, so he's usually long gone by the time I come up to get Beth. "Why are you still here?" I ask him. "Should you be at the office by now, bossing people around?"

"Good morning, sunshine," Cooper says, eyeing me from across the kitchen.

I hadn't even noticed Cooper over by the stove, which just proves how out of it I am this morning. Some bodyguard I am. I wave half-heartedly. "Hey, Coop."

Cooper pours a mug of coffee and hands it to me. "Looks like you got up on the wrong side of the bed this morning, kiddo."

"Don't call me that." At twenty-two, I may be the youngest person in the room, but I'm not a kid. I scowl at him, then take a sip of the hot black coffee and groan. Pure liquid gold. "Thanks, man."

"You're welcome." He hands me a plate of scrambled eggs, bacon and toast. "Maybe hot food will improve your disposition this morning."

"I'd better get going," Shane says, checking the time on his chunky Rolex watch. He pockets his keys and phone, then leans down to kiss

Beth's forehead. "I'm meeting Jonah Locke and his manager at the house they rented in Lincoln Park."

Beth looks at me and grins conspiratorially. "Do you need any help? Lia and I could come with you."

Shane chuckles at her less-than-subtle offer. "Thanks, sweetheart, but I think I can handle one rock star on my own."

As he heads to the foyer, Shane pauses to look back at me. "I want you here for dinner tonight, Lia. Official business. Seven sharp."

I scowl at him. He knows I hate hobnobbing with clients. "Why me?"

"Just be here." And then he heads out the door and is gone.

"Jonah and his manager are coming for dinner tonight," Beth says, as I inhale my breakfast.

I met Jonah Locke briefly in Shane's office last week, and yeah, the guy's fucking hot. Like total sex-on-a-stick hot. Surprisingly, he seemed pretty chill for a rock star who makes the headlines every time he sneezes. "Why does Shane want me here? I'm not exactly the best dinner company."

Beth shrugs. "You'll have to ask him."

I swear Beth knows more than she's letting on, but before I can pry it out of her, she hops down from her seat and runs off to brush her teeth. The traitor.

* * *

I gulp my last swallow of coffee and set my mug down with a satisfied thunk. "Thanks for breakfast, Cooper."

He nods at me, and then stands there scrutinizing me as I rinse off my plate and cup and put them in the dishwasher.

He's staring, and that makes me uncomfortable. "What?"

He crosses his arms over his chest. "Nothing."

Liar.

"Did you get enough to eat?" he says.

Cooper's old enough to be my father, and half the time, he acts like he is. It pisses me off because I don't need another parent. I have two as it is, thank you, not to mention six siblings who think it's their God-given right to boss me around.

"Yes, *dad*."

"Don't get mouthy with me, young lady." He reaches out and grasps my shoulder before I can walk away. "You doing okay, kiddo? You've seemed off the past few days. Ever since Shane's party."

I shake him off. Cooper knows damn well I'm not all right, and he knows why. He saw Logan that night at Rowdy's, and he knows exactly what that asshat did to me. He's probably even seen the video, or at least part of it, and that skeeves me out. "I'm fine."

"Don't forget, you're due at the shooting range at nine-thirty. Don't be late."

I salute him. "Yes, sir!"

"Don't be a smart ass, young lady."

2

"Are you okay?" Beth asks as we pull out of the parking garage and head downtown to her bookstore.

A couple months ago, my idiot brother bought Clancy's Bookshop for Beth – one of the largest independent bookstores in the country. This bookstore is her favorite place on Earth – her happy place. Before meeting Shane, she used to spend Friday evenings downtown by herself, hanging out at Clancy's, browsing books, especially romance novels. It's where they met, so I guess it was some kind of grand gesture of affection on his part to buy the place for her. The store's located right in the heart of downtown Chicago's main shopping district on N. Michigan Avenue. The building alone is worth a fortune. He paid cash for it and put it solely in her name, no strings attached. It was certainly one hell of a gesture on his part! His attorney gave him grief over it for weeks.

Am I okay? No, I'm not.

I look over at Beth, trying really hard not to glare at her just to shut her down, because she doesn't deserve any shit from me. She's been nothing but good to me since the day we met. She means well, but I'm tired of people asking me if I'm okay. "I really wish everyone would stop asking me that."

She smiles, but it's a sad smile. The girl wears her heart on her sleeve. "I saw what happened at Rowdy's," she says. "I saw how you reacted when you saw that guy. And I saw Jake chase him out of there. Who was he? I asked Shane, but he wouldn't tell me. He said I had to ask you, so... I am."

I grind my teeth. I really hate people knowing my personal business, and that goes double for my past. But this is Beth. She's the best friend I have. Hell, she's the only friend I have, so I can't afford to fuck this up. "The guy you saw that night – his name is Logan Wintermeyer. He was my... first boyfriend." *And last.*

"When was this?"

"High school. I was sixteen."

She looks surprised. "My God, what did he do? You looked absolutely gutted the other night."

I swallow the rock hard lump in my throat. I've never willingly told anyone about this before, never opened up to anyone other than my family and Cooper. I don't know if I can do this.

I keep my eyes glued to the street as I dodge downtown morning traffic. "He, uh... we had sex." My heart's beating so hard I think there's a chance it might burst. "I didn't know at the time, but he videotaped the whole thing. I was on top, and it was pretty raw stuff. It was my first time, and it was really awkward. I didn't know what I was doing, and it hurt. It was a disaster."

"A couple days later, when I found out he was cheating on me with another girl from school, I broke up with him. I was furious at him, and I made a scene in the school cafeteria in front of all his friends. He was really pissed at me for embarrassing him in public. He got back at me by posting the video on one of those amateur porn sites. It went viral, to say the least. It had been viewed millions of times before Shane managed to get the video taken down."

I finally muster the courage to look at Beth just as the blood drains from her face and her blue-green eyes widen. "Oh, my God," she breathes. "I remember that video – that was *you?*"

I nod. Probably half the world watched me lose my virginity and then cry about it.

"Oh, Lia, I'm so sorry. I can't believe he did that to you. Was he charged with anything? Isn't that a crime?"

"Technically, yes it was, because I was a minor. But he claimed he didn't do it – that he didn't set up the video camera. He said one of his buddies did it as a prank. Shane did everything he could, brought in all kinds of attorneys, but we couldn't make any charges stick. Shane did get a court injunction, though, ordering all copies of the video to be pulled off the Internet. It resurfaces from time to time, but Shane's IT department has bots watching for it, and when they find it, they take it down. I'm pretty sure Logan still has a copy, although the judge ordered him to delete all of the copies he had."

Beth faces forward in her seat and sits quietly, her gaze locked on the car in front of us. She doesn't look at me for the rest of the short trip. I can see the wheels turning in her head as she mulls it over. I'm sure if anyone can understand how I feel, Beth does. She's had to deal with her own painful history, and with betrayal. With Shane's help, she's come a long way.

I pull into the reserved drop-off space in front of Clancy's and put my Jeep in park. Beth sits there for a moment, saying nothing. She's gazing out her side passenger window at the bookstore's front entrance, but I don't think she's actually seeing anything. When she turns back to me, her eyes are glittering with unshed tears.

"I didn't actually see the video," she says in a subdued voice. "I heard about it, but I didn't watch it myself. I just couldn't."

I nod, unable to speak over the damn knot in my throat. I'm glad she didn't see the video. I don't want that image of me in her head.

Sam Harrison strolls out of the bookstore and does a quick scan of the sidewalk and the multitude of pedestrians passing by. He's ex-military, but you wouldn't know it looking at him. He's tall and lean, and he looks like a punk dressed in black cargo pants, a gray graphic T, and black shitkickers. His red hair is pulled up into a man-bun. With the black plugs in his ear lobes and black ink decorating his sinewy arms, he looks more like a street-wise thug than a professional bodyguard. I guess that's part of his charm.

Sam's gaze lights on Beth and he gives her a quick smile. Part of my job these days is to drop Beth off at work and pick her up at the end of the day. Sam is her official daytime bodyguard while she's in the bookstore. Even though she and Sam really hit it off well, she doesn't like all the extra security fuss now that Howard Kline is no

longer a threat to her. Kline's dead, thanks to Shane. But as the fiancée of a very wealthy man, Beth still needs protection. Shane's never
going to ease up on that. He's got more than a few skeletons in his
closet, and he'd never risk any of them showing up to cause Beth
harm.

Beth doesn't seem to be in any hurry to vacate the vehicle, so Sam
approaches the front passenger door and peers inside, rapping lightly on Beth's window with one knuckle. "Everything okay, Beth?"

Beth laughs bashfully as she wipes away her tears with the back
of her hand, then smiles up at Sam and nods. "Yes, fine. Just a sec."
Then she leans across the console and hugs me. "Are you okay?"

I hug her back, squeezing my own misty eyes. "I'm fine. Go manage your bookstore. I'll see you at five."

Reluctantly, Beth releases me and unlocks her door. Sam opens
it and helps her step down from the Jeep. At the last moment, she
turns back to me. "Call me if you need me."

Sam closes the door, and I nod to Beth as I put the Jeep in gear
and pull away from the curb.

I can't stand it when others look at me with pity.

* * *

After dropping Beth off at Clancy's, I leave downtown and head
to the company's private shooting range for my weekly mandatory
practice and evaluation. Once there, I unwind by shooting two full
boxes of ammo – fifty rounds a box – shredding a veritable army of
paper targets suspended from a wire on a pulley mechanism. Each

time I pull the trigger, I picture Logan's face. I hope he rots in hell one day. But unfortunately, he's still breathing, still walking the streets of Chicago a free man. The last I heard, he's in college and working as an intern at his daddy's prestigious downtown law firm. Figures. One day the asshole will be an attorney. He'll probably be a defense attorney, since he has so much experience at evading prosecution.

Seeing Logan the other night really set me off, bringing it all crashing back. It was all I could do to refrain from pulling out my Beretta and plugging him on the spot, right there in the bar. But if I got myself arrested for cold-blooded murder, my family would kill me. If only I could run into Logan in a dark alley in the middle of the night. I'd beat the shit out of him, record the entire thing, and then blast it across the Internet for the whole fucking world to see.

Just thinking about that asshat makes me burn. Some days it feels like I have acid running through my veins instead of blood, eating away at me day after day.

I raise my 9 mm and hold it with both hands, my grip steady despite the fact that my heart is pounding triple-time in my chest. When the paper targets shaped like human beings drop into place, I tear through the things, firing shot after shot into the center of their heads, shredding their brains. When I lower my weapon, there's not much left of the targets.

I feel a tap on my shoulder and glance back to see Cooper standing behind me. I pull off my protective ear covering. "Hey, Coop."

He leans against the partition separating my stall from the next, his arms crossed over his chest in classic Cooper style. "I'm pretty sure you got him with the first couple of bullets, Lia. A whole clip seems wasteful."

Cooper's dressed in jeans and a faded Marine Corps T-shirt that hugs his muscled torso. For an old guy, he's still pretty hot, with his short gray hair, a short salt-and-pepper beard, and steely blue eyes. He's tall and solid, muscular. Even though he's been out of the military for nearly a decade, he's still got that air of discipline about him. He was a shooting instructor in the Marine Corps, and he's still a damn fine marksman. Tough as nails. I bet he'd be bossy as hell in bed, cause he's sure bossy out of it.

I shake my head. "It's just ammo, Cooper. I can afford it."

He frowns at me. "Cut the bravado, kid. I saw him Friday night, at Rowdy's. I saw Wintermeyer. If Jake hadn't kicked him out, I sure as hell would have."

I shrug, remembering how my brother browbeat Logan out of the bar. My brothers may drive me crazy, but they've always got my back.

My jaw tightens to the point my teeth hurt. Abruptly I turn away and load a fresh clip into my handgun and face the shooting range. "I don't want to talk about it."

"I also saw your reaction."

"Yeah, well, we all have our burdens to carry, right? Mine's that asshole. I'll deal with it." A fresh target comes my way. I don my ear protection and then unload an entire clip into its head, hitting dead center and pulverizing it.

"I wish it was that easy, Lia," Cooper says before walking away.

3

After completing my weekly shoot-em-up session, I head back downtown to the McIntyre Security building, which is located on N. Michigan Avenue not far from the shopping district. When I shut off the engine, I sit in the underground parking garage for a while with my hands jammed between my thighs in an attempt to still the shaking. My hands have been shaking on and off since Friday. Seeing Logan does that to me. I want to get wasted. I want to drown myself in liquor until I can't feel anything. But I'm afraid to drink any more. I'm afraid if I actually succeed in dulling the pain with liquor, I won't be able to stop.

I need an outlet to expend all this crazy negative energy, so I head up to the third floor where I know I'll get to do some sparring today. Beating the crap out of someone – or maybe getting the crap beat out of me – is just what I need to shut down the video looping in my head.

My twin, Liam, runs the company's martial arts studio. I find him in the ring with two recent hires, Mateo and Phillip. Liam's assessing their current level of hand-to-hand combat skills. Our bodyguards all train in Krav Maga – simply because it's fast and expedient. When we're on the job, we don't mess around. We drop our opponents to the ground fast, and they stay there. I use a mixture of Krav Maga and Aikido. Krav Maga is brutal and effective. Aikido gives me an advantage over my opponents, who are usually way bigger than I am. With Aikido, I can use their size against them.

It doesn't hurt that my opponents always underestimate me. That's their downfall. Just because I'm a cute, petite blonde, they make assumptions about me and they underestimate me, which works in my favor. I can usually take down a man twice my size in less than two minutes. And they never see it coming.

I'm here today because Shane asked me to participate in a demonstration for the new guys. Actually, I'm a ringer. Because I'm female, and because I'm small, they'll assume I'm a pushover. I'm here to teach them otherwise. It's a fun lesson for everyone.

I sit on the sidelines for a few minutes watching Liam and Mateo square off. Mateo's good. He's strong and muscular, and stubborn as an ox. With his beautiful mocha skin, short twisted braids, and gorgeous smile, he's certainly easy on the eyes. And I could listen to that Jamaican accent all day long. *Yeah, mon.*

The other guy, Phillip, looks like your typical all-American white boy, a former high school quarterback with broad shoulders, a lean waist, and thighs the size of tree trunks. *Asshole.* He reminds me of Logan. He's even got the same shade of nut brown hair and brown eyes. I know I'm being irrational, but I don't like him.

Liam wraps up with Mateo, then calls me forward to officially meet the two new guys. I've already reviewed their resumes. Mateo's older, in his early thirties, and he has experience in both military and private sectors. Phillip's fresh out of college, and yeah, he's actually a former high school football player, just like Logan. Naturally I now have a deep-seated hatred of football players. I'm surprised Shane asked me to do this – he should know better.

Liam meets me halfway, scanning me with his too-perceptive gaze. His brown eyes narrow. "How's it going?"

I shrug. "Fine."

He doesn't look convinced. "Are you good?"

"Of course I am. Why wouldn't I be?" Damn it, my brothers are worse than a bunch of gossiping sissies.

I'm dressed in my typical workout clothes – black boy shorts and a black sports bra. "Let's do this," I tell him. "I haven't got all day."

"All right. Let me introduce you to the guys."

As I step up beside the ring, Liam introduces me to Mateo and Phillip. After we all make nice and shake hands, I glance behind me and happen to catch a glimpse of Shane and his newest client watching through the observation window. Great, that's all I need. Jonah Locke – God's gift to women – watching me about to get sweaty in the ring.

Shane's looking very GQ in his suit and tie. In contrast, Jonah's dressed down in a pair of seriously ripped jeans and a faded gray

T-shirt. I have to admit, I can understand why this guy has fan-girls drooling all over him. He's definitely fuck-worthy material, with his scruffy good looks, a trim beard and gorgeous, soulful eyes the color of fine whisky. His dark brown hair, which hangs past his shoulders, is currently pulled back into a ponytail. Just looking at him makes my girl parts tingle. Man, what I wouldn't give to tap that... just once. But I have a rule against sleeping with clients, so he's off limits. Too bad.

When I met first Jonah in Shane's office, he surprised me. You'd think a guy with rabid fan-girls dogging his every step would have an ego as big as his head. What guy wouldn't? But he was actually kind of quiet, pretty low key for a big heart throb. Even now, he's watching us through the viewing pane with a quiet, unassuming expression. When his gaze settles on me, a shiver courses through me and I have to turn away.

My faith in men may be shot to hell, but my body's not dead. I still have needs, and sometimes my vibrator alone just won't cut it. Sometimes I need something more. I get my needs met, but on my own terms. *Wham bam, thanks pal. Don't let the door hit you on the way out. Buh-bye!*

I'll never let myself be used again.

Never.

* * *

Forcing myself to ignore the audience out in the hallway – which frankly is not easy to do – I climb into the ring with Mateo. Mateo's trained in Karate – he's a 4th degree black belt, which I'll admit is pretty impressive. He's about six feet tall, with a slender build. He has a runner's body, long and lean, and I'll bet he's fast. His hips are narrow and his shoulders are broad, and that means he's top heavy. Good. This guy's going down hard. I almost feel sorry for him.

"Don't take this personally, okay?" I tell him, when we're facing off in the ring.

He gives me a wide, bright smile. "Doan worry, pretty lay-dee. I'll take it easy on you."

I do love the accent. It almost makes me feel bad for what I'm about to do to him.

Liam gives the signal, and we start by testing the waters. We dance around each other a little bit. I like to lure them into a false sense of security before I drop them to the floor. My objective is to teach them the consequences of underestimating their opponent. They take one look at me and think I'm a walk in the park. I'm here to teach them otherwise.

Mateo's sole objective is to pin me to the mat. As if!

I advance and retreat a little, setting up a pattern and rhythm that he thinks he can exploit. When he makes his move, lunging to lock onto me, I send him sailing right over my shoulder. He hits the mat with a loud smack, and I hear his breath wheezing in his chest. I pin him to the mat with a knee to his lower back and a hand gripping the back of his neck.

Score one for the little blond! Lesson learned, the hard way.

Mateo sits up and shakes his head, looking honestly perplexed. "How the hell did she do that, mon?" he asks Liam.

Liam shrugs his shoulders and chuckles as he pulls Mateo to his feet. "You okay?"

Mateo looks at me and chuckles, his pained expression transforming into a good-natured grin. He steps toward, high-fiving me. "Damn, girl! You kicked my ass!"

His smile is contagious, and I can't help returning it.

Phillip – the ass – is laughing his head off at Mateo's expense, and that just makes me resent the big pretty boy athlete even more.

"Lemme show you how it's done, *mon*," Phillip says as he climbs into the ring, giving me a smarmy grin as he shoulders Mateo aside.

"Your Jamaican accent sucks," I say.

Phillip winks at me, a stupid grin on his face.

I shake my head. "Don't do that. Don't *ever* wink at me."

Liam gives us the signal to go, and we move around the ring, sizing each other up. This guy is big, well over six feet, with a broad upper torso. He's big all over and at least twice my weight.

I shoot a quick glance at the viewing window and see that Shane and Jonah are still there, watching. Shane is talking to Jonah, but Jonah's eyes are on me, and I feel a surge of heat. Fine. I'll give him something to see.

Phillip comes at me hard. He's trained in Ju Jitsu, which is something my brothers use a lot, along with Krav Maga and a little kickboxing. Sure, I can easily anticipate his moves, but it's his big size that's going to be his undoing.

"Come on, sugar," he says, taunting me. "Show me your stuff."

That's the worst possible thing he could have said to me. Logan called me *sugar*. It's not cute. In fact, it pisses me off. "Get over yourself, prick. No one's impressed."

"Ah, come on, sugar! Show me you're more than just a pretty face." His jaw tightens, and I know I've gotten under his skin.

Phillip's going to make mistakes now. Sure enough, he barreling toward me like a locomotive. As he reaches for me, I grab his arm and highjack his momentum to send him right over me, and he hits the mat hard.

Now it's Mateo's turn to laugh.

Phillip jumps to this feet, his face beet red and his chest heaving. "You little bitch," he mouths under his breath. He comes at me again using sheer brute force Pissed, and ready to end this, I resort to a brutal Krav Maga move that I know will get me in a lot of trouble. But I'm past caring. As he rushes me, I shift out of his trajectory, then catch him with a two-handed blow to his nasal septum, grabbing his head and throwing him face down on the mat. I follow him down with a knee to his lower back and pin him to the floor like a bug. When he doesn't fight back, I realize he's out cold.

Well, shit. I know I'm going to get my ass chewed out over this, but it was worth it. He pissed me off, damn it.

I jump off him and step back, my hands raised in capitulation. But Phillip remains face down on the mat. Yeah, he's out for the count.

But at least he's still breathing. It's not like I killed him.

When I hear the door to the studio crash open, I flinch. I know what's coming. I turn to face Shane, who's standing in the doorway with his hands on his hips. His jaws are clenched tightly, and he looks royally pissed. "Lia! In my office, now!"

Yeah, I'm in trouble. But what's more disconcerting isn't the scowl on my brother's face; it's the look of sheer amusement on Jonah Locke's face. Jonah's still watching me through the window, and he's fighting a grin. When our gazes meet, the corners of his lips curve up in an infuriating smile.

Asshole.

4

I don't bother with a shower or change out of my workout clothes. Shane's pissed, so I decide it's better to head straight to the lion's den and get this tongue lashing over with so I can get on with my day.

When I step outside the martial arts studio, I'm relieved to see the hallway is empty. Both Shane and Jonah are gone. Good. I'll have to face Shane soon enough – I don't need to see or speak to Mr. Rockstar. I wonder what he's doing here in the building. Shouldn't he be out signing autographs?

I exit the elevator on Shane's floor and walk into the executive suite, waving at Shane's executive assistant as I stroll past her desk. Diane Hughes is a tiny little woman with short white hair and bright blue eyes. She reminds me of a fairy godmother in a business suit. All that's missing is the sparkly wand.

"Hi, Lia, honey," she says, giving me a little wave as I walk past her desk. "He's expecting you."

Shane's office door is closed, so I rap once with my knuckles, then open the door and walk in. I know he's expecting me, so there's no point beating around the bush. Immediately I scan the room, half expecting Jonah to be in here with Shane, but he's not. Shane's standing alone at one of the huge picture windows overlooking N. Michigan Avenue and the cross street. It must be nice having a fancy corner office.

I just want to get this over with. "You wanted to see me, boss?"

He turns to face me, and yeah, he's still pissed. "What the fuck did you think you were doing back there? You could have seriously hurt Phillip."

I shrug. "He asked for it."

"How so?"

"He called me *sugar*. And then he winked at me."

He shakes his head. "And you consider that justification for rendering a man unconscious?"

"He pissed me off, Shane. Besides, he reminded me of someone."

Shane frowns. Of course he knows who I'm talking about, but he doesn't say anything.

I guess I do feel kinda bad for clocking the guy. "Is he okay?"

"He'll be all right. Liam called up to say he's conscious again. Dr. Monroe will take a look at him. But he likely has a concussion."

I frown. "Sorry." *Not sorry.*

Shane sighs. "Lia, you have to learn to control your temper."

"Ha. That guy should learn to watch his mouth."

Shane shakes his head again, then walks over to the credenza and pours himself a cup of coffee. "Want some?"

"No thanks, I'm good."

"Take a seat, Lia."

Uh oh. This isn't good. This is more than a simple tongue lashing. I drop down into one of the two black leather chairs that face Shane's desk and wait for him to take his seat behind the desk. "Am I still in trouble?"

He gives me a small smile, looking more like my big brother now than my boss. "No. Just don't do it again. Besides knocking the poor guy out, you also put a big dent in his ego. It's going to take him a while to get over getting thrashed by a girl. Try to play nice with others, okay? Especially the new hires."

I ignore the little bit of guilt gnawing at me. "Whatever. Can we get to the point, please? I've got stuff to do."

"All right." Shane taps the fingertips of his right hand on the desk. "I'm reassigning you."

"What!" I sit up straight in my chair, my hands gripping the arm rests. "Why? Did Beth ask you to reassign me?"

"No! Of course not. This is my idea. I have another assignment for you. It's a high-priority client, and you're especially well suited for the job. I need you on this."

I relax a bit, relieved that Beth didn't ask for me to be reassigned. She's the only friend I've got. It would kill me if she didn't want me around. "Who's the client?"

There's a knock on the door, and Shane says, "Come in."

The door opens behind me and I hear the thud of boots hitting the polished wood floors. I know who it is without even looking.

Shane smiles over the top of my head. "Have a seat, Jonah."

I close my eyes and take a deep breath before counting to ten. This day keeps getting better and better.

"Hello, Lia," Jonah says as he drops into the chair beside mine.

When I finally open my eyes and look at him, I feel an unfamiliar tightening in my chest. *Asshole.*

I turn to Shane. "You've got to be kidding me. You know I don't like babysitting celebrities." I hate the screaming crowds, not to mention the fucking paparazzi. Publicity and I don't go well together. I've had enough publicity to last a lifetime.

Jonah snorts in amusement, and I shoot him a glare. *Shut up.*

"Jonah needs a bodyguard while he's in town for a couple of months, and you're perfect for the job. We need someone who can get in close to him, someone who can fit in with the music scene, hang out with the band. While he's here, you'll shadow him pretty much twenty-four-seven."

"The hell I will!" I jump to my feet. "There's no way I'm spending twenty-four-seven with this guy. No way."

"Lia, sit down," Shane says without heat.

Jonah's calmly gazing up at me now that I'm standing. Up this close, I see that his eyes aren't as dark as I first thought they were. They're flecked with bits of gold and amber. His long lashes are the color of fine dark chocolate. I have to admit, he really is gorgeous, but I don't have the patience for celebrities with big egos. Or any man, for that matter.

"Sit, Lia," Shane repeats, pointing at my chair.

I shake my head as my butt hits the seat cushion. "Get someone else to do it. How about Miguel? He'd be good."

"Miguel's busy on another assignment."

"What about Carolyn Palmer? She'd be great."

"She's already on another job. I want you, Lia. End of discussion."

I glare across the desk at my brother. There's no reasoning with him when he's got his mind made up.

"Jonah's going to be in Chicago for just a couple months to work on some new songs. He attracts a lot of attention wherever he goes, unfortunately, and he needs someone to keep the more aggressive fans at bay. I need someone on the inside keeping an eye on things around the clock. And that's you."

Shane looks at Jonah. "Lia's a chameleon. She'll blend right in with your crew."

Jonah glances at me. "Are you okay with this, Lia?"

I frown, surprised he even cares enough to ask me. I look at Shane. "Does Beth know about the reassignment?"

Shane nods. "She does."

"And she's okay with this?"

"Yes, we talked it over. It's just temporary, Lia, just while Jonah's in town."

"But what about Beth? Who'll be her driver if I'm not?"

"Sam will take over for you. He's already watching her during the day."

That makes sense. They already spend a lot of time together, and they've really hit it off. And Sam's a good guy – he'll take good care of Beth.

"All right," I sigh, realizing I really don't have much choice.

Shane gives me a curt nod. "Be at the penthouse this evening at seven. Jonah and his manager are coming over tonight for dinner, and I want you to join us. Bring your gear, Lia, because you'll go back to the rental house with Jonah tonight."

"Fine." I take one last look at Jonah, who's being awfully quiet. I kind of expected him to start making demands or bitching about something. But instead, he's silent.

I look at him warily out of the corner of my eye. "I guess I'll see you at dinner then."

He chuckles. "I'm looking forward to it."

* * *

On my way out of the building, I make a quick stop at the martial arts studio and find Liam setting up for his next class. "Where's Phil?"

"In the locker room." He grins at me. "Why? Are you going to knock him out again?"

I smirk. "Very funny, Liam."

I head into the co-ed locker room and find Phillip dressing. He's fresh out of the shower and wearing nothing but a towel wrapped around his hips. He's in the process of drying his chest with another towel when I approach him.

His eyes widen in mock fear when he sees me. "Ooh, should I be scared?"

"Nah." I stop a couple of feet away, feeling uncharacteristically nervous. "Actually, I came to apologize. I'm sorry for knocking you out. It was uncalled for."

He smiles. "Apology accepted."

"You pissed me off," I explain. "Don't ever call me sugar. Or wink at me."

He nods. "Duly noted. Do you by chance have anger management issues?"

"You could say that. Anyway, I am sorry."

"No problem." Phillip throws a towel around his neck. "Hey, it's getting late. Are you hungry? Can I buy you dinner? Or a drink? We got off on the wrong foot, and I'd like to make it up to you."

"No thanks. I've got plans tonight." *Never, pal.* "Anyway, I just came by to apologize."

"Sure. Maybe next time."

I shake my head, wanting to nip this in the bud. "Nope. Not going to happen. No offense, 'cause you seem like a nice guy. I'm just not interested. I make it a rule never to fraternize with co-workers."

"Well, rules are made to be broken, right?"

I shake my head. "Not in this lifetime."

5

With a clear conscience, I drive to Clancy's Bookshop and park in the VIP spot right in front of the store. I'm a few minutes early, so I go inside to look for Beth. I find her organizing sci-fi books on a cart.

I walk up behind her. "Hey, Princess. Did Shane tell you he wants to reassign me to babysit Jonah Locke?"

She turns to me and smiles. "He did. We discussed it last night. Are you okay with it?"

"Are *you* okay with it?"

She shrugs. "He's Jonah Locke, Lia. It would be criminal for me to stand in your way. Besides, it's only temporary, right? Jonah's not going to be in town for that long. Sam will fill in for you in the meanwhile."

I catch a glimpse of Sam, who's standing a few feet away. He's got one eye on Beth and the other glued to a fitness magazine. I nod. "Hey, red."

He nods back. "Shorty."

Sam's got a classic undercut – the sides of his red hair are trimmed close and the hair on top is long and pulled back into a bun. It looks good on him. In addition to the black plugs in his ear lobes, he's got some industrial hardware piercings through the cartilage at the top of his right ear. He's a good guy. He and Beth certainly get along well, which is a good thing if he's going to take over as her primary bodyguard for a while.

"Looks like you're getting promoted," I say.

He nods. "That's right. Try not to take it personally."

I smirk. "Don't flatter yourself, red. You're the B team."

* * *

I walk upstairs with Beth as she goes to her office to collect her sweater and purse. We run into Erin O'Connor, the assistant manager, on our way out of Beth's office.

"Lia!" Erin says, flashing killer dimples that make her look like she's twelve.

"Hey, Erin."

Erin's too cute for her own good, with her freckled, round face and chin-length brown hair. She's one of the original management staff here at the bookstore. She's become a good friend to Beth, and that makes her okay in my book.

"I heard you're going to be Jonah Locke's bodyguard for a while," she says. "Is that true?"

I guess news travels fast. "Yeah. Looks like it."

Erin's green eyes are as wide as saucers. "Oh, my God, you're so lucky. He's gorgeous!"

"Is he? I hadn't noticed."

Erin gently smacks my arm. "You are such a liar! If he performs while he's here in town, please promise you'll get me a ticket."

"I'll see what I can do."

* * *

We drive back to the Lake Shore Drive apartment building where we live – a building Shane owns. I escort Beth in the private elevator that exclusively services the penthouse. On the ride up, she's practically vibrating with excitement over the evening's plans.

I have mixed feelings about my new assignment. On the one hand, shadowing Jonah will be interesting to say the least. But at the same time, I'll miss Beth. Right now I see her at least twice a day, and we often have lunch together if our schedules permit. With my new assignment, I don't know when I'll see her. I have no idea what kind of insane schedule Jonah keeps. And I'll be leaving the apartment building to move into his rented house in Lincoln Park for the duration. It's not that far away, but our paths won't likely cross very often while he's in town.

Beth squeezes my hand. "What's wrong?"

I shake my head. "Nothing's wrong."

"Lia, come on."

"I'm going to miss you, Princess." There, I said it. I've never had someone to miss before.

As the elevator comes to a gliding stop, she throws her slender arms around me and squeezes. "Don't be silly. I'll always be right here if you need me. Think of this as an adventure! You're going to be living with Jonah Locke!"

* * *

After dropping Beth off, I make my way down to my own apartment. Compared to the penthouse, my apartment is tiny – two bedrooms, a living room and kitchen, and two bathrooms. Its best feature is that it offers a perfect front-row view of Lake Michigan. It's not much, but it's all mine.

Stripping, I head for the bathroom to take my second shower of the day, wanting to wash off all the sweat and grime from the workout in the martial arts studio. The hot water feels good on my back as the pulsating massage unit does its job.

After showering, I towel-dry my hair, run a comb through it, and head to my bedroom to get dressed for dinner. I'm sure as hell not getting dressed up for Jonah Locke. I put on my grungiest pair of ripped jeans and a black T-shirt with white printing on it that says, *Sorry I'm late. I didn't want to come.* I pull on my black shitkickers just in case the guy gets out of line tonight and I'm obliged to kick his ass.

It could happen. You never know.

After packing a couple duffle bags of clothes, personal items, and a small arsenal, I head back up to the penthouse. I dump my bags on the floor in the foyer, just outside the elevator, then head into the apartment.

I realize I'm sorely underdressed for the occasion when I walk into the great room and see Beth dressed in a form-fitting black dress with matching flat-heeled shoes.

She gives my outfit a quick once-over and smiles at me without a single word of reproach, bless her heart. "Aren't you excited, Lia?" she says, coming forward to give me a quick hug. "Jonah and Mr. Peterson came home with Shane after work. They're in Shane's office right now."

I shrug. "He's just a guy, Beth, like any other. He puts his pants on one leg at a time."

"I know, but have you noticed how nicely he fills them out?" Her blue-green eyes are fairly glittering with excitement.

I raise my eyebrows, shaking my head in mock condemnation. "Beth, I'm shocked. I thought you had eyes only for Shane."

She grins. "I love Shane, but I'm not blind."

The sound of footsteps draws our attention to the archway leading into the spacious living area. Shane leads the way, followed by Dwight Peterson, Jonah's manager. I met Peterson once already, in Shane's office last week.

Shane looks relaxed in gray slacks and a white shirt sans tie, and Peterson's got on a navy-and-white pinstriped suit. Yep, I'm definitely underdressed. Too bad I don't give a shit.

Shane's gaze lands on my outfit and he frowns. Yeah, I know, I'm underdressed. So what? I don't care about making a good impression, and Shane knows it. He gives a rueful shake of his head, suppressing a grin. "Dwight, you remember my sister Lia. You met her once before in my office."

Dwight Peterson eyes me from head to toe, frowning as he takes in my appearance. He looks at me like I'm something the cat dragged in off the street. I can tell we're going to hit it off swell.

He nods at me like he's a head of state graciously acknowledging a peon. "Yes, I do recall meeting Ms. McIntyre."

Frankly, I'd like to punch him. He rubs me the wrong way.

Jonah steps out from behind them. "Hi, Lia."

I give Jonah a curt nod. "Hey."

Jonah's wearing what he had on earlier at the office – jeans and a T-shirt. Apparently, he's underdressed too. I'm just now noticing how badly scuffed his boots are. The guy's got to be rolling in money. Surely he can afford new boots.

For the first time, I notice a frayed length of braided twine tied around his wrist, looking like it's been there for years. Mentally, I shake my head. I don't get this guy. His band is giving all the top acts a run for their money on the charts right now, and yet Jonah looks like he could easily pass for a hobo. He's such a contradiction.

I feel a sudden urge to reach up and release his hair from its ponytail. I want to thread my fingers through those waves and see how long his hair is. But I immediately squelch the impulse. Jonah's a client. Even if he was on board with the idea, I can't just bang him and walk away. For starters, it would get messy. And there would surely be repercussions, especially if Shane found out. Still... damn. This guy oozes sex appeal. No wonder the fans-girls are throwing themselves at him.

He looks me over, his eyes dwelling on the slogan on my T-shirt, and grins. "So glad you could make it."

We're interrupted by a young woman dressed in a catering uniform as she presents a tray of chilled champagne flutes.

Shane takes a glass and tastes it. "Excellent, thank you." Then he picks up a second glass and hands it to Beth.

As Peterson takes a glass of the bubbly stuff, I excuse myself and head across the great room to the bar, where I help myself to a bottle of ale from the fridge beneath the bar. Champagne's not my thing.

"You got another one of those?"

I look up, surprised to see Jonah leaning across the bar, peering down at the bottle of beer in my hand. "Sure." I hand him a bottle. "Not a fan of champagne either?"

"Nah. It's too pretentious." He pops off the cap and takes a long swig of my favorite beer and nods in approval. Then he reads the label and chuckles. "Zombie Dust, huh?"

"I dare you to produce a better ale."

"Don't think I can." Jonah takes a seat on one of the barstools opposite me and surveys the mahogany bar with its brass fittings and vintage lights, shaking his head in disbelief. "Why does Shane have a bar – *a real bar* – in his apartment?"

"He and my brothers used to hang out at a tavern in Old Town. A couple years ago, when they found out it was about to be demolished to put in a shopping center, they bought the bar and its fixtures and reassembled it here."

I glance behind me at the ornate mirror that spans the 10-foot length of the bar counter, the wooden racks of glasses hanging over-head, and the glass shelves holding scores of bottles of liquor. It is pretty cool, I have to admit.

Jonah props his elbows on the bar, the bottle of Zombie Dust dangling from his fingers. My eyes gravitate to those fingers. They're long and agile, tipped with neatly trimmed, blunt nails. I can just picture them stroking the strings of his guitar, plucking notes out of the air.

I wonder what type of guitar he plays.

"Acoustic or electric?" I ask.

"Acoustic."

My eyes skim across the black tattoos peaking out beneath the sleeves of his T-shirt, intricate scrolls combined with geometric shapes. He's got a band of black triangles circling his biceps. I can't help wondering where else he's inked. Or maybe even pierced? He's got multiple piercings in his ears, so it stands to reason he may be pierced elsewhere on his body. Unfortunately, I find that proposition very intriguing.

"So, you're going to babysit me," he says. He takes a long swig of his beer, and I watch the muscles in his throat contract as he swallows. His skin is golden, as if he spends a lot of time in the sun. His dark hair bears streaks of highlights only the sun can produce.

"It looks like it," I say, taking a drink of my beer.

"I've seen what you can do – in the boxing ring, I mean. I admit it's impressive, especially for a girl."

My hackles rise immediately, but by the glint in his eyes, I know he's just trying to get a rise out of me.

"I saw what you did to those two guys today, in the martial arts studio. You don't look like someone who can toss around men twice her size."

"That's the point. Everyone underestimates me because of my size and my looks." I shrug. "It works to my advantage."

"I won't underestimate you," he says, his steely gaze on mine. His voice had dropped, low and rough, like his singing voice.

I know damn well what he sings like. His sound is reminiscent of Nickelback, another band I like. And Seether. Imagine Dragons. His band is part of that set, although Locke's hits have been dominating the charts for the past couple of years, ever since they came on the music scene. They've barely given any ground to any other rock band.

His gaze is still on me, intent and heated. I'd be lying to myself if I denied the frisson of awareness pulsing between us. I realize I know absolutely nothing about this guy. Does he have a girlfriend? A lover? Does he sleep around? Hell, maybe he's married.

I mentally shake myself, disgusted by the direction of my thoughts. He's a *job* to me, and I don't mess around with my jobs. He could have a wife and ten kids back home in LA for all I know. Not that I care. Because I don't.

Before I can even ask him, Shane call our names. "Dinner's served, guys!"

"Shall we?" Jonah says, standing. He heads to the dining table without sparing me another glance.

And that's fine with me, as it lets me admire his fine ass as he walks away.

Damn.

6

My brother's completely out of his mind if he thinks it's a good idea to pair me up with Jonah. He thinks he knows what's best for me, his poor dysfunctional sister, but he's dead wrong. I know exactly what he's up to. He could have easily assigned any of a dozen bodyguards to Jonah, but he chose me. Jonah is God's gift to women, a fan-girl-magnet to end all magnets. When Jonah walks into a room, ovaries explode. And for some crazy-ass reason, Shane thinks Jonah and I would be good together. What the hell is he up to?

It's not going to happen. Jonah may be easy on the eyes with his lean, muscular build and the tribal tats, but I'm no pushover. And besides, why does Shane think Jonah would want to waste his time on me? I'm a nobody. This guy could have his pick of women in any room he walks into. He probably has fan-girls lined up outside his rental house right now, hoping to catch a glimpse of him when he arrives home this evening. I'm sure they'd all love a chance to get lucky. I realize I'm going to have to walk through that gauntlet of screaming girls tonight. After our dinner here, I'll be heading back to Jonah's house with him. As of tonight, I'm on the job for as long as he's in town. Hopefully, it won't be for long.

As I walk to the dining table, the succulent aroma of beef brisket and pulled pork hits me, and I have to smile. Our catered dinner this evening is barbecue. Awesome. I was afraid we'd be eating escargot or pâté. But I should have known better. Shane may be wealthy as hell, but he's also down to earth.

The table is huge – designed to seat ten. Shane's seated at the far end, with Beth to his right and Dwight Peterson beside her. Jonah takes a seat across from Peterson, and that leaves me only one choice: between Jonah and Shane.

Jonah takes a swig of his Zombie Dust and smiles at me. "This is good stuff. We'll have to stock some at the house."

I nod, dismissing his attempt at small talk. I'm here to do a job, not socialize. It's time to switch to work mode. "So, this is the part where we get to know each other," I say to Jonah, helping myself to some of the beef brisket. "So start talking. You married? Got a girl-friend? Or a boyfriend?"

Beth chokes on a sip of water, and Peterson glares at me. Oops. I have a feeling this guy's gonna be a problem.

Peterson turns to address Shane. "No offense, Shane, but is she really the best you have to offer? At the rate we're paying for your services, I would expect someone a little more... professional."

I suck in a breath, astonished at the gall of that man and ready to rip him a new one, but Shane steps in before I can respond.

"Dwight, I assure you Lia is exactly what you – what Jonah needs."

Peterson shakes his head. "I disagree. I think we need someone... bigger. More intimidating. I don't see how she can provide the type of security Jonah requires. He's hounded by fans and paparazzi everywhere he goes. I'm not a big guy, but I could take Lia with one arm tied behind my back."

"Oh, really?" I say, setting my beer bottle down on the table. I look Peterson in the eye. "Would you like to test that theory? Because there's a boxing ring in this apartment, and I'd be only too happy to let you try."

Peterson blanches at my challenge. "Well, I – I – I'm not dressed for physical activity." He gestures to his pompous pinstripe suit, which makes him look like an overgrown kid wearing his daddy's clothes.

But I'm not about to let him off the hook that easily. "Then whose ass would you like for me to kick? I'll be happy to give you a demonstration."

"How about mine?" Jonah offers, turning to face me. His expression is implacable. "I did a little boxing back in high school. I'm not completely helpless, you know."

I smirk. Like I would risk hurting the client on the first day on the job. Although, I have to admit the idea of putting my hands on him is tempting.

Shane clears his throat. "I'm sure a demonstration can be arranged, Dwight. I'd be happy to join Lia in the ring."

I'm tempted to jump across the table and give Peterson a demonstration right here he won't soon forget.

Peterson crosses his arms over his chest. "Actually, I'd like a demonstration, because honestly, I don't see how a girl her size could possibly protect anyone."

"Oh, you're on!" I say, pushing my chair back as I rise. "How about I start with you?"

"Sit down, Lia," Shane says.

Jonah points his beer bottle at his manager. "Dwight, trust me, this isn't necessary. I've seen what she can do. I watched her put two guys twice her size on their backs today. Lia can handle herself."

I don't know what pisses me off more... Dwight and his attitude or the fact that Jonah is vouching for me. I don't need Jonah fighting my fights.

The conversation flows around me after that, with everyone enjoying their meals and chit chatting about everything from Beth's bookstore to Chicago baseball. After the meal, Shane opens a bottle of red wine, and he and Peterson each have a glass. Jonah opts for another bottle of Zombie Dust. Beth and I both opt for water. Beth's not much of a drinker to begin with, and I'm essentially on duty now, so no more alcohol for me tonight. One beer's my limit.

At the end of the evening, as Jonah and his manager are heading to the foyer, Shane pulls me aside and hands me two sets of keys to a black Cadillac Escalade. "Use the Escalade for official business. I'll have your Jeep delivered to the house in the morning."

"Okay."

"And Lia? One more thing." He lays his hands on my shoulders and leans in. "I know Peterson can be a challenge. I'm counting on you to keep your cool and not go ballistic on him, okay?"

I nod, frowning.

"Lia?"

"What?"

"Please. Don't let him get to you, okay?"

"I said okay!"

Shane releases me, looking skeptical.

"I promise, all right?" I say.

"Good luck," he says, as I head toward the foyer and my new client.

* * *

After I collect my two duffle bags in the foyer, Jonah, Dwight, and I take the elevator down to the parking garage. Dwight stands right in front of the elevator doors, as if he's impatient to get out. Jonah and I are behind him. Standing this close to Jonah, I'm painfully aware of the difference in our heights. He's easily six feet tall, if not a little more, and he towers over me. Jonah's close enough that I can feel the heat radiating off his body. I detect a faint cologne, as well as the scent of men's deodorant. I also detect *him*, the scent of his heated skin, and it does something to me.

I'm used to working around men. Most of my coworkers are men. I'm used to their smells and their colognes and their sweat and often their funk. But none of them ever smelled this good. I don't like it.

As the elevator descends to the parking garage, I crouch down and open one of my duffle bags to pull out my chest holster and 9 mm Beretta. After strapping on the holster, I check the chamber of the handgun and the clip, then engage the safety, and stow the gun in my holster. Jonah watches as I pull on a jacket to conceal the weapon. So does Peterson, a perpetual scowl on his narrow face. I'm not sure the guy has any other expression other than dour.

"I'm officially on the clock, gentlemen," I say as I rise. "If I tell you to do something, you do it. Without hesitation or argument. Is that clear?"

"Crystal," Jonah says, but Peterson turns away, facing the elevator doors. I'm not sure what his problem is, but Peterson definitely has issues with me. I glance at Jonah, and he rolls his eyes at Peterson's behavior, and I have to bite back a grin.

The Escalade is parked in the reserved spot closest to the penthouse elevator. "Here's our ride, guys," I say, using the key fob to unlock the doors.

Jonah walks around to the front passenger seat and climbs in, and Peterson gets into the back. I climb up into the driver's seat and start the ignition.

"Where to?" I ask Jonah. "The house?"

He nods. "Yes, if you don't mind."

Jonah has leased a house in Lincoln Park, as well as a private recording studio not far from there. I pull out onto Lake Shore Drive and head north.

After a few minutes of blessed silence, I hear Peterson's whiney voice in the backseat. "If you don't mind me asking, Lia, how old are you?"

Yes, I do mind. But I'll try not to be a dick to this guy, even though he rubs me the wrong way. I glance in the rear view mirror to catch his gaze. "Twenty-two."

Peterson shakes his head in dismay.

Jonah tosses a recriminating look back at his manager. "Dwight."

"I was just checking to make sure she's old enough to drive," Peterson mutters under his breath.

I burst out laughing. "Is that the best you've got?" I shake my head. "Surely you can do better than that. If you've got a problem with me, Peterson, at least make it interesting."

"I wish you wouldn't call me that," he says. "You can call me *Mr. Peterson* or *Dwight*, but don't call me *Peterson*. It's disrespectful."

I roll my eyes, but bite my tongue. Jonah's looking straight ahead, his eyes on the car in front of us as he pretends to ignore us. But I can't help noticing the slight twitch to his lips as he tries not to smile.

No man should have such kissable lips, damn it.

Asshole.

~~9~~ 7

The house Jonah leased is huge. There are three floors above ground, plus a finished lower level. There are eight bedrooms and six bathrooms – more than enough space for Jonah, the three other band members, Peterson, the housekeeper, the audio engineer, and me.

The house is located on a quiet, tree-lined residential street. The front exterior is traditional, red brick colonial with a door in the center and lots of windows. There's a six-foot red brick wall surrounding the property, providing some degree of privacy from prying eyes and eager photographers. In the rear of the property is a four-car detached garage and a smaller building that will house additional security staff. My job is to protect Jonah. Shane has other security staff on the premises to chauffeur the others around as needed and to keep the crowds outside the gates in check.

Apparently, Jonah's presence in Lincoln Park is public knowledge already, because there are about forty teenage girls clustered on the sidewalk in front of the house, most of them standing on their tiptoes in mini skirts and high heels in a futile attempt to see over the wall. I'm sure they're posting pics on social media like crazy, which is only going to feed the frenzy.

"Well, shit," I say, slowing the Escalade as we near the property. The girls are blocking the drive, as well as the remote-controlled gate that leads to the parking area behind the house. I radio to the security staff on duty that we're here.

As we approach the crowd, I double-check to make sure all the vehicle doors are locked and the windows are up. Then I flash my lights at the crowd as I slowly inch my way toward the gate. The girls don't seem to take the hint – or maybe they just don't care if I run them over – so I tap the horn a few times.

Impatient, I lower my window. "Move it, girls!" I yell, although I doubt they can hear me over the chanting. I wouldn't be one bit surprised if the neighbors call the police because of all the ruckus.

I continue to inch forward at a painfully slow crawl. I'm tempted to gun the engine and scare them out of the way. The vehicle's windows are darkly tinted, so they can't really see inside, especially not this late at night, but that doesn't stop them from pressing their pert little noses against the glass, trying to see if they can spot Jonah inside. These girls have no shame.

As we stop right in front of the ornate wrought iron gate, a couple of photographers jump in front of the Escalade and start snapping pictures through the front windshield, where the tinting is far lighter. *Asshats.*

"Give me a break," I mutter, inching the vehicle forward.

The gate ahead of us opens just enough for one of the security guards to slip through it. He pushes the photographers aside, as well as a few of the girls who sneak around to the front of the vehicle. It'll be a miracle if one of them doesn't get run over. Once the entrance is cleared of bodies, the gate swings open just enough that I can drive through.

I turn to Jonah, who's in the front passenger seat. "Will we have to deal with this every time we come and go?"

He nods, smiling apologetically. "Yeah. Sorry."

"How do you stand it?"

He shrugs. "It comes with the territory, I'm afraid. Don't worry, you'll get used to it."

Just as the gates are closing behind us, one of the photographers manages to slip inside, but the guard catches him and pushes him back.

Peterson opens his door and practically falls out of the rear passenger seat. I don't say a word as he stalks toward the rear entrance to the house without a word and disappears inside.

I head to the rear of the vehicle and open the door to retrieve my stuff. As I reach for my duffle bags, Jonah beats me to them, hauling them out. One's full of clothes, and it's not too heavy. But the other one has a small arsenal in it and some electronic equipment. It's quite heavy.

"Good God," he says, hefting the heavier of the two bags. "What did you pack in here? Bricks?"

Trying not to allow myself to be distracted by his biceps, I take the heavy bag from him and sling it over my shoulder. "You're such a baby."

I don't look back as I walk toward the house. I've practically got eyes in the back of my head, and I can feel the heat of his gaze on me as he follows me across the driveway. The girls are still milling around out in front of the house, their chatter a low buzz, like a hive of persistent bees. I hope they get tired soon and go home.

The rear door to the house opens into a mud room, which leads into an expansive gourmet kitchen. The house is dark and quiet, and there's no sign of Peterson. He apparently high-tailed it out of sight, which is fine with me. I quickly survey the kitchen, with its fancy cherry cabinetry, granite countertops, and stainless steel appliances. The kitchen has a large eat-in table that seats six people. Through an open arched doorway, I can see a long dining table that seats even more. It's definitely a big house.

One of my first tasks will be to learn the layout of the house and plan emergency escape routes. I know my brother Jake and his team have already been here to install a proper security and surveillance system. There's a control center in one of the downstairs bedrooms – that will be my room.

I have a lot of work to do tonight before I can call it a day.

"So, how about a quick tour of the place?" I say.

"After you," he says, extending his hand toward an arched opening that leads to the central hallway.

After I drop my bags off in my room, we head downstairs to the lower level. It's what you'd expect in a swanky place like this. There's a media room with an enormous flat-screen TV, a well-outfitted rec room with a pool table and pinball machines, a fitness room, and a bar. I walk through room after room, looking for means of ingress and egress, and making mental notes on what I find.

The ground floor is pretty traditional – a kitchen, dining room, formal living room, an office, a bathroom, and three bedrooms – one of which is my command and control center. I luck out and get the bedroom with an en-suite bathroom. On the second floor, there are four bedrooms and two bathrooms. The third floor is the master suite, with a huge bedroom and private bathroom. This is the bedroom Jonah has claimed for himself – it's quiet up here, well off the beaten path. I certainly don't blame him for wanting some peace and quiet.

Besides his empty suitcases stowed in the large walk-in closet, he has clothes in here, sneakers, boots, and four acoustic guitars lined up on stands, arranged against one empty wall. I glance at the large, unmade bed with its dark wood headboard. The blankets are a jumbled mess, as if someone spent a restless night in here, tossing and turning. Several pillows are stacked on top of each other at the head of the bed, and I can picture him lying there reading or surfing the net on his phone. I can't help wondering what he would have been wearing – if anything.

"Sorry," he says, looking at the messy bed. "I don't see the point in making the bed if I'm just going to mess it up again in a few hours."

I chuckle. "I'm your minder, Jonah, not your mother. I don't give a damn if you make your bed or not." Unbidden, the image of Jonah lazing around naked in that big bed comes to mind, and I mentally shake myself. No matter how much of a temptation he is, I could never go there with him. He's a job, and I don't tap jobs. Shane would have my head on a pike if I did.

"So, when does the rest of the band arrive?" I say, trying to redirect my slutty thoughts back to reality.

"Tomorrow. The guys are flying in to O'Hare in the early afternoon, along with Esperanza and Ruben."

"Esperanza's your housekeeper-slash-cook?"

"Yeah. Honestly, we couldn't function without her."

"And Ruben is your audio engineer?"

"That's right."

I nod. Seven people living in this house, plus me. But really, Jonah's the only one who matters as far as I'm concerned. He's my client. If push comes to shove, I've got his back. The rest are on their own.

* * *

It's nearly midnight, so I leave Jonah to his own devices up in his attic retreat and head back down to the first floor to secure all the doors and windows. I wouldn't put it past the paparazzi to climb up into one of the huge trees that border the property to get a shot through a window.

Once that's taken care of, I head to my own room to check out the control center. Jake configured this surveillance system himself, so I know it's top-notch. My brother's a wiz with the electronic gear.

It doesn't take me long to realize there's a video camera in every room of the house... every room. I flip through the video feeds and spot Peterson lying on his bed, reading on a tablet. I spot Jonah seated on his bed with a guitar on his lap, gently plucking the strings. Spying on people isn't my thing, so I switch the monitors over to the public spaces on the ground floor, like the kitchen, living room, and office. The other monitors display video feeds from various vantage points around the exterior of the house and the garage. Jake is certainly thorough. The house is locked up tighter than a drum, so I set the security system for the night. Then I unpack my bags and hang my clothes in the walk-in closet.

I brought a small arsenal with me in the form of a portable handgun safe. Inside the safe are two spare handguns and a good supply of ammo. Honestly, I'm not expecting any real trouble. I think the worst I'll have to deal with is unscrupulous paparazzi or obsessive fan-girls attempting to get a little grabby. I can handle all of that without any firepower. The guns are just a precaution.

It's late, but I know better than to try to sleep. I'm too restless to settle down, so I head to the kitchen to check out the provisions. The fridge and pantry are well stocked, and I help myself to some pretzels and a cold Pepsi. Then I make my rounds through the ground floor again, rechecking the doors and windows even though it's unnecessary. I have to do something to keep myself occupied.

I check out the home office, which is nicely furnished with a cherry desk, leather chair, and bookcases filled with expensive books in matching leather covers. I peer out the window at the front of the house, surprised to see girls are still out there loitering in small groups on the sidewalk. I can see a few of them peeking through the bars of the wrought iron gate. Don't these girls have any sense? They should be home in their warm, cozy beds, not camping outside in the frigid night air. It has started drizzling, and the temperature has dropped. These kids are crazy.

After I finish my tour of the ground floor, I'm heading to my room when I hear the faint strains of a guitar coming from upstairs. Curious, I climb the stairs to the attic and walk quietly down the short hallway that leads to Jonah's suite. His door is closed, but I can still make out the sound of the guitar and his low voice. Frequently he stops and starts, singing the same phrases again and again, each time just a little bit differently. He's writing a song, I realize. It's a slow song, a ballad, which is unlike most of the hard-driving songs he usually sings.

I return to my room, and after a quick check of the exterior surveillance monitors and shooting off a status report to Shane, I turn off the lights in my room and fall into bed. My eyes are aching and I'm suitably tired. I read on my phone for a while, then watch a bit of a movie until my eyes grow heavy. I shut off my phone and lie still in the night, waiting for sleep to overtake me.

I dream about footsteps in the attic and the faint strains of an acoustic guitar.

8

Someone's rattling around in the kitchen making enough noise to wake the dead. I groan, forcing my eyes open, then grab my phone and check the time. Six-thirty. Really? Who the hell is up at six-thirty in the morning? It's not like either of these guys has anywhere he needs to be anytime soon.

I drag myself out of bed and head to the kitchen, PJs, bed head, and all. I find Peterson dragging pans out of a cabinet.

"What the hell are you doing, Peterson?"

He straightens and scowls at me. "What are we supposed to do for breakfast?" he says. "Esperanza's not here."

"What, you can't feed yourself? Dude, this kitchen is well stocked."

He rolls his eyes. "It's her job to cook for us."

"Yeah, well, she's not here yet, so make do."

"Why don't you make me breakfast?"

Dwight reminds me of a petulant, spoiled child. Obviously, he's never had to fend for himself. He expects everything to be done for him.

"I'm not making you breakfast."

"Well, I don't cook," he says, sounding exasperated.

"Then make some toast, or eat a bowl of cereal. You can pour milk out of a carton, can't you?"

He scowls at me, and I ignore him. Now that I'm up, I need coffee, so I make a cup using one of those fancy single-cup coffee makers. I poke around in the cupboards until I score a box of protein bars. I hop up on the kitchen counter and enjoy my coffee and protein bar.

Dwight watches me take a bite of my protein bar. "What are you eating?"

I shrug. "A protein bar. There's a box of them in that cupboard over there. Help yourself."

Frowning, Dwight grabs a mug from the cabinet and makes himself a cup of coffee. "Look, you work for us," he says, staring at me with pale, watery blue eyes. "So make yourself useful. Fix me some eggs and bacon, something more substantial than a protein bar. I'm hungry."

I smile at him. "Let's make one thing clear, Peterson. Hash tag, I'm-not-cooking-for-you. That's not in my job description."

"*Mr.* Peterson," he growls. "Or, Dwight."

"Okay, *Dwight*. I don't work for you. I work for McIntyre Security, and my sole reason for being here is to make sure no one fucks with Jonah." I glance around the empty kitchen. "Since I don't see Jonah up yet and in imminent danger of being fucked with, that means I can sit here on my ass and eat my protein bar and enjoy my damned cup of coffee without any grief from you."

Dwight scoffs. "It's a miracle you can even keep a job, Lia. Really. Besides, Jonah sleeps half the day away. He won't surface until early afternoon. Since you have nothing to do right now, you can make me some breakfast."

"Make it yourself, Dwight," I say, as I hop down from the counter and take my coffee and protein bar back to my room. Dwight can fend for himself.

* * *

Apparently, my new client is a night owl who likes to sleep in. As of midmorning, I haven't heard a peep from the upstairs suite. That means I have some time to kill this morning. I head outside for some sunshine and fresh air and take a stroll around the perimeter of the property just to check things out. I hear a few cars drive by out front, and I hear the chatter of little kids playing in a yard nearby. It seems like a nice, quiet neighborhood. I wonder how the neighbors like having one of the houses on the street leased out to a rock 'n roll star and his entourage.

The brick wall that encloses the half-acre property is topped with a wrought-iron extension that provides additional security, but allows some visibility over the top. There's a smooth, stone path just inside the perimeter, meandering through lush groundcover.

Every few steps, I come across what looks like a child's paper airplane. As I pick them up and unfold them, I have to smile when I see all the girls' names and phone numbers scribbled on the pieces of paper, along with photos, vows of undying devotion, and sometimes a description of the creative things she can do with her mouth.

Most of the notes are addressed to Jonah, but a few of them are addressed to the three other members of the band: Dylan, Travis, and Zeke. I wad up the invitations and toss them in a garbage can. It's not that I think some random fan girl would pose a risk to one of the members of the band. But if Jonah or the guys in his band want to score with underaged fan-girls, too bad. That's not happening on my watch.

My phone chimes with an incoming message from Shane:

Liam and Miguel will drop off your Jeep this morning.

I text him back:

Thx

I receive an immediate reply:

Try not to get in too much trouble, ok?

Gee, thanks. Such confidence.

* * *

After finishing my outside tour, I head back to my bedroom and change into black bike shorts, a matching sports bra, and my boxing gloves, then head down to the fitness room on the lower level.

This place is nicely outfitted with quality workout equipment, including free weights, two treadmills, and a professional-grade punching bag. There's even a top-of-the line TRX suspension training system. After warming up with some free weights, I hit the treadmill and quickly work up to running three miles at full bore. I love running. I love pushing myself to my limits. I love pushing myself until it hurts.

I save the best for last – the punching bag. There's something very cathartic about beating the shit out of a punching bag. You can easily pretend it's someone you hate. After wrapping my hands and pulling on boxing gloves, I attack the bag with everything I've got, imagining that it's Logan. I punch and kick, finding a good cathartic rhythm, until my muscles are screaming for mercy and my lungs are desperate for air.

A low voice shatters my concentration. "Damn. What did that bag ever do to you?"

I stop mid-kick and pivot to face the open doorway. Jonah's standing there looking like he just rolled out of bed, in sweats and a wrinkled T-shirt. He's barefoot, and I find even the sight of his feet hot.

I try to reign in my pounding heart. "It's about time you woke up. I thought you were going to sleep the day away."

He shrugs. "I'm a night owl. What can I say?"

His unruly dark hair is pulled back in a haphazard ponytail, as if it was an afterthought because he couldn't be bothered to brush it. I have a sudden urge to take it down and thread my fingers through it. Jesus, he looks good.

"I'm starved," he says, running his hand over his trim beard. "What do you say we go out for lunch? My treat."

"Okay." At least he doesn't expect me to cook for him. If he'd even suggested it, I would have decked him. "Sounds good. I just need a quick shower."

He steps into the room and reaches for my gloved hands. "Here. I'll help you."

Of course I can do this myself – I don't need his help. But for some unfathomable reason, I bite back a snarky retort and instead watch his long fingers undo the Velcro straps of my gloves. I feel a little self-conscious standing here dripping with sweat, hot and in definite need of a shower. But why should I care what he thinks about me? He's the one who stepped into my personal space, not the other way around.

After pulling off my gloves and unwrapping my hands, he sets my protective gear down on the mat and reaches for my hands, inspecting them as if looking for damage. Seemingly satisfied that I'm still in one piece, he peers down at me intently, a ghost of a smile on his face. "Did you sleep well?"

I nod. "You?"

He shrugs, his eyes becoming guarded. "As well as can be expected."

"I thought I heard you up in the night."

"Yeah, that's typical for me. As I said, I'm a night owl." He releases my hands, looking a bit distracted. "Go get changed. I'll meet you in the kitchen." And then he simply walks away.

* * *

We step out the back door of the house just as Liam and Miguel Rodriguez arrive. Liam's driving my Jeep, and Miguel is right behind him in his black Mustang.

After parking my Jeep behind the house, Liam tosses me the keys.

"Perfect timing," I say, glad we can take my Jeep instead of the Escalade.

Liam nods, reaching out to grasp my chin. "You settled in okay?"

I pull away, embarrassed by his concern. "Sure. Piece of cake."

"Holler if you need anything. I'm just one text away, right?"

I nod. "Jeez, cut it out before you make me blush."

Liam rolls his eyes at me. "Cooper's picking up the rest of the band and two staff members this afternoon at O'Hare. He'll bring them here."

"Good. One of those staff members is the cook-slash-housekeeper. Dwight needs her if he's not going to starve to death, because I'm sure as hell not cooking for him."

Liam grins. "And why does that not surprise me?"

Liam and Miguel take off. I find Jonah already buckled into the front passenger seat of my Jeep. He looks the same as he did a little while ago, except he brushed his hair, and now he's wearing shoes – well-worn sneakers that look like they've seen better days. The guy's rolling in money, but he dresses like a bum. I kinda like that.

Jonah glances at me as I start the engine. "Who's that guy you were talking to? I saw you with him in the martial arts studio yesterday."

"Liam, my twin."

Jonah's eyebrows shoot up. "You two look nothing alike."

He's right, of course. Liam's six feet tall. I'm five-two. Brown hair versus blond. No one would ever take us for siblings. "Yeah, I know. I'm the cool one."

Jonah bites back a chuckle as we approach the gate. I point at the garbage can where I tossed all the fan-girl notes I collected earlier in the morning. "I threw out about twenty offers for blow jobs, and a half-dozen offers for ménages, if you're interested. You have quite a loyal following."

He chuckles. "That's okay, I'm good."

I look over at him. "You could have a different girl every night if you wanted. Or several a night, if you had the stamina to keep up. I doubt there's ever a shortage of girls throwing themselves at you, is there?"

He shrugs. "It's not all it's cracked up to be, Lia. I play music because I love it, not to get laid. Besides, I don't need to rely on a guitar or a mic to get laid."

"I'm sure you don't." Of course he doesn't. Jonah's beautiful, like a fallen angel. Who wouldn't want a piece of him?

I face forward in the driver's seat and pull through the gates as the security guards open it and push back the crowd, which is now twice the size it was yesterday. Several of the girls come right up to the Jeep to peer inside the front passenger window. They start squealing when they make out what they assume is the shadowy figure of Jonah through the darkly tinted window. Photographers are snapping pics right and left through the windshield. I pull out into the street, successfully avoiding running over any of the girls.

Out of the corner of my eye, I see he's still watching me.

"In case you were wondering," he says, "I have plenty of stamina. Never doubt that."

I'll be damned if I wouldn't like to test his assertion.

9

S o, what's good to eat around here?" Jonah says, switching on the radio. He zeroes in on a rock station and turns up the volume.

"Can you be a little more specific? What are you hungry for? I can eat just about anything except for sushi. I'm not a big fan of sushi."

"How about a really good burger and fries?"

I smile, nodding with approval. "I know just the place."

I take him to one of my favorite local burger joints. It's just a little hole in the wall, very nondescript, but the locals know the food here is off the charts. The dining room is packed as we walk up to the counter to order.

Jonah hangs back. "Ladies first."

I'm thrown for a minute by his chivalrous attitude – frankly, I'm not used to it. My brothers treat me like one of the guys, which is what I prefer. As I place my order, I'm hyperaware that Jonah's standing right behind me, close enough that I swear I can feel the gravitational force of his body. It's unsettling. I have to fight the urge to lean back against him.

The guy taking my order does a double-take when he looks up at Jonah, but he plays it cool. After Jonah orders, the cashier gives him the total for both our orders, and Jonah digs in his back pocket for his wallet.

"Whoa," I say as he hands the cashier money. "I'll pay for myself."

"It's okay. I've got it."

Before I can protest, the cashier takes Jonah's money and gives him change. No one's ever paid my way before, I realize, and I don't like that he's doing it now. This isn't a fucking date. It's just two people getting a bite to eat, that's all. But I don't want to make a scene in public, because I don't want to draw attention to Jonah. So I walk away from the order counter, needing a moment to center myself. When the hell did our little lunch outing turn into a date? It's not a fucking date. I'm here for one reason, and one reason only... because it's my job to keep rabid fans from molesting my client. Otherwise, I'd be outta here so fast, Jonah's head would spin.

"Mister Locke? Would you sign this for me?"

I turn back, mentally kicking myself for spacing out on the job. But it's just a little girl, probably around eight years old, holding out a restaurant take-out menu and a ballpoint pen as she asks Jonah for an autograph. Behind her, a woman, presumably the girl's mother, squeezes the little girl's thin shoulders with nervous hands. The mom's eyes are bright, and I'd bet money she put the little girl up to asking for the autograph.

"Sure, I'd be happy to," Jonah says, taking the menu and the pen from the kid. "What's your name?"

"Can you make it out to Kaitlyn and Becky?" The little girl glances nervously back at the woman behind her, who nods in approval. "I'm Kaitlyn, and that's my mom, Becky. We love your music. I've seen all your videos like a thousand times on YouTube."

Jonah makes out their names and adds his in a heavy, masculine scrawl. "Here you go, Kaitlyn."

"Are you on vacation?" the kid asks, craning her head up to look at him.

"Yeah." He nods, shooting me a grin. "I'm on vacation."

She smiles at him. "I hope you have a nice one." Then she turns and hands the autographed menu and the pen to her mom.

The mom has never once taken her eyes off Jonah.

"Okay, show over," I say, breaking the spell. "Let the man sit down and relax." I grab a handful of the back of Jonah's T-shirt and maneuver him toward one of the few empty tables in the room.

Kaitlyn and her mom rush out the door, both of them giggling like teenagers.

"Does that happen a lot?" I ask him.

He shrugs. "Yeah. It's no big deal. At least they were polite. They're not always polite."

* * *

"So, Lia, do you have a boyfriend?"

As I chew a fry, I eye him warily. *None of your effing business, pal.* I swallow. "That's really not relevant."

"Just trying to make small talk." He takes a sip of his Coke. "What's the big deal?"

I shake my head. "There isn't one. It's just not relevant to our working relationship."

"So, you do have one then?"

"No!" *Damn it!* "I'm not answering that. Forget it." And I know by the triumphant gleam in his eye that he knows he tricked me. The bastard. "What about you?" I counter. "Got a steady girl back home in LA? You never did answer me last night."

Jonah's face is routinely plastered on the covers of gossip magazines and on the Internet, paired up with one female celebrity after another. Most of the photos are obvious hack jobs, but not all. He certainly has more than his fair share of admirers in the celebrity world.

"Nope. I'm officially single."

"I read on the Internet that you're dating Makayla Hendricks."

His smile falters. "Was. We broke up a few weeks ago."

"She's pretty hot." That's an understatement. Makayla Hendricks is not just gorgeous, but she dominates the pop charts. She's the queen of divas.

He shrugs. "She's beautiful, yes, but it wasn't working out. She thrives on publicity, while I do everything in my power to avoid it. My idea of a good time is to stay in and watch a movie, while she just wants to go to red carpet events. It wasn't a good match."

"Yeah, but you two looked damn good together in the press. You, the king of rock, and Makayla, the princess of pop. Sounds like destiny to me."

He makes a face, then bites into his burger. When he's done chewing, he says, "What you read in the press isn't always true."

"Well, I can't argue with that."

Just before we leave the burger joint, I get a text from Cooper. He's on his way to the house with the rest of the party, their ETA twenty minutes. *Oh, joy.* We're about to have a house full of rockers. I can't wait.

"The others are on their way to the house," I tell him, pocketing my phone.

I notice then that Jonah's reading a text on his phone. "We'd better get back there to supervise, or all hell might break loose."

* * *

We arrive back at the house before Cooper and the others. Someone must have notified Dwight, too, because he's standing outside on the circular drive, fidgeting as usual. For a moment, I wonder if Dwight's a drug addict. That would explain so much.

Cooper pulls into the drive right on our heels, and the security staff open the gates for him. I help the security guys shoo the girls out of the way as Cooper drives through the gates. A photographer sneaks in behind Cooper's Escalade, and I take great pleasure in strong-arming him right back out.

Cooper parks near the rear door to the house, and all four doors pop open simultaneously. Three hotties who look like they're barely old enough to have graduated high school jump down from the vehicle, followed by a middle-aged woman and a beatnik in his early 30s.

The woman has to be Esperanza, of course, although she's nothing like what I expected. She's basically their housekeeper, but she doesn't fit any stereotype I had in my head. She's tall and elegant, with a lovely oval face and a friendly smile. She looks cool and collected in a beige pant suit and white silk shell – she looks more like an attorney than a housekeeper-slash-cook. Her long black hair, streaked with faint threads of silver, is pulled back in a sophisticated, twisted bun.

Ruben, the sound engineer, is definitely a throw-back to the 60s. Dressed in black slacks and a black turtleneck, wearing a pair of round black-frame glasses perched on his nose, he totally looks the part. His hair is black, trimmed very short, and his skin is a rich shade of mocha. I'm not sure exactly what his ethnicity is. He's also a little unsteady on his feet, and one of the guys from the band steps up to offer him a shoulder to lean on as they walk up the steps into the house.

Cooper appears beside me. "Good luck, kiddo," he says, patting me on the back. "Keep an eye on the sound guy. He's drunk."

Jonah passes us, carrying a suitcase in each hand. "Ruben's deathly afraid of flying. I'm sure he had a few drinks before and during the flight."

Cooper watches Jonah carrying luggage into the house. "He hardly acts like a big star rocker, does he?"

* * *

I head inside to face a whole lot of commotion. There's a small mountain of luggage piled up on the central hallway floor at the base of the staircase. Upstairs, there's a lot of noise and heavy footsteps.

Jonah comes down the stairs, chuckling as he picks up two suitcases. "They're fighting over the bedrooms. I'd wait down here until it's over, if I were you. You might get trampled."

"You'll have to introduce me." I have a feeling this place is going to turn into a frat house.

"That depends," he says. "You never answered me back at the restaurant. Do you have a boyfriend?"

"I told you, it's irrelevant."

He leans forward, gazing into my eyes. "I don't think it's irrelevant."

I look at him like he's crazy. "Trust me, it is. I don't fraternize with clients. Even if I wanted to – "

"Do you? Want to, I mean."

I huff, exasperated. I'm not about to answer that question. "I was going to say, even if I wanted to, I couldn't. It's against company policy."

He laughs. "Since when do you give a shit about company policy?"

True, but he doesn't need to know that. "You're nuts." Shaking my head, I leave him to it and go in search of the new housekeeper-slash-cook. She's probably the only sane one in the group.

ꙮ 10

I find Esperanza in the kitchen reorganizing the pantry.

"Hello, I'm Esperanza," she tells me, reaching out to shake my hand.

Her fingers are long and slim, the nails painted a deep dark red that contrasts nicely with her black hair. She's soft-spoken, calm, and courteous, quite the antithesis of her annoying boss.

"Dwight was at risk of starving to death this morning," I tell her, hopping up on the counter to watch her inventory the spice rack. "The man's incapable of feeding himself."

Esperanza smiles at me. "Good. That means job security for me, right?"

I can't help but return her smile. "True."

She works quickly and efficiently, and I already like her.

"Do you have a room yet?" I ask her.

"Yes. On the first floor. I travel light, so there wasn't much to unpack."

It looks like Dwight didn't exaggerate her culinary skills. She informs me that dinner will be a pot roast with roasted vegetables, mashed potatoes and beef gravy, freshly-baked rolls, and salad. For dessert, she's making a pineapple upside-down cake, which apparently is one of her specialties.

I leave Esperanza to her work and find Ruben unpacking his suitcase in one of the remaining ground floor bedrooms. He's quiet and methodical as he hangs his monochromatic wardrobe in the closet. Apparently, all the grown-ups – Esperanza and Ruben – will be bunking on my floor. The three newly arrived band members have staked out bedrooms on the second floor, along with Dwight, and Jonah is king of the castle up in the attic. While everyone is busy unpacking and settling in, I grab an opportunity for some alone time and slip outside to walk the perimeter of the property.

I can tell by the swelling drone of voices coming over the privacy wall that the crowd has grown. I also catch glimpses of several photographers pacing the sidewalk in front of the house, hoping to get a chance shot of one of the band members – preferably Jonah, I'm sure.

When I circle back to the front of the house, I peer through the bars of the front gate at the crowd of hopeful fans and shake my head. Don't these girls have anything better to do than stand around in the hope that they'll catch a glimpse of one of the band members?

I hear footsteps approaching from behind and I turn, surprised to see Jonah. He's dressed up, at least for him, in a pair of black jeans and a black button-down shirt, and he's wearing a half-way decent pair of black boots. His hair is brushed and pulled up into a tidy man-bun. I guess this is him cleaned up. While I have to admit it looks really good on him, I find myself preferring the scruffy hobo look. I have a feeling he did it on purpose, to thrill the fan-girls. The times I've seen him performing on television, his hair's been up in a bun. I guess it's part of his image.

Jonah peers through the bars of the gate. "I guess now's as good a time as any. Before the crowd gets any bigger."

"A good time for what, exactly?" I ask him, although I already have my suspicions.

"To make an appearance."

The guy's got to be crazy! "You're not going out there, Jonah."

"I have to. I can't hide from them all the time. It's autograph time. Let's do this."

I shake my head, peering out through the wrought iron gate. "There are at least fifty or sixty girls out there who don't get the concept of personal boundaries, not to mention the photographers. No way am I letting you go out there."

"It's all part of the job, Lia." His whisky-colored eyes are warm as he gazes down at me. "If it weren't for the fans, there wouldn't be a band. I'd still be mopping floors at an auto factory. I owe them everything."

"Don't you have any grown-up fans?"

He chuckles. "Of course I do. But you won't find them camped out in front of my residence. Come on, let's get this over with."

Against my better judgment, I punch a code into the electronic control panel to unlock the front gate. Jonah moves to walk through it, but I stop him. "I'll go out first. But you have to promise me, if I tell you to get back inside, you do it, got me?"

He nods. "Gotcha."

I have a suspicion he's just humoring me.

The girls hush expectantly when they see me come through the gate, and the atmosphere is fairly buzzing with anticipation. When Jonah steps out behind me, they erupt in deafening squeals of ecstasy, and the crowd moves in closer. Their faces are flushed and many of them are actually sobbing, copious amounts of tears streaming down their cheeks. Good grief! Bobbing up and down, they clutch each other, holding on for dear life as they wave photos of various band members and other paraphernalia, ticket stubs, glossy photos, T-shirts with the band's logo. Nearly all of them are holding out phones and snapping pics and selfies left and right. It's absolutely insane. I don't know how he can stand it.

Jonah smiles as he waves at the crowd, and the noise level increases. In a solid wall of screaming enthusiasm, they press forward, boxing us in against the wall. This is a recipe for disaster – not so much for us, but I'm afraid some of the girls in the front might get knocked down and trampled by the overeager crowd. I do what I can to push them back, trying to create a small buffer between us and them. The last thing I want to do is get in a situation where I have to drop a teenage girl to the ground. And no matter how tempting it might be, I sure as hell can't shoot any of them. Although I haven't ruled that out where the paparazzi are concerned. Those idiots are old enough to know better.

I'm glued to Jonah's side as the girls start to press forward in a wave of excitement, ready to step in if needed. I doubt any of these girls mean him any harm, but a riled up crowd can get ugly fast. I can hear the rapid clicks of cameras and the flash of smartphones going off everywhere, as both the girls and the paparazzi angle for shots of Jonah, who's signing everything thrust at him: CD cases, T-shirts, glossy photographs, magazine covers. One girl asks him to sign her arm with a permanent black marker – I doubt she'll bathe in the foreseeable future. It's a bit of a feeding frenzy, but Jonah seems to be taking it all in stride. The girls are half hysterical, many of them in tears as they gawk at him.

"Jonah!" screams a petite brunette, who latches onto him. She's clinging to him for dear life, and he's trying hard not to lose his balance and topple into her.

"Okay, that's enough," I tell her, forcibly prying her arms from around his waist. "Please don't maim the rock star."

She glares at me, and if looks could kill, I'd be dead.

"Hey, Jonah, who's the blond?" one of the paparazzi shouts, turning his camera lens on me.

Immediately, my heart starts racing. I avoid publicity like a vampire avoids the sun. I notice a lot of cameras are directed at me for a few uncomfortable moments, but Jonah ignores the question, and soon the photographers turn their attention back to him.

Another girl throws herself – literally – at Jonah. He catches her, mostly to prevent her from getting hurt. She's sobbing as she goes up on her toes as if to kiss him.

I step between them and push her back a few feet, none too gently. "Back off, sister."

"Jonah, I love you!" she cries over my shoulder, gazing at him with desperate, pleading eyes.

"That's nice," I tell her, holding her at arm's length. "But you've still got to stay back."

The crowd presses in closer and the pushing and shoving gets increasingly out of hand. Somebody's bound to get hurt. I figure Jonah has signed enough publicity photos and souvenirs for one day. "All right, stud. That's enough. Get back inside."

The crowd erupts in boos and jeers at my pronouncement, and more than a few colorful slurs are thrown my way, but I'm dead serious. I physically edge him back toward the narrow opening in the gate.

"Inside," I growl, pushing him through the opening. Once we're inside, I lock the gate and breathe a sigh of relief. "Well, that was loads of fun."

He laughs. "Don't worry, you'll get used to it."

* * *

As we're heading back inside the house, Jonah stops me on the threshold. "I want to go to the recording studio this evening. I need to work."

The studio's only a ten-minute drive from the house. "Okay. What time?"

"Around eight."

Inside the house, we're met with the very enticing aroma of dinner, accompanied by a lot of exuberant voices. We head to the dining room, which is right off the central hallway, adjacent to the kitchen. In the center of the room is a long mahogany table that seats ten. Dwight is already seated at the head of the table – that figures. Everyone else is in the kitchen, so we head that way.

Esperanza apparently has the band members well trained, because they're all washing their hands at the kitchen sink. Then she hands each one a dish to carry in to the dining room. Ruben digs chilled bottles of beer out of the fridge, as well as a bottle of red wine, and carries the bottles to the table.

After we wash our hands, Esperanza hands Jonah a huge salad bowl. Then she hands me a basket of warm dinner rolls. When Jonah and I step into the dining room, everyone has settled into their seats at the table and begun passing the platters of food around. This reminds me of when I was a kid living at home. With a family of nine, meal time was always a group event. My mom made sure of it.

I can't help noticing five curious pairs of eyes on me.

Jonah pulls out a chair and motions for me to sit. "Guys, this is Lia McIntyre. She's my bodyguard."

I get curious stares from the three band members, a scowl from Dwight, and absolutely nothing from Ruben, who completely ignores us as he butters a roll.

I smile as I sit. "Hi, everyone."

"Your bodygyard?" one of the guys says. He's blond, with gorgeous, Caribbean blue eyes and surfer-boy good looks. "Excellent! I was afraid you were going to say she's your date."

"Forget it, Dylan," another guy says. This one has brown hair and brown eyes. He's good looking, in a boy-next-door way. "You don't have a chance with this girl."

Esperanza smiles warmly at me from the doorway. "Welcome to the family, Lia. Please, help yourself. There's always plenty to go around."

I smile back. "Thank you."

"I hope you're hungry," Jonah says. "Esperanza's an incredible cook."

A giant salad bowl makes its way around the table, as well as the platter of pot roast and vegetables. Obviously these guys eat well. There's a happy, low hum around the table as the guys discuss the flight from LA, how long it was, how bad the snacks were, how many drinks Ruben had on the flight. And then there's a loud discussion about the guy who hogged the bathroom for much of the flight.

As we eat, Jonah points everyone out by name, starting with the hot blond. "Dylan is our drummer. Travis plays guitar. And next to him is Zeke, who plays bass guitar." Zeke has midnight black hair and dark eyes. "Ruben's our sound engineer. And last but not least, of course, is Esperanza, who takes good care of us all."

The guys are all in their early twenties, considerably younger than Jonah, who's twenty-eight, and far younger than I would have expected. But with all their tattoos and piercings, they sure look the part of the rocker.

The guys all talk over each other as they stuff their mouths and drink a lot of beer. Esperanza presides over the table, always hovering, always on the ready to jump up and get anything for anyone.

She gets up from the table at least a half-dozen times to run back to the kitchen for something. She's like a dorm mother to them all, which is fitting since the guys remind me of college frat boys, care-free, living the good life, mostly out to have a good time. The only one I can't read well is Ruben. He's far too taciturn and brooding.

Esperanza is clearly the mothering type. She'd changed out of the tailored pantsuit that she wore on the plane into a loose-fitting maxi-dress with a vibrant red-and-black geometric pattern.

After we indulge in a delicious meal, Esperanza brings out the pineapple-upside-down cake, which is still warm, to a very appre-ciative audience. I swear, these guys must eat their bodyweight in food. If they eat like this all the time, it's a wonder they're all in such good shape.

When the meal ends, the guys take off to the media room in the basement to play video games. Dwight remains at the table, settling in with a fresh cup of coffee and a copy of the *Chicago Tribune*, while Jonah and I start carrying the dirty dishes to the sink.

"Oh, you don't have to bother yourselves with that," Esperanza says when we carry in our first load. "I'll take care of the dishes. You two go, have fun."

"It's the least we can do," I say, setting down a stack of dirty plates on the counter near the sink. "Thank you for a delicious meal."

Her face lights up with pleasure, and her dark eyes sparkle. "Thank you, dear."

I get the feeling this woman doesn't hear those words often enough. While she starts rinsing off the plates and loading the dish-washer, Jonah and I make short work of clearing off the dining room table. Dwight's still seated at the end of the table, engrossed in the newspaper he has spread out on the table in front of him. He'd shoved his plate and utensils aside, and his hand is wrapped around his steaming cup of coffee.

"You missed one, Lia," he says, turning the page and smoothing out the paper. He tips his head at his discarded plate and silverware, then peers up at me expectantly. I swear, would it kill him to get off his ass and help?

I think this guy takes way too much pleasure in pushing my buttons. "What's wrong, Dwight? Are you too good to take your own plate to the kitchen?"

He frowns at me, his lips thinning in a compressed line. "You're costing me a fortune, Lia. Make yourself useful."

Oh, he did not just say that. I cross my arms over my chest and glare down at him. "Are you serious?"

Jonah walks into the dining room. "Serious about what? What'd I miss?"

I scowl at Dwight, but bite my lip. I don't need anyone fighting my battles for me. "Nothing. You missed nothing." I pick up Dwight's empty place setting and brush past Jonah to carry it into the kitchen.

I half expect Jonah to follow me, but he doesn't. Curious, I glance through the open door into the dining room and see Jonah having a quiet word with Dwight. I can't hear what he's saying, but Dwight's face is flushed, and he's glaring defensively up at Jonah. When Jonah catches me watching them, he smiles, then claps Dwight on the back in a friendly good-old-boy gesture. Dwight doesn't seem to appreciate the overture and he shrugs away from Jonah, his jaws tight.

Esperanza comes up behind me and lays a hand on my shoulder. "Don't take it personally, Lia. Dwight's an ass to everyone."

I snort with laughter. "I can't help it. He rubs me the wrong way."

"He rubs everyone the wrong way."

Jonah joins us in the kitchen, an innocent smile on his face. "If you're free, Lia, let's head to the studio. I just need to run upstairs and grab a guitar."

I nod, only too happy to put some distance between myself and Dwight. "Sounds like a plan."

11

The ride to the recording studio is uneventful, once we make it past the gate. Thank goodness for the security guys manning the property. Otherwise, we'd never be able to get through the gate without running over a few fans, and that would be bad.

"So, how long have you all known each other?" I ask Jonah. "You and the rest of the band?"

Jonah fiddles with the radio, checking out the local stations. "The record label hired the guys about two years ago, when they signed me. They're young, but they're good guys, all of them. We have a good time together, and they're excellent musicians."

"Tell me about Makayla. Is she someone I need to worry about?"

"I hope not. She's back in LA. She's the reason I wanted to get out of there. Her behavior had become increasingly inappropriate. And I caught her leaking personal information about me to the tabloids."

"Define *inappropriate*."

"I found her naked in my bed a few times after we broke up. The guys and I share a house back in LA, and she'd sweet talk them into letting her in. I got tired of kicking her out of my bed. She just wouldn't take no for an answer."

"She didn't handle your break-up well?"

Jonah chuckles. "She claims we're just *taking a break*. She's in total denial."

We park in the rear lot behind the recording studio and walk to the door at the back of the building. Jonah presses a doorbell to alert the security guard to our arrival.

"At least there's some security," I murmur, looking around the empty parking lot.

The door opens and a white-haired man pokes his head out and smiles. "Good evenin', Mr. Locke."

"Hi, Bob," Jonah says as we step inside.

The building is quiet and most of the lights are out. There are four recording studios in the facility, one of which Jonah has rented for the duration of his stay in Chicago. It looks like the place is empty right now, except for Bob.

The four recording studios branch off a central hallway, two studios on the left and two on the right. We walk down the dimly-lit corridor to the second studio on the right, and Jonah punches a code into an electric keypad to open the door. The door opens into a small vestibule, and through that doorway we enter the main control room. One wall is filled with an electronic control panel with what looks to be hundreds of little switches and slider bars. Over the control panel is a large picture window that overlooks the sound booth.

Jonah flips on the overhead lights and the place lights up, revealing a rather outdated space. The floor is covered in an olive green carpet that surely dates back to the '70s. There's a well-worn brown leather sofa, a pair of upholstered arm chairs and a large wooden coffee table with names carved into the top. The place smells old and musty, tinged with the odor of old cigarette smoke.

"Ugh! You couldn't find anywhere better than this dive?" I say.

He chuckles. "I know, it's rough. But the acoustics are great. Make yourself at home. There's a small kitchenette with a vending machine and a restroom through that door there. I'll be in the sound booth, here." Jonah points through the window at a padded room with several mic stands, stools, and sheet music racks.

I take a seat in a large, overstuffed black leather chair at the recording console. While Jonah gets comfortable in the sound booth, I check out the control panel, which is a confusing mess of electronic switches. But the boards are not on, so apparently he's not planning to actually record anything this evening.

After dimming the lights in the recording room, I return to my chair and get comfortable. I have a feeling we'll be here for a while. Jonah sits on the other side of the viewing pane on a tall wooden stool in a pool of warm light shining down from an overhead spotlight. He pulls a music stand close, which holds a pad of paper and a pen. He props his guitar against his thigh.

I figure I have the best seat in the house because I have a direct view of him. Since the control room is dark, and he can't really see me through the glass, I'm free to look my fill. He's not hard to look at. In fact, I can't help staring. Watching him sitting there on that stool, tuning his guitar, does things to me. I feel warm suddenly, as my body responds to him. I feel an unfamiliar ache down low in my belly.

The microphone must be open, because I can hear him plucking the individual strings on his guitar as he tunes them by ear. Then he strums a few chords, testing his work. Apparently, he's satisfied with the results, because he starts playing a familiar song.

It's one of my favorites of theirs, one of their slower songs. It's almost a ballad, but it still has enough rough edge on it to avoid being sappy or sweet. It's an earthy song about a man in love, a man in pain because the woman he wants doesn't return his affections. The song sounds so different with just Jonah on the acoustic guitar. Without the drums and the bass, and his band members singing back up, it's almost a different song altogether... more intimate, more sensual.

I love watching the expressions on his face as he sings. My gaze zeroes in on his mouth, and I watch his lips form the words. I watch his arms as he plays the guitar, as those sinewy muscles and tattoos bunch and flex. A shiver courses through me, and I mentally shake myself.

He runs through a few more numbers, all of which I recognize because they're all sitting on the music charts right now, in the top twenty. Eventually, he starts tinkering around on his guitar, trying out different chords and different notes. I can hear him trying to tease a melody out of a variety of notes, and I realize he's writing something new. Occasionally he stops to make a notation on the pad of paper propped up on the music stand at his side. He's alone in there, with just his guitar and a pad of paper, and he seems quite content. Cooper was right. Jonah doesn't seem to fit the mold of a rock star, whatever that mold is supposed to be. He seems more like a loner. Like me.

I'm perfectly content to sit in my swivel chair, with my feet propped up on the control panel, and listen to the music coming through the speakers. Jonah seems lost in his own world, and he pays me no attention, which is fine. Having some quiet time to spend alone with my thoughts is a good thing. The melody he's working on starts to come together, and I begin to recognize pieces and parts of it as he repeats them in different combinations. It's a ballad with a poignant, simple melody. I'm curious to find out what the lyrics will be.

My musings are interrupted by the sound of muffled voices in the hallway outside our door. I can make out two voices – a male and a female – in heated discussion. The male voice is that of the elderly security guard, Bob. The voices grow louder, and the woman starts to get shrill.

"Jonah! Jonah, where are you? I know you're here, damn it! Open the door, right this minute!"

Since the sound booth is soundproofed, Jonah's oblivious to the woman's outburst in the hallway. But I can certainly hear her. I have a sinking suspicion that whoever she is, her presence can't be good news.

I can hear someone working their way down the hallway, systematically knocking on doors. Whoever she is, she sounds determined.

"Jonah! I know you're in here somewhere! Open up!"

I consider simply ignoring her, hoping she'll go away. I really don't want to deal with any drama – and this woman is definitely drama.

Finally, she pounds on the door to Jonah's studio. "Jonah, open the door! I'm not leaving until you talk to me."

I reach down to my ankle holster and pull out my handgun and tuck it into the back waistband of my jeans.

When I rise from my chair, Jonah's head snaps up and he looks at me. I shrug at him and point toward the door. When I open it, I come face to face with someone I never thought I'd see in person. Makayla Hendricks. Shit! What's she doing here in Chicago? She's supposed to be back in LA.

Behind her, Bob bounces on the balls of his feet, completely flustered. "I'm sorry, miss," he says, peering at me from behind Makayla. "I tried to stop her, but she just wouldn't listen."

Behind Bob is a young woman with long black hair, straight as a stick, and a huge bruiser of a bald muscle guy – apparently Makayla's own bodyguard.

My gaze returns to Makayla Hendricks. She's gorgeous, I have to give her that. Her long, sleek brown hair which normally hangs down to the middle of her back, is up in a high ponytail that looks like it's sprouting right out of the top of her head. Her complexion is the color of cafe au lait, soft and smooth, and her dark eyes are lined with kohl. She's beautiful, exotic, and apparently spoiled rotten – according to the tabloids. She's dressed in a glittery halter top, a black leather mini skirt with black fishnet hose, and black knee-high boots with wickedly pointed heels. Around her slim neck is a stunning diamond choker that surely costs more than most people make in a year.

I look past her at the security guard. "It's okay, Bob. I'll handle this."

Makayla's eyes narrow as she glares down at me. With her spiky, fuck-me heels, she's at least five-ten. "Who the hell are you?" she says, propping her hands on her half-naked hips as she stares down her nose at me.

I smile, enjoying this way too much. "Who the hell are *you*?"

She frowns. "Don't get smart with me. Answer the question. Where's Jonah? I know he's here." She peers over me into the studio. "Jonah!"

"How do you know he's here?"

Her dark eyes narrow. "That's none of your business. Where is he?"

Jonah reaches over my shoulder from behind and opens the door wider. "Makayla, what are you doing here?"

Makayla breaks into a beatific smile at his appearance. "Hi, baby!"

"Why are you in Chicago? You shouldn't be here. We talked about this."

Her smile transforms into a sex-kitten pout, her glossy lips plump and poised for attention. "Don't be silly, baby. Of course I'm supposed to be here. Dwight arranged everything. He *invited* me. You and I are going to perform our duet at the show Friday night. We're going to do *our song*."

I look back at Jonah. "What show? No one said anything about a show."

Jonah exhales a rough breath. "It's news to me, too," he says, clenching his jaw.

"Don't be silly, baby," Makayla says as she pushes past me and wraps her bare arms around Jonah's neck. "The two of us, together on stage again... it'll be perfect. The fans will go nuts. We'll be Jakayla again, just like before." She leans forward and plants a wet one on him before he can react.

I can't help chuckling. "*Jakayla?* Seriously? You mean like *Brangelina* or *Bennifer?*"

Jonah pulls back from her and glares at me, clearly not amused. "Shouldn't you be doing something about this?" he says to me.

I smirk at him. The woman's clearly not armed – I can practically see every fucking inch of her barely-clad, svelte body – so she's no physical threat to Jonah. I suppose I could intervene on his behalf, put some distance between them, but watching him squirm is far more entertaining. "You act like this is my fault."

She moves toward him again, in hug mode.

"A little help here, Lia," he mutters.

I smile and bat my eyes at him. "I don't know. I think you're handling her just fine... *baby.*"

Makayla frowns at me. "Jonah, who is this bitch? I don't like her." She studies me for a moment, cocking her head, her expression pensive. "Do I know you? You look familiar."

My heart skips a beat, and for a moment I can't fucking think straight. Recognition is my biggest fear – that someone will recognize me from the damned video, even six years later. The thought that Makayla might put two and two together makes me ill.

Jonah lays his hand on my shoulder. "Lia's my bodyguard. Watch how you talk to her."

Makayla's eyes widen. "*She's* a bodyguard? Are you kidding me? She's just a child." She raises her hand imperiously. "Seriously, Jonah, I don't like her. Get rid of her."

"Makayla, you need to leave." Jonah walks the pop diva back to the doorway, where Bob and her entourage hover anxiously. "Bob, Makayla was just leaving. Would you see that she and her companions find their way to the nearest exit? Thanks."

"Jonah, we need to talk, baby," she says, as Jonah carefully, yet firmly, pushes her through the door.

"No, we don't. We've done all the talking we're going to do. You need to leave."

"You have to talk to me, silly," she pouts. "We need to rehearse. We're performing Friday night at some stupid club downtown – it's some surprise thing Dwight set up."

"Apparently, this little plan slipped Dwight's mind, because he's not mentioned it to me or the guys."

"Well, it's on," she continues, "and it's being advertised all over social media as we speak, so you can't back out now."

As he shuts the door in Makayla's face, Jonah makes a noise that sounds awfully like a growl.

"Well, that was fun," I say. "You're just full of surprises."

He looks down at me, far from amused. "Let's go. I need to talk to Dwight."

12

We lock up and head out. The hallway is quiet once more, and there's no sign of Makayla Hendricks and her people. On our way out the rear door, Bob apologizes once more for letting her in the building.

"It's okay, Bob," Jonah says, patting the man on the back. "I know how persuasive she can be."

On the way back to the house, Jonah's pensive.

"Did I mention that was fun?" I say, hoping to pull him out of his reverie. But Jonah's lost in his own thoughts. "You know, all levity aside – and trust me, that was the most entertainment I've had in a long time – the security at the studio sucks. No offense to Bob, but he should never have let her in. I'll have to tell Shane. He'll either have to augment their security while you're there, or you'll have to find new studio space."

Jonah nods. "The less I have to deal with her histrionics, the better."

* * *

It's late when we get back to the house, and Dwight's in bed for the night. So are Esperanza and Ruben. We find the rest of the band members in the lower level, playing video games in the media room. It's a sweet set-up down here, with a huge, flat panel TV that takes up half the wall, Surround Sound speakers, and comfy leather sofas. It's a gamer's playground. The guys are playing a first-person shooter game, and the sound of gun fire and explosions is deafening. It's a good thing this place has really good soundproofing.

The guys plead with Jonah to join them, but he begs off, telling them he wants to finish working on some ideas for a new song. They challenge me to join them, but I beg off too. I've got work to do this evening if there's really going to be a performance Friday night. That won't give us much time to plan the security.

Jonah and I head back upstairs, and Jonah walks me to my bedroom door.

He reaches out and absently tucks a strand of my hair behind my ear. "It's late. You should go to bed. I'll see you in the morning."

He's standing a little too close for comfort, and I find myself reacting to the scent of his skin and a faint whiff of his cologne. It's an intoxicating mix. I reach behind me for the doorknob to my bedroom. "Yeah, see ya in the morning."

"Thanks for today, Lia."

"For what? I was just doing my job."

The corner of his mouth twitches, and I swear he's suppressing a smile. "Well, it didn't suck for me to spend a few hours with you, so thanks for that."

"I never suck, Jonah." I was just trying to be funny, but the joke backfires on me as a wave of heat rushes through me and I feel my cheeks turn pink.

His eyebrows lift in amusement. "Never?"

I chuckle. "Go to bed, Jonah."

"Goodnight, Lia."

I watch him as he heads upstairs, thinking of him all alone up there in his private retreat. I get the feeling he's a bit of a loner. He's nothing like what I expected of a rock star. He doesn't appear to be chasing the spotlight. On the contrary, he tries to keep a low profile.

After grabbing a quick shower to cool off my overheated body, I put on a pair of comfy knit shorts and a T-shirt, then sit down at the surveillance console and review some of the day's footage. Nothing unusual shows up.

After a quick trip to the bathroom to brush my teeth, I climb into bed and listen to music for a while, hoping it will help me relax. My pulse is still racing – it has been ever since Makayla asked me if she knew me.

Millions of people saw that damn video before Shane managed to get it pulled off the Internet – which took some serious doing. It took a court order and an entire cyber forensics team to hunt down every copy they could find. Of course they didn't get them all, and occasionally the video resurfaces on some obscure video file server. But Shane's IT folks diligently watch for the video to reappear, and when they find it, they delete it. The thought of Makayla, or Jonah, or any of these guys seeing that video makes me sick.

I lay here listening to my favorite playlist, my heart still racing. After an hour of this, I accept that I'm not going to be able to sleep. The fucking video is playing in my head now, caught in an endless loop, and it makes me want to gouge my eyes out. I keep seeing the image of myself on top of Logan, rocking on him, looking awkward and so damn unsure of myself. Hell, I was just sixteen years old – far too young to be doing what I was doing. I had long hair back then, and it's up in a ponytail, bobbing along with me as I move on him. His big hands grasp my hips, squeezing them as he holds me in place. His hips rock as he thrusts up into me. I was so out of my league with him, trying to act cool and pretend I wasn't scared shitless and hurting.

I was just a sophomore, and he was a senior. He was the golden boy who could do no wrong. He played every sport known to man, and he played them all well. He was the football team's starting quarterback, the starting pitcher on the baseball team. He played basketball and soccer. Everyone liked him – the teachers, the students, the parents. And I was a nobody.

That night, when I glanced down and saw a smear of bright red blood on his abdomen, *my blood*, I panicked and tried to get off of him. But he rolled us so that he was on top and finished himself off, slamming into me with the force of a jackhammer as his bruising hands held my legs wide open. He ignored my tears and my pleas for

him to stop. And while the physical pain was bad enough, the sense
of betrayal hurt even more.

I thought it was just my imagination when the other kids started
staring at me, whispering behind my back. Some of them blushed,
some of them snickered. It wasn't until a girl cornered me in the
bathroom during lunch and told me about the video that reality
began to sink in. At first I didn't believe her, but by the end of the
day, I knew she was telling the truth. All the looks and snide comments and innuendos made it impossible for me to remain in denial.

The final straw was when the principal called me into his office to
read me the riot act. Me! He lectured me for an hour on personal ac-
countability and personal conduct. He never once said a critical word
about Logan. I was sent home in tears, feeling sick, and my mother
had to pry the story out of me. She'd called Shane immediately.

God, I want a drink. I want to drown out all the noise, the sick
fear of discovery that I feel even now, years later. I'm not that naive
little kid anymore. I'm not! And yet I still can't seem to escape the
sick sense of dread, the hopelessness, the sense of violation. I need
to dull the pain. I need to shut it down.

There's alcohol in the house – there's a bar in the library stocked
with dozens of unopened bottles of top shelf goods – and I'm so
tempted to help myself. But I know that way lies disaster. I've turned
to alcohol too many times to dull the noise in my head, and each
time it gets easier and easier to drink my way to oblivion. I saw first-
hand what abusing alcohol did to my brother Jake a few years ago,
and I don't want to go there.

It's two o'clock in the morning now, and Jake's probably asleep, but I pick up my phone and call him anyway. He made me promise I'd call him if I ever felt myself wanting to slide down that slippery slope.

Jake answers on the second ring, his rough voice sharp and alert. "Lia? What's wrong?"

Of all my brothers, Jake is the hard ass, the tough guy. I guess pain and loss and betrayal have made him that way. For a long time, he lost himself in alcohol, trying to self medicate and almost got himself killed in the process. But somehow, he made it through. If he can do it, so can I.

"I want a drink." I huff out a breath. "I *need* a drink."

He sighs heavily. "What happened?"

I shrug helplessly, but of course he can't see that over the phone.

His voice is low and comforting. "Lia, talk to me, honey. Tell me what happened."

"I thought someone might have recognized me tonight. She's an ex-girlfriend of Jonah Locke's. She asked me if we'd met before."

He's silent for a moment. "Do you think she put it together?"

"I don't know. She said I looked familiar."

"That doesn't mean she connected you to the video. Don't worry."

"I know. It's just – I don't want Jonah knowing. If she makes me, she'll tell him. She's already made it perfectly clear that she doesn't like me."

"Shane says he's a nice guy. I wouldn't worry."

"Jonah? Yeah, he is. I just don't want him to know."

"So, what are you going to do in lieu of drinking? Because you're not going to do that, *right*?"

I laugh. "Right. There's a workout room downstairs. I guess I could spend some quality time with a punching bag."

I remember watching Jake pummel a punching bag time after time until his knuckles were shredded.

"Good choice," he says. "Call me back if you need me. I'm always here for you, you know that, right?"

"Yeah. Thanks, Jake."

ᥱᏅ 13

T he fitness room in this place is nicely outfitted. Besides the spacious bathroom, there's every piece of workout equipment known to man in here, including a regulation punching bag hanging from a reinforced steel beam in the ceiling.

I put on hand wraps, but forego the gloves. Gloves are for pussies. Jake hits the bag without gloves, so can I.

I slam my left fist into the bag, which has hardly any give to it at all, and pain shoots up my arm to my brain, setting off fireworks. Good. I superimpose Logan's face on the bag and start delivering calculated blow after blow. I immediately slip into a familiar rhythm, with a jab, right hook, then four undercuts in rapid succession. As I beat the bag, I focus on the strain of my muscles and the pain in my knuckles, the feel and the sound of my breathing as my lungs suck in air. I alternate between hitting the bag and kicking, letting my mind go and giving myself over to the sheer joy of grueling physical exertion. The harder I hit the bag, the worse the pain in my hands and shoulders, the quieter my head, the better I feel.

I lose all track of time as I pummel the bag, my fists flying in a comforting routine. Sweat runs down my forehead, burning my eyes, and I brush it away with the back of my arm. My fists are slipping on the bag now, and I realize it's because my hand wraps are smeared with fresh blood. So is the bag. The thick, viscous fluid trickles down the bag and drips onto the floor. My knuckles are bathed in blood, the red strikingly bright against the white wraps, and I revel in it.

I learned years ago that external pain masks internal pain. I know some people cut themselves for the external pain, for the distraction, but I can't do that. My brothers would see the cut marks, and they'd kill me. But I can beat the bag senseless – batter my fists ragged – and no one will question my motives. They'll just chide me for overdoing it.

I beat the bag repeatedly in a finely choreographed dance of jabs and crosses, my numb fists flying as fast as humanly possible, connecting with the heavy bag with as much force as I can muster. My arm muscles are screaming in agony now, starved of oxygen. My lungs burn as they strive to draw in more oxygen. But my muscles are burning up the oxygen faster than my lungs can replace it. The more searing the pain, the better. Pain radiates up my arms, swamping my brain with warning signals.

Strong arms snake around me, long arms with taut, golden skin stretched tightly over sinewy muscles and decorated with intricately designed black tattoos. Long fingers encircle my wrists, surprisingly gentle as they slow my blows.

"Lia, stop."

His voice is low, his breath ruffling the hair near my ear. I know who it is without looking. Not only do I recognize the low, resonate timbre of his voice, but I can smell him – his cologne, the warmth of his body heat, his skin. My gut clenches in recognition, and I exhale on a harsh breath, knowing I've accomplished nothing now in trying to still my mind. He's ruined it all.

"Let go!" I try to pull away from his hold, but his fingers are like manacles locked around my wrists and I can't easily shake him off – not without hurting him.

Wrapping his arms around me, he forces my arms to cross over my chest. Then he leans in closer from behind, his head dipping down so that his mouth brushes against my left ear. "Jesus, Lia. You're bleeding."

I glance down at his big hands, which are now smeared with my blood. "Mind your own business, Jonah!" I hiss, trying half-heartedly to pull free. "Let go!"

"No."

His voice sends shivers down my spine. My knees go weak, and I just want to melt into his arms. And that pisses me off even more, because I don't want his help. I sure as hell don't want to feel what I'm feeling right now – a mixture of anger, embarrassment, and... arousal. I'm tempted to toss him across the fucking room just on principle, but Shane would be furious if I hurt him. And the truth is, I don't want to hurt him.

Jonah turns me in his arms, stepping back to get a good look at the damage. He holds my hands in his, studying the shredded wraps and my torn, bloody knuckles. "Why aren't you wearing gloves?"

I ignore his question. "What are you doing here?"

"Probably the same thing you're doing. I couldn't sleep. I thought I'd come down and work out a bit."

I can't help wondering if the unexpected appearance this evening of Makayla Hendricks has anything to do with his inability to sleep tonight. Maybe he's not as immune to her plentiful charms as he claims he is.

He circles one of my wrists with this long fingers and pulls me with him. "Come with me."

Curious, I follow as Jonah leads me into the bathroom. After flipping on the light switch, he lifts me up onto the cool granite countertop, then turns on the water to let it warm up while he grabs a couple of hand towels and the first-aid kit from the cabinet beneath the sink.

"Here, let me," he says, gingerly unwrapping the bandages from my hands. He tosses the bloody wraps into a waste basket.

He rinses the blood from my hands, then pats my knuckles dry with a pad of sterile gauze. "Jesus, Lia."

I'm struck by the pained expression on his face, and my chest tightens. "It's nothing. I've had worse." I know I sound defiant, but I can't help it.

He lifts his gaze to meet mine. "It's not *nothing*."

After dabbing antibiotic ointment on the cuts and abrasions, he carefully wraps the knuckles of both my hands in clean gauze.

While he's busy doctoring my hands, I stare at his deft fingers. These are the fingers of a musician, I remind myself. And yet I can't help noticing the multitude of scars and nicks on his own knuckles. He certainly didn't get those scars from playing a guitar.

I glance up at him. "Looks like I'm not the only one who didn't always wear gloves."

He smiles ruefully. "Let's just say I've been in my fair share of fights."

His voice is low, rough, almost hypnotic. His hands come up to cradle my face, and he peers down at me. His hands feel good against my hot face, and I lean into his touch despite my intention to keep my distance. Neither one of us needs this kind of complication.

"Jonah – "

"You are such a fierce little thing," he says, brushing my hair back.

His hot gaze drops to my lips, and he swallows hard. Oh, my god, he's staring at my mouth. The realization is both shocking and tantalizing, and something flutters low in my belly, like tiny little butterflies awakening from a deep slumber. Startled by my reaction to him, I knock his hands away. "Don't patronize me, Jonah."

"I'm not. I've never met anyone as fearless as you. I'm in awe of you." His thumb brushes across my lower lip, sending a pang of unwelcome need coursing through me. His eyes darken with something that looks an awful lot like desire, and he leans toward me, his gaze still on my mouth.

I push him back and hop down from the countertop. I can't do this with him. When I reach the door, I glance back. "Do us both a favor, Jonah. Save it for the girls lined up outside. They may fall all over you, but I'm not going to. You're nothing more than a job to me, and it's going to stay that way."

* * *

Damn it, I still can't sleep. Although this time it's for a completely different reason. I'm back in my bed and now, thanks to Jonah, my body is a raging mess of hormone overload. The moment I realized he looked like he was about to kiss me, I couldn't get out of there fast enough. The problem is, I wanted him to kiss me. I wanted to lick and suck and drink him in. I wanted to taste him. And now my body's punishing me for sending it mixed signals. My traitorous body is hot and flushed and throbbing, and I'm squirming like a worm on a hook. *Stupid celebrity asshole.*

For a split second, I tease myself with what might have been. I can't help wondering what it would be like to kiss him. When I first saw him in Shane's office, I thought yeah, I'd tap that. But I never dreamed then that I'd be assigned as his bodyguard. Now that we're essentially in each other's back pocket, my words are coming back to haunt me.

I strip off my panties and shorts and slip my hand between my legs, to that lush warm place that's demanding some attention tonight. The only way I'll get any sleep now is if I get myself off and then crash in the lonely, post-orgasmic glow.

E arly the next morning, I head to the kitchen in search of
coffee, where I find Esperanza already hard at work.

She greets me with a smile. "Good morning, Lia. There's
coffee and a hot breakfast on the buffet in the dining room. Help
yourself, dear."

I could definitely get used to living like this. "Thank you."

As I walk into the dining room, my good mood is spoiled by the
sight of Dwight seated at the far end of the big table, engrossed in a
newspaper. After I fill a plate with food, I take a seat at the opposite
end of the table. "So, Dwight, what's this about a performance Friday night?"

He looks up from his paper. "Since when do I have to inform you
of my every decision?"

I snort with laughter. "Since you hired McIntyre Security to provide security for Jonah. A concert is a pretty big deal, *pal*."

"Don't call me that."

I honestly have to wonder why Shane assigned me to Jonah in the first place. Surely he knew that Dwight and I could never get along. Dwight is a pompous ass, and I don't take shit from anyone. I'm baffled, but I know Shane doesn't do anything without a good reason.

"Isn't it kind of obvious?" *Pal*. "We'll need to secure a suitable venue, and we'll need to schedule extra security that night. Don't you think you should have let us in on this? Does Shane even know?"

He shrugs. "It's only been in the works a few days. I wasn't even sure if Makayla would agree to do it."

"Oh, she's agreed all right."

"How do you know that?"

"Because she told me last night. She waylaid Jonah at the recording studio. You told her where to find him, didn't you?"

At that moment, Jonah walks into the dining room looking a bit hung over. His jeans hang low on his hips and his plain white tee is wrinkled. He looks like he just rolled out of bed.

"Yeah, Dwight," Jonah says. "What's Makayla doing here? We talked about this. The reason I came out here was to get away from her, and you invited her out here?"

Dwight sets down his paper and picks up his cup of coffee, cradling it in both hands. "It'll be a media sensation, Jonah, so don't worry. Locke performs an impromptu concert here in the city, and Makayla strolls out on stage – a total surprise – and you two sing your hit duet together. The public wants you two back together.

This surprise performance will take social media by storm... it'll be an instant viral hit. You've got contract negotiations coming up next week, Jonah. The buzz from this event will give you greater leverage in negotiations. It's a win-win."

Jonah pours himself a cup of coffee. "Stop encouraging Makayla, Dwight. I'm trying to make a clean break of it with her, and you're not helping."

"You dating Makayla was the best thing that's ever happened to you or this band."

"That's debatable."

"The publicity alone keeps you at the top of the media feeding frenzy."

"But I don't want to be at the top of the media feeding frenzy!" Jonah says. "That's the whole point!"

Dwight picks up his fork and stabs his eggs. "Don't be ridiculous, Jonah. Stars don't just happen – they're made. And I'm making you a star – that's my job. This concert is going to happen. End of story."

I'd really love to smack Dwight upside the head. "I repeat, does Shane know about this?"

Dwight shrugs and resumes eating his breakfast. "I can't remember if I told him or not."

"Where is this supposed event taking place?"

Dwight shrugs. "I'm sure we can find a venue. It doesn't have to be anything fancy – we just need an adequate stage and an audience, decent lighting, and a good sound system. It's just for the PR. And I've arranged for a video crew to be there. I want to make a music video out of it."

I get up to pour myself a second cup of coffee, hoping caffeine will get me through the morning. As I graby my plate and walk out of the room to go call Shane, I ponder the fact that Jonah didn't say a single word to me. Hell, he didn't even look at me. I guess I got my message across last night.

I know I should be grateful, so why do I feel like a total ass instead?

* * *

Shane answers on the second ring. "Lia. What's up?"

"Did douchebag tell you he's planning a performance Friday night?"

"What? No, Dwight hasn't said anything about a performance."

I have to grin at the tinge of annoyance in Shane's voice. Apparently I'm not the only one who finds Dwight Peterson a pain in the ass.

"*This* Friday?" he says, trying not to sound incredulous. "That doesn't give us much time."

"No, it doesn't."

"All right. I'll meet with Dwight this morning, and we'll figure something out. We'll have to keep it relatively small and tightly contained, because we don't need a fan mob on our hands. Rowdy's will work. They can seat two hundred. I'll arrange to rent the bar for the night. Thanks for the heads up."

* * *

I head back to the dining room to give Jonah an update, but both he and Dwight are gone. Esperanza's still in the kitchen, though, peeling a small mountain of Granny Smith apples.

"Hello, Lia," she says, when I hop up on the counter to watch her work. "Did you get enough for breakfast?"

She peels apples with surgical precision, wasting not one bit of the white flesh. "Yes, thank you. It was delicious. What are you making?"

"An apple pie. Jonah loves apple pie." She smiles, her dark eyes crinkling at the corners. She has a multitude of tiny crow's feet framing her eyes, and her face is softly lined with age. In a lot of ways, she reminds me of my mom.

I watch her work, her fingers nimble as she rolls out dough and forms a pie shell. She prepares the apple filling, then she braids strips of dough to make a decorative, latticed top for the pie. I'm impressed – no easy shortcuts for Esperanza.

"You take good care of him, don't you?" I say, as she puts the pie in the oven. We both know who I'm talking about.

"He's a good man. And he's easy to care for."

"Where is Jonah, by the way?"

"I believe he took his breakfast and coffee upstairs with him."

Jonah's an introvert, like me. No wonder he and Makayla are ill-suited for each other. I also can't help wondering if he's avoiding me now, after our interlude in the fitness room last night.

There's a knock at the rear door and one of the security guards opens the door and pokes his head inside. "Mr. McIntyre just arrived."

Shane's here. Awesome. I can't wait to watch him manage Peterson. I head out the back door just as Shane gets out of his vintage silver Jaguar. He's looking all bad ass in his dark suit and tie and a pair of dark sunglasses.

I meet him halfway across the drive, and he gives me a fist bump. "Hey," I say.

He slips his phone inside his suit jacket pocket, then slips his arm across my shoulders and pulls me to him. "How's it going?"

"Fine."

"Things going all right with you and Jonah?"

His question surprises me. "Sure."

"So, what's this about a performance?"

"Dwight invited Jonah's crazy ex-girlfriend to come out here from LA so she can perform with Jonah Friday night. It's a PR stunt, and Jonah's not happy about it. He's avoiding his ex."

Shane frowns. "The reason Jonah left LA in the first place was to get away from Makayla Hendricks, and now she's here?"

"Yeah. She showed up at the recording studio last night demanding to see him."

We head inside, and Shane removes his sunglasses as he greets Esperanza. "Ms. Lopez," he says, shaking her hand. "Shane McIntyre. It's a pleasure to meet you, ma'am."

She smiles. "Mr. McIntyre, welcome."

"Call me Shane, please. I'm here to see Dwight. Is he around?"

She points toward the central hallway. "Check the library, left down the hall. He's using it for his office."

I follow Shane to the library, not wanting to miss this. Dwight is seated in a high-back leather chair behind a large mahogany desk, tapping away on his laptop.

Shane pauses inside the open doorway. "Dwight."

Dwight glances up from his computer. "Oh, Shane, good. You're just the person I need to see."

Shane walks into the room. "What's this about a performance Friday night?"

"I'm throwing together an impromptu performance for the band. It'll be a small event, but we need somewhere nice."

Shane takes a seat in one of the chairs in front of the desk, motioning for me to take the other. "It would've been nice if you'd given us more warning about this event. We need time to make the preparations."

Dwight shrugs. "As I said, it's a small event. I'm sure your people can manage it."

"I'll handle all the arrangements," Shane says. "I'll rent a venue for the night, and I'll handle the security arrangements. I'll also provide the guests. The bar seats two hundred. We'll fill it with my employees and some of Beth's to eliminate risk."

"Fine." Dwight waves his hand dismissively. "As long as the place is full, I don't care who attends. I just want a good photo op and some good video footage of Jonah with Makayla Hendricks. I'll invite the big social media outlets and some popular YouTubers."

Shane frowns. "Dwight, Jonah came to Chicago to get away from Makayla and the media."

"That's too bad. Media coverage is part of the deal. He doesn't have a say in the matter. And as for Makayla, she's publicity gold. Jonah needs this."

I've heard enough. Listening to Dwight plan Jonah's life with a complete disregard for the guy's feelings is sending my blood pressure through the roof. I stand in protest. "Sounds to me like what Jonah really needs is a new manager."

Dwight's jaw snaps shut and his face flushes a deep red. "Maybe what he needs is new security."

"What I need is for people to stop talking behind my back."

We all turn to see Jonah standing in the open doorway, his hands on his hips. "What the hell is going on?" he says, coming into the room. He nods at Shane. "Hey, thanks for coming."

"No problem," Shane says.

Jonah turns his gaze on Dwight. "You should never have invited Makayla to Chicago."

"It's not up to you, Jonah. As your manager – "

I butt in, eyeing Jonah. "You need a new manager."

"Shut up, Lia," Dwight says, practically growling. Then he turns back to Jonah. "Need I remind you that you have contract negotiations coming up next week? Your first contract was crap, because you were an unknown then. Now you're a household name. We need to capitalize on that fact to get you the best terms. You need to be at the top of the heap. That means owning social media, trending, viral, the whole nine yards. The livelihood and welfare of everyone in your organization depends on the contract you can negotiate."

There's a knock on the open door, and we all turn to see one of the security staff standing behind Jonah.

"What is it?" Dwight snaps.

"Makayla Hendricks is outside the gates, asking to come in."

"Well, let her in!" Dwight says. "Don't keep her waiting."

"For fuck's sake," Jonah says, glaring at Dwight. He turns and stalks out of the room. "You deal with her, Dwight. I'm not here."

I run after Jonah. "Jonah, wait!"

He pauses, but doesn't turn around to look at me. "What is it, Lia?"

I come around him to face him. His expression is tight and he's radiating tension.

"Why do you let that douchebag call the shots? In case you haven't noticed, the band is called Locke. As in Jonah Locke. You are the band. You don't have to let him make all the decisions, especially when they're counter to your own needs."

"He's right. There are a lot of people on my payroll. I can't just leave things to chance. People depend on me. The guys, Esperanza, Ruben, the stage and road crews. Even Dwight."

"Look, Makayla's going to be here in about three minutes."

He shakes his head. "I need to get out of here. I need some fresh air, and I don't want to deal with her drama right now."

"Then let's go." I grab his hand and lead him down the hall to my room. We slip inside and I close the door. After grabbing my keys and wallet, I crack open the door and wait until Makayla and her little entourage walk past my room, escorted by one of the security staff. Once they pass, Jonah and I sneak out through the kitchen and take off in my Jeep.

Getting through the gate and past the growing crowd out front takes some doing, but before long, we're on the road.

"Where to?" I ask him.

"I don't know. I'd say the studio, but she knows where that is now.

She'll probably come there looking for me. So, I don't know. This is your town. Where do you suggest? I just want somewhere quiet, no crowds, no photographers. Just fresh air and sunshine."

"I know just the place."

15

"Where are we?" Jonah asks, when I exit the highway and turn onto a paved two-lane drive that meanders through the woods.

"This is Shane's place. Well, one of them. No one will bother you here, I guarantee it."

We drive a half-mile through the woods before coming to a tall wrought-iron gate. I stop the Jeep and open my window. "It's me. Lia. Open up."

The gate promptly opens, and I drive through. We approach a second gate a few minutes later, and it opens for us automatically.

"Jesus, this place is like Fort Knox," Jonah says.

The lane continues on for another half mile, as we pass a huge pond on the left and pastures on the right where half a dozen horses graze. Turning a bend in the road, we come into view of the house. It's an impressive sight, I must say. It's huge, with over a dozen suites. Shane fashioned it after a ski lodge our family visited once years ago in Aspen, Colorado.

"Whoa," Jonah says. "This is Shane's house?"

I chuckle. "Beth calls it a hotel."

I park in front of the main entrance, and we walk inside the two-story foyer, which is well lit with large picture windows and sky lights. I lead him down the hallway to the great room at the rear of the house, to show him the view out back. The two-story great room overlooks a wide expanse of lush green lawn, and at the bottom of the slight hill is a private sandy beach and Lake Michigan.

"This is one hell of a view," Jonah says.

From here the docks are visible, too, off to the right, as are the boats.

Jonah looks around the great room, with its soaring stone hearth and a fireplace large enough for a man to walk into. Several comfortable sofas and chairs are arranged in conversational groupings. There's a full bar on one side of the room, and through an open archway is the kitchen.

"Is anyone here?" Jonah asks. "It's so quiet."

"There are about a half dozen people who live here all the time. Ellie runs the house, and her husband, George, manages the estate. There are four security staff members here at all times. Sometimes Shane has clients stay here, whenever extra security is required. He's had all kinds of visiting dignitaries stay here, even the President and visiting royals from the UK and other European countries. My brother Jamie used to live here full time, but he recently moved into an apartment of his own in Wicker Park."

"It's a beautiful place," Jonah says, sounding almost wistful. He turns his gaze toward the beach. "Can we walk down there?"

"Sure. Come on."

The lawn slopes gently downward toward the lake, and before long, the well-trimmed grass transitions into tall grasses lining the beach. We follow a well-worn foot path through the grass down to the beach, where the surf rolls in gently onto the sandy beach. The water here is clear. Off in the distance, there are a few yachts and a large charter boat out on the horizon, cutting through the white-capped waves.

Jonah pulls off his sneakers and socks and folds up the legs of his jeans so he can wade into the waves as they roll onto the beach.

"The water's cold," I warn him. "It's not like the beaches you're used to in California. Lake Michigan never really warms up, not even in the summer."

"I've never even made it to the beaches in LA," he says. "I was always too busy with all the events Dwight scheduled. I was running nonstop. This is the first time in a long time that I've been able to just chill."

"I know it's none of my business, but why do you keep Dwight around? He seems like an ass, and he obviously doesn't listen to you. Why do you put up with him?"

"He's the one who discovered me through some videos I posted on YouTube of myself performing. He pitched me to the record label. I owe him, Lia. And I guess I'm stuck with him."

"That's bullshit. You're the talent, not Dwight. Surely you can insist on a new manager. The guy's a total douchebag."

Jonah chuckles. "That may be true, but he gets results. I've had a song in the top ten every single week for six months now. Dwight knows the industry, and he understands the public well. He's never been wrong."

"But you're not happy, are you?"

Jonah stares out at the horizon. "Happy was never part of the deal."

I shake my head. "It doesn't have to be one or the other, Jonah. You don't have to sacrifice your happiness – or your soul, for that matter – just to be successful in the music business. I'm sure there's another way. There has to be."

He frowns at me. "What do you know about the music business?"

"Nothing. But I'm not stupid. You're incredibly talented. You should be the one calling the shots. Do things your way. Fuck Dwight. Fuck the record label."

"I can't, Lia. I'm under contract."

"A contract that's about to expire, right?"

He nods. "Yes, but we'll negotiate a new one soon."

"Let it expire. You're wickedly talented, Jonah, and you have a ravenous following of devoted fans. Set your own terms and do it your way. Go indie."

Jonah walks down the beach toward the docks where the boats are moored. I follow him at a distance, feeling sorry for the guy. Despite his millions, he's essentially trapped.

We step up onto the boardwalk and head down to the pier, which extends out into the lake. Shane has two speed boats moored here, a couple of small sailboats, and a pontoon. He keeps his big yacht moored at the Chicago Yacht Club, near downtown, where it's better protected from the harsh winter weather.

"My family often hangs out here on the weekends," I tell him, following him to the end of the pier. "We have camp fires and cookouts and take the boats out. It's a lot of fun."

"You're lucky to have such a close family," he says, turning to head back.

* * *

Ellie meets us at the back door when we come inside. Her long silver hair is up in a messy ponytail, and she's wearing dusty riding clothes and boots. She must have just come in from the stables. When she's not tending the house or spoiling us, she's babying her horses.

"Hello, Lia, dear," she says, smiling as reaches out to hug me. "I didn't know you'd be stopping by today or I would have prepared something for you and your guest." She smiles politely at Jonah, and it's obvious she has no idea who he is.

"No problem, Ellie. It's just an impromptu visit. This is Jonah Locke. He's a client. I was just showing him around."

"Welcome, Mr. Locke," she says. "I'm sorry I wasn't here earlier to greet you. Can I get you something to eat or drink? It's nearing lunch time."

"Oh, no, but thank you," he says. "I wouldn't want to make work for you."

"Nonsense!" she says. "I can have a luncheon ready in no time at all. You and Lia could sit out on the back deck and eat while you enjoy this lovely day."

"That would be great, Ellie, thanks," I say, before Jonah can refuse her offer. I have a suspicion he's not had much to eat today. And I'm starving.

* * *

"What now?" I ask Jonah, after we finish our deli sandwiches, fresh fruit, and lemonade.

Jonah doesn't seem to be in any hurry to get back. He's probably avoiding Makayla, and maybe Dwight as well. But if he and Makayla are going to perform together in three days, they're going to have to spend some time together.

"I saw horses as we drove in," he says. "Can we go see the barn?"

"Sure."

We carry our dishes into the kitchen and thank Ellie for lunch. Then I walk Jonah outside and down the path that leads to the barn. The barn is cool and dimly lit inside, and it smells of leather, grain, and fresh cut hay.

Jonah strolls the length of the barn, looking into the empty stalls. "This brings back a lot of good memories." He has a bittersweet smile on his face. "When I was little, we'd visit my grandparents' farm on the weekends and ride horses and swim in the pond."

I get the feeling that happy childhood didn't last. "What

happened?"

Jonah shakes his head. "Nothing. Never mind." He reaches for my hands and raises them for inspection. "How are your knuckles?"

I pull my hands back, feeling self-conscious. I don't have pretty hands like other girls. My nails are cut short, and my knuckles are scarred. "They're fine."

His gaze searches mine. "Why did you hurt yourself last night? Working out is one thing, but beating a bag until your hands bleed is something else."

"I guess I overdid it, that's all."

"Come on, Lia. That wasn't overdoing it. That was self-inflicted damage. Why?"

I shrug. "We all have our issues to deal with. I'm sure you have a few of your own."

He steps closer, and I take a step back. "We should head back now," I say.

He takes my hand again, and his touch sends shivers up my arm. "Don't go," he says.

He moves toward me, and I back up. I can tell by the heat in his eyes what's on his mind. Before I know it, he's got me backed into a stall door, and his gaze is locked on my mouth. He's thinking about kissing me again, but it can't happen. I can't let it happen, because if he does, I'm not sure I'll want him to stop.

I raise my hand to his chest and hold him back. I can feel his body heat through his T-shirt, his chest warm and solid beneath my palm. The need to explore his body, to touch him, is overwhelming. "No."

"Why not?"

"I told you, I'm not interested."

"Yeah, I know. I'm just a job, right?"

"That's right." *No, you're not.*

His hands come up to cup my face and he leans closer. I can feel his warm breath on my cheeks.

"I don't believe you," he whispers.

I shake my head. "It doesn't matter what you believe, Jonah. I'm not going there with you, so give it up." But he keeps coming, leaning closer. "You know I could put you on your ass in about two seconds if I wanted to," I tell him.

He grins. "I know you could."

"Then stop pushing me."

"No."

He entwines his fingers with mine, and suddenly we're holding hands. He presses our joined hands right over his heart, which is thundering in his chest. God damn it, he's going to do it. He's going to kiss me. I have about two seconds to decide if I'll let him, or not. But my curiosity gets the best of me. I want to know what his mouth feels like, what he tastes like. It won't kill me to kiss him, just this once.

"Fair warning," he says. "I'm going to kiss you in about five seconds. If you don't want me to, then stop me. You certainly know how."

I roll my eyes at him. "You are so melodramatic."

"I'm just giving you a heads-up so there are no recriminations later. If you don't want this, you know what to do."

"Yeah, knock you on your ass. You see, the thing is, if I injure you and you can't perform Friday night, Dwight will kill me."

He laughs. "Since when do you care what Dwight thinks?"

Good point. "Shut up, Jonah." *Stop talking about it and just do it.*

And then he kisses me. Pressing me into the stall door, he lowers his mouth to mine. I gasp at the feel of him, his lips warm and firm on mine. I really should knock him on his ass, just to teach him a lesson. But his lips feel too good, and he smells so damn good, a combination of soap, a hint of cologne, and warm skin. I feel my insides soften.

His lips nudge mine open, and for the time being I'm willing to go along with this. When his tongue slips inside, sliding against mine, I suck in a sharp breath. I've kissed more than a few guys since Logan, but kissing has never felt this good before.

As he leans into me, enveloping me in his heat, his mouth seduces mine, stroking and licking. And before I know it, my hands are in his hair, grabbing fistfuls, and I'm kissing him back. He groans deep in his throat, and the raw sound makes me shiver.

Jonah presses closer, aligning our bodies fully, from our lips to our hips. His erection, which is hard as a rock, presses insistently into my belly. He groans again when I reach down and press my palm against him, measuring the heat and length and thickness of him. He breaks our kiss and lays his forehead against mine, his breath coming hard and fast.

When I continue exploring the outline of his erection through his jeans, he dips down to kiss my neck where it meets my shoulder, and I shudder as a tingle ripples down my spine.

He groans, pressing himself into my hand. "Lia, fuck."

His hand comes up to cover my left breast and he brushes my nipple through my clothing with his thumb. Lightning courses through me, and I can feel myself growing warm and flushed between my legs as all my blood heads south. I feel lightheaded, almost dizzy.

Gasping for air, I push him back. "We can't do this." I'm breathing hard now, too, my chest heaving, and every inch of me is on fire.

"Why not?"

I shake my head. "We can't. You're my client."

"I don't care."

"Well, I do. It's unprofessional. Shane would kill me." But the truth is, I don't trust myself with Jonah. I've never felt like this before, never wanted someone like this, and I'm afraid to give anyone that much power over me. I won't let *anyone* use me ever again.

"Lia – "

Both of us jump when Jonah's phone chimes with an incoming text.

"Aren't you going to get that?" I say, hoping to distract him.

"No."

His phone chimes a second time, and still he ignores it.

Then my phone chimes with an incoming message, and I'm pretty sure it's related. I check mine. "It's Dwight." I frown as I read the message. "Apparently, you're taking Makayla out to dinner tonight."

"What?" His expression turns grim, so I show him the message. "Shit!"

"Just say no. Tell Dwight to fuck off."

"It's not that easy, Lia," he says, replying to Dwight's text on his own phone. "If we're performing together on Friday, then I'll have to see her so we can plan. But you're coming with me."

"She's not going to like having me there."

"I don't care. You're coming."

I chuckle, anticipating the pleasure of seeing Makayla again. I don't work for her, so I'm under no obligation to kiss her ass. If she gives me any grief, I'll give it right back to her.

୬ 16

O n the drive back to Lincoln Park, Jonah's gaze is focused outside his passenger window, and he stares at the passing scenery. I'm not sure what's weighing so heavily on his mind... whether it's our kiss in the barn or the prospect of facing Makayla again.

The more I contemplate him spending time with her, the less I like the idea. He's not mine, and he never will be, so I have no right to start feeling territorial about him. And yet, the thought of those two together makes my blood boil.

* * *

It's only two o'clock in the afternoon, and we don't have pick up Makayla until eight o'clock that evening, so we have some time to kill. Jonah wants to go back to the recording studio to work, so that's where we head. Mostly, I think he's avoiding going back to the house in case Makayla's still there. That's fine with me. I don't feel like running into her a moment sooner than I have to.

Shane has upgraded the security at the recording studio, temporarily augmenting the existing staff with McIntyre Security employees. No more security breaches. He must have made some kind of deal with the building's owners.

When we arrive, we use the intercom to request entrance, and then we're vetted by a security guard dressed in black slacks and a black button-down shirt and jacket with the white McIntyre Security logo on it. He's armed and wearing an electronic listening device in his ear.

I know this guy. Joe Kramer. "Hey, Joe. How's it going?"

"Hi, Lia. Come on in."

Joe admits us to the building, and we head down the hallway to Jonah's studio.

"This place is depressing," I say, gazing down at utilitarian carpet that's a dull olive-brown color. It has to be at least fifty years old. The walls are paneled with dark, cheap fake wood that's just as old. "They could at least update the place."

Jonah laughs. "The acoustics are great, and that's all that matters to me. I'm not here for the ambiance."

We enter Jonah's studio, and he pauses just inside the control room. "This may take awhile," he says. "I'll be fine here if you want to take off. I hate that you have to babysit me all the time. You've got to be bored out of your mind."

"Nope, I'm staying. Don't worry about me. I'll entertain myself. You go do your thing."

"Are you sure? I really don't mind. And I don't think I'll get any unauthorized visitors here with Joe on duty."

"Jonah, shut up and stop worrying about me. This is my job. Let me do it, and you go do yours."

Jonah rolls his eyes at me, then disappears into the sound booth, where he turns down the lights to a low glow and picks up a guitar. I sit down at the main control panel, kick my feet up, and watch him through the window. He looks relaxed, happy even, as he sits on a tall stool and starts tuning his guitar. I've never seen him so happy as when he has a guitar in his hands. I suspect he likes writing and playing music more than he does performing.

Before long, he's lost in his music, strumming chords and picking out notes on the strings. He makes notations on his little pad of paper, then crosses things out and writes more. It's a long, tedious process as he plays little bits of music over and over again, but I enjoy watching him do it.

While Jonah's working on his music, I check text messages and e-mails on my phone. That takes a whole ten minutes. I have one text message from Shane reminding me to play nicely. There are two from Beth – nothing important, just saying hi. One from Jake – just checking in on me. And one from Cooper – also reminding me to place nicely. Cooper must have talked to Shane.

The sound of Jonah's voice draws my attention away from my

phone, and I look up. He's playing actual music now, a real song, and he's singing. God! The sound of his voice does something to my girl parts... they start tingling. His voice resonates so beautifully – it gives me goosebumps. This man was born to sing. He doesn't need any auto tuning gimmicks or special effects.

> *Let me be there for you*
> *Through your highs and your lows*
> *Let me be there for you*
> *I'll catch you when you fall*

It's a snippet of a love song, and the words flow through me like warm honey. I close my eyes and lay my head back in my chair and just listen to his voice as he works this stanza, playing with the notes, with the phrasing, the chords. I've heard his voice on the radio countless times, but hearing it like this, so intimately, makes me realize what a truly gifted artist he is. There's no artifice here, no engineering magic or tricks. It's just Jonah's voice and an acoustic guitar. I lose all track of time as I listen to him. He plays so effortlessly, his long fingers deftly navigating the strings and the frets.

Perfection.

Oh, God, I sound like a fan-girl.

* * *

"Sorry," Jonah says, coming out of the sound booth two hours later. He tucks a folded-up piece of paper in his back pocket. "I tend to lose all track of time when I'm in the studio."

"It's okay. I enjoyed listening. How'd it go?"

He nods. "Pretty well. I'm making progress."

"Good. Where to now?"

"Back to the house. We can hang there until it's time to pick up Makayla."

He frowns, and I can tell he's not happy about the plans for tonight. He's silent – preoccupied – as we lock up the recording studio and head down the empty hallway to the rear exit.

* * *

I'm not sure what to make of Jonah. He's certainly nothing like I expected. He's surprisingly normal for a celebrity, but he's clearly not happy. I don't understand why he lets Peterson call all the shots. Why doesn't he just put his foot down and say no?

The crowd outside the house is larger than usual, and they seem rather worked up this evening. I can't help wondering if this has something to do with Makayla being in town. If it does, now we're not just dealing with Jonah's fans, but with hers as well.

As I pull into the drive, a teenage girl throws herself against the passenger door, her face and hands pressed against Jonah's window, sobbing incoherently. Another girl jumps on the rear bumper of the Jeep. Two photographers are standing in front of the Jeep, rapidly snapping pictures through the windshield. I have to stop the vehicle.

I turn off the engine and unbuckle my seat belt. "Stay in the vehicle."

"Lia, you can't go out there."

I radio the guards inside the gate. "A little help out here would be nice."

The gate opens just enough for one guard to step through. He chases off the two photographers, while I go to the back of the Jeep to pry the girl off the bumper. It's not easy, because she's clinging to the luggage rack like a little monkey. I finally get her off, then get back inside the vehicle just as the security guard peels the sobbing girl off of Jonah's window.

Once we're finally inside the house, Jonah grabs a bottle of beer from the fridge and heads upstairs to his suite without a single word to me. Moody artist, much? Part of me wants to follow and make him talk to me. But I suspect he needs some alone time right now. So I head to my room and check my work e-mail. Shane's sent me some info on Friday's performance. He succeeded in renting Rowdy's bar for the night – although it cost him a fortune – and he's got some of his employees and some of Beth's lined up to attend the event. That will simplify security greatly.

With Jonah holed up in his room, and Dwight and Esperanza nowhere to be seen, I'm bored. So I go in search of the boys. It doesn't take me long to track them down. The sounds of explosions and gunfire coming from the media room in the lower level is a dead giveaway. I recognize the tell-tale sounds of a popular shoot-em-up game.

I find the guys sprawled out on the sofa with their booted feet propped up on a long, low coffee table. There are empty pizza boxes and empty beer bottles littering the room.

"Hey, Lia!" one of the guys says, jumping to his feet. He's got a game controller in his hand, and when he steps in front of one of the other guys, he gets shoved out of the way. "Hi," he says, grinning.

"Hi." I smile at him, embarrassed that I don't know which one he is. He's the blond. I think his name is Dylan.

"I'm Dylan," he says, offering me his hand. "Drums."

"Hi, Dylan." He reminds me of Justin Bieber – cute and full of energy. I'm sure the girls go gaga over him.

"So, you're Jonah's bodyguard?" he says, sizing me up.

"That's right."

"How come we've never seen you before? Did you come out here with Jonah? From LA?"

"No. I'm from around here."

Dylan peers around me, out into the hallway. "Where's Jonah?"

"He's upstairs."

I glance at the dark-haired one sprawled on the sofa, his eyes glued to the flatscreen monitor as he manipulates his game controller. His avatar is walking down a dark alley holding an automatic weapon.

He glances up just long enough to make eye contact. "Hey, Lia."

"Zeke, right?"

He nods. "Bass."

That means the other guy on the couch with muddy brown hair has to be Travis. "Hi, Travis. Guitar, right?"

"That's right," he says, his character joining Zeke's on the hunt.

"Why don't you join us?" Dylan says, offering me his controller. "Do you want to play? Are you hungry? There's more pizza."

"I'll pass on the food, but I'll watch you guys play." I grew up playing video games with four older brothers. I know my way around a gaming console.

The three of them are boisterous and just plain fun to be around. It's clear that they're a tight-knit group. I wonder why Jonah doesn't join in.

Dylan hands me his controller. "Don't you want to play?"

The one called Zeke snorts. "She wouldn't stand a chance."

"Oh, yeah?" I drop down on the sofa between Dylan and Zeke. "Prepare to get creamed, fellas."

I lose all track of time goofing around with them as we hunt down mutant aliens that have taken over the city. It turns into a race to see who can bag the most aliens. I also admit to drinking a beer or two. When I feel a pair of eyes on me, I glance at the doorway and see Jonah leaning against the door jamb, his arms crossed over his chest as he observes us. He's dressed up for a change, in black slacks and a white button-down shirt. His hair is tied back in a loose pony tail, and he looks very debonair.

"I see you guys are getting acquainted," Jonah says.

"We like her, Jonah," Dylan says, laughing as he nudges my shoulder. "This one's a keeper."

"I'm glad you approve," Jonah says, but his smile is flat. His gaze lands on me. "If you can tear yourself away from video games, Lia, it's time for you to do your job. We've got to leave soon to go get Makayla, and I imagine you need to change first."

"Sorry, guys," I say, rising from the sofa and patting Dylan on the head. "Duty calls! You'll have to muddle through without me."

As I head out the door, I'm serenaded by a chorus of boos and groans from the guys. I shut the door behind me, then plant my hands on my hips and glare at Jonah. "What the hell is your problem?"

"You're my problem!"

"Me? What the hell did I do?" I narrow my eyes.

"I'm not paying you to fraternize with my band."

"We were playing a video game, not having an orgy. Anyway, you couldn't get away from me fast enough earlier, and I was bored." His eyes narrow, and I can tell he's pissed. *Oh, my God. Is he jealous?* "Are you pissed at me for putting an end to your groping in the barn?"

"Groping? Is that what you call it? If I remember correctly, you had your hands all over me too. Yeah, I'm pissed. Our kiss was incredible, and you know it. I felt it, and you felt it. And yet you ran. You're so tough on the outside, but inside, you're a chicken. What are you afraid of, Lia?"

I'm so mad at him, all I can see is red. "I should have tossed you on your ass in that barn instead of letting you kiss me. This is what I get for being nice." My heart is practically in my throat.

This is exactly why I don't let myself get close to anyone. They always end up wanting more, and I'll never want more. Not with anyone. I'm incapable of trusting anyone that much.

"Go screw yourself, Jonah!" I say, as I head upstairs to change my clothes.

🌀 17

Since this is official business, we take the Escalade to pick up Makayla. Jonah glances at me and says, "I'm sorry. I was out of line. And I didn't mean what I said. I was... frustrated, and I took it out on you."

Frustrated, or jealous? I shrug. "Don't worry about it. I'm sorry too."

As we approach Makayla's hotel, I scowl at the huge crowd gathered outside. And I do mean huge. There have to be a couple hundred girls milling around in front of the hotel, taking pictures and video, swarming with excitement. A half-dozen uniformed security guards keep the fans confined behind a barrier, to keep them from blocking the drive and the main entrance. I pull the Escalade up to the front revolving doors.

One of the doormen comes around to my window and peers inside the vehicle. His gaze fixes on Jonah momentarily, then he looks at me. "Name?"

"Lia McIntyre. We're here to pick up Makayla Hendricks." I flash him my McIntyre Security ID.

He glances at my badge and nods. "Good luck with that," he scoffs, stepping back as I open my door. "The natives are restless."

I glance at Jonah. "Maybe you should wait in the vehicle. I'll bring her out." Thanks to the darkly tinted windows, Jonah should be able to lay low here in the vehicle. But that hope is quickly vanquished when the crowd presses forward against the security barrier. Dozens of phones are directed our way, and I see camera flashes going off like fireworks on the fourth of July. Some of the girls are holding banners and handmade signs with Jonah's name on them, decorated with red hearts and declarations of undying love. Jonah's name, not Makayla's.

I frown. "They knew you were coming."

Pissed, I bring up Twitter on my phone and look at Makayla's feed. Sure enough, she tweeted an hour ago that she was waiting for Jonah Locke to pick her up at her hotel for their dinner date tonight. And of course she supplied the name of the hotel, as well as the name of the restaurant where they have reservations tonight.

"She broadcasted your plans all over social media." I shake my head.

Jonah shrugs. "I told you, she lives for publicity. She needs the adoration, like a crack addict needs her fix. She can't go five minutes without it. When we were together, she'd Tweet our every move. We had absolutely no privacy."

"You should wait here."

"No, I'll go up. I need to have a talk with Makayla."

I study him, analyzing the relative risk of letting him go into the hotel versus waiting here in the SUV. The bottom line is, I don't want to let him out of my sight. The hotel seems to be a little understaffed for dealing with such a large crowd. "All right. I'll get out first and run interference, while you head straight inside the lobby. Got it?"

Sure enough, as soon as I open my door and step out of the vehicle, all the cameras turn in my direction, flashes going off in rapid succession. I know my face is going to end up all over the Internet tonight, and that pisses me off. I go out of my way to avoid publicity – I have for years. The last thing I want is for someone to recognize me. But right now, there's no avoiding it.

Jonah slips out the other side of the vehicle, partially hidden from the view of the crowd by the big SUV, and two security guards escort him inside the hotel. By the time the crowd realizes they've been pointing their cameras in the wrong direction, Jonah is safely inside the lobby. I follow him in.

"Wait here," Jonah says, as he heads for the elevator. "This won't take long."

"Ha!" I chuckle, following him into the elevator. "You're not going up there without me."

I escort Jonah upstairs to Makayla's top-floor suite. We step out of the elevator into an elegantly appointed hallway with burgundy carpet and subtle, gold and white striped wallpaper. Gold-accented light fixtures adorn the walls. Jonah locates her room and knocks, and a moment later it opens. Makayla greets us at the door in a barely-there lingerie ensemble – a black lace push-up bra, a black lace thong, and a pair of black thigh-high boots with five-inch heels. There's a large diamond stud twinkling in her belly button. And her thong is so skimpy, it's obvious she's waxed bare. She's left absolutely nothing to the imagination.

For a moment, Jonah stands there gaping at her. I can't help wondering if he's had a sudden change of heart about their break-up. Makayla's obviously offering herself up to him on a silver platter.

I should keep my damn mouth shut, but I just can't. "It's unclear to me what look you're going for, Makayla. Hooker or dominatrix? I can't tell. I think it's the boots. Honestly, they could go either way. Maybe if you added chains or a whip...."

Makayla glares at me. "What's she doing here?"

"She's with me," Jonah says to Makayla, finally shaking himself out of his stupor.

And I swear to God, he actually steps between us, as if he's protecting me from her. Or maybe it's the other way around.

His voice hardens. "Put some clothes on, Makayla. This isn't a booty call."

She scowls. "Well, pardon me. I didn't know you were bringing the help with you." She smirks at me. "This is a *date*, honey. Jonah doesn't need you. I have my own security."

I see a burly, muscled guy seated on a dainty sofa across the room. He's perusing a *Playboy* magazine.

Jonah sighs. "This isn't a date, Makayla. I told you that. We're just –"

Makayla grabs his shirt and pulls him into the room, then tries to shut the door in my face, but I wedge my boot in the doorway so she can't shut me out. I'll be damned if I'm going to leave him to the mercy of this barracuda. I shove the door open and step inside, letting it close behind me.

"Sorry, honey, but this is a private party," she says, eyeing me like I'm something she found stuck to the bottom of her boot. Then she turns her large, brown eyes on Jonah. "Tell her to wait in the car, baby."

"She stays," he says.

Makayla smirks at him. "Fine. Let her watch then." She steps into Jonah's personal space, standing nearly eye to eye with him in her high heels, her brightly painted red lips barely an inch from his. Her voice drops to a breathy whisper. "You know I don't mind if someone watches."

"There's nothing to watch, Makayla."

"Baby, I've missed you." She brings her long, slender fingers up to his face. "So much."

Makayla leans forward and kisses him with her glossy, plumped up lips. I watch Jonah's reaction, after all she does look fucking hot – even I can admit that. But he doesn't react. Nothing.

Jonah eases her back, steadying her when she loses her balance on those ridiculous heels. "No, Makayla."

She pouts prettily, but when he keeps her at arm's length, her sultry pout turns into a real frown. "Jonah, baby."

Jonah shakes his head. "Finish getting dressed so we can go. The sooner we get this charade over with, the better."

"It's not a charade! I want to see you, be with you. We haven't spent any quality time together since – "

"Get dressed." He points toward the bedroom door. "This is a publicity stunt, not a date. Don't confuse the two."

"Fine!" Makayla stalks off in a huff to her bedroom and slams the door behind her.

Jonah turns to me. "Sorry about that."

I shrug. "Don't mind me. I'm just along for the ride. And to keep Ms. Diva from molesting you."

The muscle guy across the room snorts in amusement.

Jonah grins at me. "I appreciate your dedication to your job."

* * *

Makayla saunters out of her bedroom dressed to kill in a black mini skirt that barely covers her butt and a diamond-encrusted top that's little more than a glorified sports bra. Her flat midriff is bare, and the diamond stud in her belly button is clearly visible. Her lustrous long brown hair is pulled up into a top-knot ponytail, and the thick length of it hangs down over her shoulder. She looks stunning.

I open the door to the suite for them, and Makayla sashays through it after telling her muscle guy he can stay behind. Jonah follows more sedately. The elevator ride down is beyond awkward, and rather entertaining, at least for me. Makayla steps between me and Jonah and edges me back into the corner of the elevator car.

When we step out into the lobby, the hotel manager is there, bowing and scraping to Makayla and Jonah. Camera flash from the street fills the lobby. The manager, a short, rotund man with thinning brown hair, is clearly frazzled by the media circus out front.

"Ms. Hendricks!" he says, scurrying over to her.

Makayla catches a glimpse of the Escalade parked outside the revolving doors and stops abruptly. "Where's my limo? I said I wanted a limo."

The manager – his name tag says "Mr. Roberts" – scurries over to Makayla. "Oh, my God, I'm so sorry! Were we supposed to arrange for a limo?"

Makayla glares at me, as if this is all my fault. "Where's my limo? I told Dwight I wanted a limo."

"We don't need a limo," Jonah says. "Lia will drive us in the Escalade."

Makayla looks stricken. "An SUV? Are you kidding me? I don't ride in SUVs. I need a limo!"

I try to keep a straight face as Makayla flushes a deep red. She really does appear to be stressed by her mode of transportation. You'd think we were asking her to take public transportation. Surely a bullet-proofed Cadillac is acceptable transportation, even for her.

To avoid completely losing my cool, I push ahead through the revolving doors and head outside. The hotel staff have created a makeshift corridor from the front doors to the Escalade, and it looks like we'll have to run the gauntlet. I move out in front amidst a barrage of camera flashes and shouting paparazzi. Jonah's right behind me, with Makayla, not quite steady in her towering heels, in tow.

The crowd is shouting Makayla's name, as well as Jonah's. There's all manner of screaming, and some of the girls are downright hysterical. The paparazzi press closer, their camera flashes nearly blinding us as they shout random questions.

"Makayla! Are you and Jonah back together?"

"Jonah! Are you seeing someone new?"

"Jonah! Who's the blond?"

Several cameras point my way, firing off volleys of shots like automatic machine guns. It takes everything I have not to cover my face and dive into the vehicle. I sure as hell don't want to get mixed up in the Makayla-Jonah drama fueled by the desperate hopes of teenage girls who have their hearts set on a sweet reunion between the two of them.

Having reached the end of my patience, I open the rear passenger door of the SUV and practically shove Makayla inside. She scoots over to the far side, making room for Jonah to sit beside her.

I look at Jonah. "Front or back?"

He answers without hesitation, and I have to bite back a grin. "Front."

When I close the rear door and open the front passenger door for Jonah, Makayla leans forward between the two front seats, clearly annoyed. "Jonah! Why aren't you sitting back here with me?" As he's buckling his seat belt, she strokes the back of his neck with a glossy red fingernail. "You should be back here with me, baby, not up front with the chauffeur."

"She's not a chauffeur, Makayla," he says, pulling away from her touch.

She's still complaining as we pull away from the hotel entrance, moving at a painfully slow crawl as the hotel security guards try to move the crowd out of our path.

"Why are there so many people here?" I ask Makayla, meeting her gaze in the rear view mirror. I'm sure it's not a coincidence. "How did they know you were staying in this hotel? I thought your presence in Chicago was supposed to be a secret until Friday."

Makayla leans back in her seat, huffing indignantly. "I have no idea. I guess someone leaked it to the media."

"And who could that someone be?" I say.

"How in the world would I know?" she says, pouting as she glares out her window.

18

This restaurant had better be good," Makayla says as we pull up to the front entrance of the towering glass and steel office building that houses Renaldo's.

"It is," I tell her. "Five stars, all the way."

Renaldo's is located at the top of a high-rise office building downtown, with an unimpeded view of N. Michigan Avenue and Lake Michigan in the distance. Beth's former roommate, Gabrielle, works here as a sous-chef, and the owner – Peter Capelli – is a close friend of Shane's. I almost feel bad bringing Makayla there, because I know she'll turn the event into a circus somehow. Peter's a nice guy, and he doesn't deserve that. But the clientele here is upscale and used to seeing celebrities in their midst, so they won't go crazy over seeing Makayla and Jonah here.

A valet opens Makayla's door, and then Jonah's, while I let myself out and walk around the front of the vehicle to join them on the sidewalk. I hand the valet a spare key. We're escorted by restaurant staff into the building and to the express elevator that goes directly up to the restaurant.

The elevator opens into a grand vestibule. A gold-accented, crystal chandelier hangs from a high ceiling, casting sparkling light on burgundy velvet papered walls. A number of sleek black sofas and chairs give guests a comfortable place to await their coveted reservations. I walk right up to the host's podium, where a girl who barely looks like she's out of high school stands. Her long, curly black hair is pulled back into a loose pony tail, and she's dressed in black dress slacks and a white tailored blouse, with a fine gold choker around her slender neck.

Our hostess gives us a polished and professional smile, but her widening gaze quickly drifts to Makayla, and then to Jonah. She makes a valiant effort to act as if these guests are nothing out of the ordinary. Finally, she transfers her gaze to me, and her voice is a little shaky. "Mr. Locke's table is ready, ma'am."

The hostess hands three menus to a young man who is hovering at her elbow, a tall young man with red hair and freckles who's fairly vibrating with suppressed excitement. "If you'll follow me," he says, flourishing a hand toward the curtained entrance to the dining room.

Makayla steps in front of me and grabs my arm in a bruising grip. "You are NOT coming in with us," she hisses in my face. "Wait out here."

Just as I'm weighing how much trouble I'll get in if I break her wrist, Jonah grabs her hand and pries it off me. "Leave her alone, Makayla."

"No!" Makayla hisses back at him. "She can wait out here or in the kitchen with the rest of the staff. She's not coming in the dining room with us! This is a dinner for two, not three."

"Don't worry, Ms. Diva," I say. "I wasn't planning to sit with you in the restaurant. But I will be close by."

"Why? We don't need you – "

"Because it's protocol. How can I do my job if I'm not near him?"

"What could he possibly need from you in there?"

"You never know – he might need help buttering his bread. I take my job very seriously."

Makayla scowls at Jonah. "This girl is crazy. Why you hired her, or even put up with her, I'll never know."

Our server is bobbing nervously on his feet, watching Makayla and me face off like we're wild animals that could attack at any moment. He looks at Jonah, a desperate plea on his face. "Sir? If you could follow me?"

Jonah pulls Makayla away from me and pushes her gently toward the dining room. "Can we please just get this over with?"

He glances back at me as they walk through the doorway, looking completely exasperated. I watch through the curtain as they are seated at a cozy table for two along the edge of the dining room, intended, I'm sure, to give them a little bit of privacy.

"So, that's Makayla Hendricks."

I smile when I hear the cultured voice of Peter Capelli, the owner of Renaldo's.

Peter Capelli is a good looking man, with a trim, athletic build, short, prematurely silver hair, and piercing blue eyes. He looks very debonair in his black suit, white shirt, and a cobalt blue tie that really makes his eyes pop.

"Yep, that's the princess of pop. She's a royal pain in the ass."

Peter smiles. "I don't doubt your ability to handle her, Lia."

"I'd like to handle her, all right."

"And the gentleman? Jonah Locke. He's your client?"

"Yes."

Peter lays a hand on my shoulder. "Rest easy, Lia. My staff know better than to fawn over celebrities, and the clientele are too sophisticated to act like the rabid fans that have amassed outside the building."

I snicker. "Don't worry, Makayla will find a way to make a scene. She lives for publicity."

After Peter leaves me to my spying, I decide to stay out of sight, for Jonah's sake. I don't want to give Makayla an excuse to make a scene. I notice Jonah scanning the dining room a few times, and I can't help wondering if he's looking for me.

A side access door opens and out steps Gabrielle Hunter, dressed in her white sous-chef uniform. Despite the plain simplicity of her chef's uniform, with her blazing red hair – which is currently confined to a long, thick braid – she makes one hell of an impression. The bridge of her nose and the top edges of her cheeks are sprinkled with cinnamon-colored freckles, and her eyes are a vibrant green. She's at least a head taller than me.

"Hey, Lia," she says breathlessly, giving me a quick hug. "Peter told me you were out here. Do you want to come back to the kitchen with me? I'll feed you."

Because of Beth, Gabrielle and I have become friends of a sort. Since I don't have many friends, I appreciate the ones I do have. I peek through the curtained doorway at Jonah's table. Their server is taking their orders, and everything looks relatively quiet. I can monitor things from the kitchen just as easily as I can from here. Besides, I am hungry. "That sounds great. Thank you."

I follow Gabrielle down the corridor that leads to the kitchen, where I am assailed with delicious aromas of Italian cuisine. Having friends in the restaurant business does have its perks, especially when it's a five-star restaurant.

Gabrielle sets a stool in front of a window that acts as a one-way mirror overlooking the dining room. From here, I can watch Jonah and Makayla comfortably without anyone seeing me.

Gabrielle pats my shoulder. "How about a platter of appetizers while you decide what you want to eat? I'll be right back."

A few moments later, Gabrielle returns wheeling a cart that holds a crazy assortment of appetizers. There's enough food here for three people.

"What would you like to drink?" she says. "Wine? A soft drink?"

"Coke is fine. No alcohol for me tonight."

"Oh, right! Sorry." Gabrielle returns with my soft drink, which she sets on my cart. "Would you like to order an entree?"

"This is way more than I can eat, Gabrielle," I tell her. "I won't need anything else. Thank you."

She glances out the window at Jonah and Makayla and sighs heavily. "My goodness, he's gorgeous. No man has a right to look that good. I could eat him up, you know?"

I chuckle. "You'd have to go through Makayla first." *Not to mention me.*

"I thought they broke up."

"They did. But she keeps forgetting that. Anyway, it's his manager who organized this little spectacle tonight. They're putting on a surprise performance Friday night at Rowdy's. It's mainly a PR stunt."

Gabrielle's eyes light up. "A concert here? Really?"

"You want to come? It's by invitation only. You're welcome to come. Beth will be there, and I think she's bringing a bunch of her employees."

"Of course I want to come! Thank you!" Gabrielle gives me a one-armed hug. "Enjoy your food! If you need anything else, just let me know. I'll be at my station."

I enjoy my sampler feast while watching Jonah and Makayla. They're seated directly across from each other, and Makayla keeps leaning toward Jonah, putting her ample cleavage on display. I can practically see her nipples, even from where I'm sitting. More than once, she reaches out to take his hand, her fingers bedazzled with more diamond rings than a Tiffany display case. And each time, he manages to pull his hand away discretely. Jonah's far too nice for his own good. If I were him, I'd slap her.

Makayla pours herself a glass of red wine and downs it quickly, and then pours another. I'm thinking she'd better pace herself until she's eaten something.

When their entrees arrive, Jonah focuses on eating, while Makayla talks nonstop, gesturing animatedly and laughing. I think the wine's hit her bloodstream before the food. She pours another glass and takes a sip.

Jonah looks miserable, and I can't help feeling sorry for him. Part of me wants to go in there and rescue him. But I can't. He's a big boy. He has to deal with this – with her – himself.

Finally, their meal comes to an end, and while Jonah pays the check, I wait for them in the front lobby. As they come out, I can tell immediately that Makayla's had a little too much to drink. She looks flushed and unsteady on those ridiculous spiked heels.

As we head down in the elevator, Makayla leans into Jonah and whispers loudly to him. "Do you wanna go dancing?"

"No," he says.

She runs her index finger in little circles on his shirt. "We could go to a club, have a few drinks. Just the two of us."

"No," Jonah says, removing her finger. "We're taking you back to your hotel."

Makayla pouts. "Baby..."

"Please don't call me that. And stand up."

"I'm not sure she can," I say, coming around the other side of her. "Did you notice how much wine she drank and how little she ate? I'd say she's officially drunk."

Makayla laughs, the sound overly loud in the confines of the elevator. "I am not drunk! Tell her I'm not, Jonah."

"Yes, Makayla, you are." Jonah looks past Makayla at me. "Did you get something to eat?"

I nod. "I ate in the kitchen."

The elevator doors whoosh open and Jonah helps Makayla out. She's getting less and less steady on her feet.

I head for the revolving doors. "I'll get the Escalade. Can you get her out the door?"

Jonah nods. "I'll try. Let's get her back to the hotel before she falls down."

19

J onah leads Makayla out of the building with both arms around her, and I think he may be the only thing holding her up. She has her arms around him, too, and her face is pressed against his shirt. I can't tell if she's really drunk or if she's playing him for attention. I wouldn't put it past her to fake it.

I open the rear passenger door, and Jonah maneuvers her into the back seat.

"Sit with me," she begs, holding onto his shirt with a death grip. She pulls him into the vehicle with her, and he acquiesces, climbing in beside her. He gives me a pained look as I close his door and then walk around the front of the vehicle to the driver's door.

For the entire drive back to her hotel, I'm forced to listen to her pleading with him. I'm pretty sure she really is toasted, because why else would she humiliate herself like this?

"Jonah, please," she whines, wrapping her arms around his waist and snuggling into him. Her slurred, sultry voice is muffled against his shirt. "You can't break up with me. We belong together. Everyone can see that. Why can't you?"

Jonah meets my gaze in the rear view mirror. "Makayla, please," he says, trying to remove her arms from around his waist. "Sit up."

"No!" She tightens her hold on him. "I've missed you so much, baby." She tilts her face up and kisses the side of his throat. Her voice drops and she attempts to whisper to him. "Come back to my hotel room with me. It's been so long, and I need you." She sits up, and her lush, painted lips nibble their way toward his mouth. "Please, I'll do anything you want."

This is getting downright awkward and embarrassing for everyone.

Jonah dodges her kiss and sets her back in her seat, buckling her in to keep her there.

"Please hurry," he says to me.

I would be tempted to laugh if the situation weren't so pathetic.

* * *

Jonah closes Makayla's hotel door and leans back against it, looking absolutely wiped. All the drama has taken quite a toll on him. I had to help him get her up to her room, where we left her in the capable hands of her personal assistant, Stacy, who promised not to let her leave the room before morning.

I lean against the wall just a foot away from him. "Are you okay?" It must have been hard on him to see her like this.

He's staring at the blank wall across the hallway. "This is why I left LA. To get away from this, all the melodrama."

"Makayla loves you, in her own twisted way. I feel sorry for her."

Jonah reaches out to touch my arm where Makayla grabbed me earlier, leaving behind traces of a faint bruise. "Did she hurt you?"

I laugh. "No, I'm fine."

His fingers slip down my arm to grasp my fingers. "I'm wiped. Let's go home."

I feel an odd tightening in my chest at his words. It's just a rental house, a temporary place for him to stay while he's in Chicago. And yet, the way he said home makes it sound like a whole lot more.

* * *

It's late, and the house is quiet inside when we come in through the back door. The lights are off, but someone left a nightlight on in the kitchen. Probably Esperanza.

As we reach the main hallway, Jonah pauses a moment to look at me, his gaze searching mine. His expression is impassive. "Good night, Lia."

As I watch him walk away, I feel oddly bereft. "Good night."

I'm doing the right thing by keeping him at arm's length. I am! There's no point in us getting any closer. I don't do clients. So why does my chest feel tight, like it's being squeezed in a giant vise? I suck in a deep breath, steeling myself against going after him. For a self-indulgent moment, I wonder would he'd do if I followed him upstairs to his suite. That's his private domain up there, where he hides from the world. For the millionth time, I think Jonah's not cut out for the music industry. At least not for the crazy world of the rock star. He's more the suffering artist type. The thought makes me smile. I think I'd prefer a suffering artist over an egomaniac any day.

With a sigh, I head to my room to check e-mail. Shane has sent me some logistical information about Friday's concert, and it looks like everything's under control. Jake's in charge of security that evening. All we have to do is show up.

Despite the late hour, I'm too wired to sleep, so I change into my workout clothes and head downstairs to burn off some energy. Halfway down the stairs, I see flashing lights coming from underneath the media room door. I pause outside the door for a moment. The room is well sound-proofed, but I can feel the vibrations from the Surround Sound system beating against the door. I open the door and step in, and find the trio kicking back on the sofa watching a movie on the big screen. Empty beer bottles and Chinese food cartons are everywhere – it looks like a disaster zone.

I shake my head. "Shouldn't you boys be in bed by now?"

All three heads turn my way, and Dylan flashes me a big grin.

"Lia!" he says, jumping to his feet. "Hey! I'm glad you're home. Come hang with us."

Dylan makes room for me between himself and Travis, and pats the empty sofa seat. "Come watch Iron Man versus Captain America."

I shake my head, smiling. "Thanks, but I've got a date with a treadmill. Maybe next time."

"Oh, come on, Lia!" Dylan grabs the remote to pause the movie, then he dashes over to me, more than a little unsteady on his feet. I can smell beer on his breath. He grabs my hand and pulls me into the room. "Hang out with us. Just for a while."

I have to admit, Dylan's really easy on the eyes. His eagerness is infectious, and watching the three of them together reminds me so much of my childhood, when all my brothers lived at home. The nostalgia I'm feeling must show on my face, because Dylan gives me a triumphant grin and pulls me over to the sofa.

"Sit!" he says, pushing me down on the sofa. He drops down beside me and lays his arm across the back of the sofa, just inches from my shoulders and neck.

Travis pauses to look at me, a superior smirk on his handsome face. His brown eyes are lit up with a mixture of excitement and perhaps a little too much alcohol. He grabs his beer and takes a long pull. "Want one?"

"Yeah. I'm off the clock, and that sounds great." I eye the open cooler on the floor at Travis' feet and have to chuckle. Several bottles of Zombie Dust stick up out of the ice. "I'd love one of those."

Travis grabs a bottle and twists off the top, then hands the bottle to me.

I take a swig of the cold, crisp beer. "Where did this come from? The Zombie Dust?"

Travis shrugs. "We found several cases of it upstairs in the pantry. Why? Don't you like it? It's good stuff."

I shrug. "Yeah, it's great. I was just curious." It just happens to be my favorite beer, only I didn't bring it here. And Jonah's the only one in this house who knows I like it. Did he arrange to have it brought here?

We've been watching the movie for about an hour now – and I admit that my one beer turned into two – when the door opens, letting the hall light flood the media room, blinding us.

"Jesus, Jonah, shut the door!" Zeke yells, shielding his eyes.

Jonah steps inside the room and kicks the door shut with an ominous thud. "What the hell are you guys doing?"

Travis raises his bottle to Jonah – it's the third one I've seen him drink since I joined them. "Isn't it obvious, dude? We're having a foursome with Lia."

Jonah's wearing gray sweat pants and nothing else. He looks haggard and on edge. "Leave her alone, guys. She's not here for your entertainment."

"Come on, Jonah!" Dylan says. "She's off the clock. She can hang with us if she wants."

Jonah stands with his legs braced apart and his hands clamped on his hips. His expression is tight, his jaw clenched, and he looks like he's ready to rumble, although I can't imagine with whom or why. We're not doing anything wrong. We're just watching a movie, for God's sake.

Jonah glares at me. "Can I talk to you, please?"

I step over Travis's and Zeke's legs, which are propped up on the coffee table, to get to Jonah. "What's your problem?" I hiss.

Jonah looks down at me, his eyes narrowing. Then he grabs my arm and drags me out into the hallway, shutting the door behind him.

I roll my eyes at him. "Seriously, what the hell is your problem?"

"This is my problem!" He pushes me up against the wall, his hands framing my face, and leans into me, his mouth covering mine.

"What the fuck!" I gasp against his lips, half-heartedly pushing at his chest. I don't know whether to laugh at his audacity, slam my knee into his balls, or kiss him back.

"Just shut up and kiss me," he growls, as if reading my mind.

ᶜᶦ 20

J onah kisses me like he's starving for it, his lips hot and hard
on mine, and my belly does a somersault, leaving me feeling
lightheaded and off balance.

"Jonah – "

My words are cut off when his tongue slips into my mouth, finding mine with unerring precision and stroking it. Suddenly I'm
burning up, as heat blooms between my legs. I know I should drop
him on his ass, and I'm so tempted to do it. I'm not used to being
manhandled like this. But before I can strike, he moves closer, his
body coming up flush with mine, pinning me to the wall. His thick
erection presses into my belly, and I swallow hard.

Jonah groans, the sound low and harsh in the otherwise deserted
hallway. One of his hands slips down to cover my breast, and when

his thumb brushes across the tip, my nipple contracts so quickly it hurts. I gasp in surprise, and his lips gentle on mine, the kiss becoming one of exploration as his tongue strokes mine.

"Lia."

The longing in his voice sets up an ache deep inside me, where my insides are going soft and I'm tumbling in a freefall. I can feel my blood converging on my sex, making things down there hot and wet. This ache is an unfamiliar sensation, and I don't like it. I don't want to ache like this for anyone.

Jonah pulls back and looks at me beseechingly, as if waiting for the answer to an unspoken question.

I have to close my eyes, because looking at what I can't have hurts too much. When I open them again, I resolve to put a quick end to this. "You're wasting your time, Jonah. I told you, I'm not interested."

His eyes narrow. "You're lying."

Now he's pissing me off. I shove him hard, knocking him off balance, and he has to catch himself before he falls. "Your ego is showing, asshole. Here's the thing, Jonah. You don't get to decide what I want. *I do.*"

I expect anger from him, resentment even. Instead, he's got a stupid grin on his face.

I'm completely baffled. "Why are you smiling?"

He shakes his head, laughing. "Everyone in my life wants something from me. They either want money, or publicity, or they want to control me. You're the only person I've ever met who doesn't give a flying fuck about any of those things. I'm literally throwing myself at you, and you couldn't care less."

He takes a step closer, and his voice drops an octave. "I'm in awe of you, Lia."

His gaze is hot as he raises his hand to my face and gently brushes his thumb across my lower lip. "You're fierce and you take no prisoners." His gaze searches mine. "But here's the thing. I think you're lying, both to me and to yourself. I know desire when I see it, Lia. You want this as much as I do, so what gives? And please don't give me any crap about company policy, because when do you ever follow company policy when it doesn't suit you?"

I have to smile at that – he's right. I've never let company policy stop me when I wanted something.

Before I can say a word, he adds, "And don't tell me you don't sleep with clients, because I don't think you'd let anything stand in the way of what you want. Hell, I'll fire McIntyre Security right this second, if that's what it takes. I'll call Shane and tell him his services are no longer needed, so don't use the company as your excuse."

His warm hands cradle my face, and he gazes into my eyes, his dark eyes seeming to see right through me. Slowly, he leans down and kisses me, a soft gentle kiss that speaks of desire and need. "I want you, Lia." His lips brush mine. "I've never wanted anyone so much in my life."

He pulls back and pins me with his gaze, and I can barely breathe. "Give us a chance," he says. "Give *me* a chance. Please."

Tears spring into my eyes, prickling and stinging, and I swipe an angry fist across them. I resent the fact he's made me weepy, that he's made me want to *try*. "You're such a jerk," I say, my voice wavering as I stifle a reluctant laugh.

"Is that a yes?"

"It's a maybe."

"Close enough."

Jonah sweeps me up into his arms and carries me down the hallway to the fitness room. He shoulders open the door and carries me inside, then closes the door with his foot. The heat from his body radiates outward, filling my senses. I can smell him, his warm skin fresh from a shower, the faint hint of soap. It's a tantalizing mixture of scents, and it does something to my insides.

When I feel one of his hands on my face, his fingers gently searching my face in the semi-darkness, my knees go weak. He could be grabbing my tits or my ass, but he's not. He's touching my *face*. As if it's really *me* he's interested in, and not just getting his rocks off.

There's a faint bit of light coming through the blinds, just enough that I can see the tension in his expression, how his jaw is clenched tightly, his nostrils flaring with arousal. He's breathing heavily, his chest heaving as he watches me, waiting for something. For what? A signal?

Can I do this? God, I know it's a mistake, but right now my body is so on board with the idea, I'm finding it hard to shut him down. I tilt my head up to see his face, studying the curve of his lips, the straight line of his nose. His hair is loose around his shoulders and a bit damp from a shower. I reach up and finger a wavy strand, wrapping it around my finger, just like Jonah's trying to wrap himself around my heart.

My heart's off limit, but my body... it has needs. And Jonah's doing a damn good job of stoking them.

I do want him. At least I can be honest enough with myself to admit that. "All right, fine."

His eyebrows rise, as if he's surprised.

Taking a deep breath and mentally steeling myself, I whip off my T-shirt and drop it to the floor. I'm no prude, nor a shrinking violet. This is sex, pure and simple. I want it, he wants it, so there's no point in drawing this out and turning it into something it's not. My sports bra follows my T-shirt to the floor with a light thud. Jonah's staring at me in the flickering moonlight as if enthralled.

"Is there a problem?" I say, reaching down to pull off my boots and socks.

"No." His voice sounds incredulous. And then his hands go to the waist band of his sweats and he shoves them to the floor, leaving him naked. The fact that he was commando underneath just makes me that much hotter. Just the sight of his naked body makes my sex clench hotly.

I rid myself of my cargo pants and undies just as quickly.

My hands find his cock unerringly as it bobs in the air between us, already stiff as a rod, thick and hot against my fingers. I latch onto him, drawing him closer, and he makes a gruff sound low in his throat as he takes a step toward me, bringing our bodies flush. The heat and the substantial size of him feel so good in my hands.

He has an incredible body, with broad, well-muscled shoulders, firm biceps covered in tats, and strong forearms. His hands snake around my torso, pulling me close. I groan at the feel of my bare breasts brushing against his lightly furred chest. His cock stirs eagerly between us.

He runs his hands down my back, then lets them slip farther down to cup my buttocks. When he draws me closer, I feel his erection nudging my belly. I groan at the contact. The truth is, I've been thinking about this a lot, wondering what he would feel like, what he would taste like. And now it appears I'll get to find out.

I sink to my knees, padded by the pile of our discarded clothing on the floor, and wet my tongue before flicking it out to swipe the head of his cock. I catch a taste of his pre-come.

He jerks, and his cock kicks hard in my hands. "Lia!"

But I'm not here for conversation. I'm here to fuck. And that's what we're going to do – that's *all* we're going to do. I keep reminding myself, this is just a hook-up, pure and simple, nothing more. I won't let it be anything more.

Whatever he was about to say ends up a garbled mess when I suck him deep into my mouth, one hand stroking his length as the other cradles his heavy sac.

He shudders. "Jesus, Lia!"

I pull back and look up at him, shocked by the intensity in his heated gaze. Then I proceed to blow his mind, using my lips and tongue and hand to stroke, lick, and caress every inch of him, from the bulbous head, down his thick stalk, to the root of his cock. Breathing hard and fast, he strokes my hair as he murmurs mindless praise.

I've learned to take control of sexual encounters, doing this on my terms. If I drive him crazy right off the bat, he'll be desperate to get inside me, desperate to come. And while I'm driving him over the edge, I can easily take care of myself in the process, then quietly make my escape. It's a win-win for both of us. And afterward, we can pretend it never happened. We can go right back to the way things were.

I walk him back toward the sofa and push him down, then kneel between his legs. His erection is impressive, lifting up from the thatch of dark hair between his legs. A shaft of light hits him right on his chest, and I'm treated with a visual feast. His chest is a work of art, with its beautifully defined pectoral muscles and crisp dark hair. His arms are rugged, with sexy tendons leading down to his strong, long-fingered hands. Those hands, so gentle now, are stroking the sides of my head and he's watching me swallow his cock with an intensity that takes my breath away.

Our gazes connect, and I can't look away. With his gorgeous body on display, and his wild, dark hair down loose on his shoulders, he looks like a fallen angel. I want him like this, not all tidy and neat, but raw and exposed.

His skin is tan, bronzed by the sun, and his abdomen is ridged with taut muscles. His chest hair converges into a thin dark line that leads down to my destination. He spreads his legs to make room for his heavy sac.

I stroke his cock from root to tip with one hand, while my other hand slips between his thighs to gently massage his balls. I lean forward to take him into my mouth again, when he stops me.

"Come here," he says, trying to pull me up onto the sofa with him.

I imagine he thinks this is about hearts and flowers, cuddling and kisses. But that's not what I'm looking for. I use my mouth and my hands to short circuit his brain, licking and sucking him in deep, with the sole purpose of driving him wild. Soon his hips are bucking as he lifts himself, mindlessly trying to shove himself deeper into my mouth. He's breathing hard, gasping, his hands cradling my head.

"Lia, my God! Please!"

I'm not sure what he's asking for. Please what? Stop? Keep going? Make him come? When his balls tighten and draw up, and I know he's close. I can feel the blood pounding through his length, a thick vein pulsing in time with his rapid heartbeat. He's so close! He's pulling on me now, trying to get me to come up onto the sofa with him.

It dawns at me that we're missing something crucial. "Shit! Condom!" I rise to my feet and make a run for the bathroom, where I know there's a stash of condoms in the cupboard. I grab one and return to the sofa, ripping open the small packet. I roll it down his erection, then crawl up next to him on the sofa. I open my legs to make room for him, then pull him down on top of me.

"Wait," he says. "What's the rush?"

His lips mold themselves to mine, and his kiss is unexpectedly sweet, taking me by surprise. I was expecting something quick and frantic, not this tenderness. When I suck in a shaky breath, he takes advantage and deepens the kiss, sliding his tongue inside my mouth, stroking me and setting my body on fire. As if he can tell what he's doing to me, he slips his hand down between us and touches me, slipping his fingers between my flushed folds.

I chuckle. "Don't worry, I'm ready."

I know I'm ready because I can feel the wetness between my legs. My sex is tingling, throbbing with need. I take hold of him and guide him to my opening. He groans as the head of his cock nudges inside me, sinking into wet flesh.

But he takes his sweet time, rocking gently into me, one slow inch at a time.

I lift my hips and urge him deeper inside. He thrusts, and I gasp at the sudden fullness. He's a big guy. A *really* big guy. I can't remember ever being stretched like this before. It steals my breath.

Jonah lifts my leg over his hip, opening me up so he can settle more fully between my thighs. I can't help moaning at the sensation of being filled like this.

"Are you all right?" he says, searching my gaze.

"Yes. Just... yes, I'm fine."

Coated with my arousal, he moves more easily now, stroking inside me with a rhythm and angle designed to make me come. I lift my hips, meeting him thrust for thrust, urging him to move faster, harder.

"Lia."

I close my eyes, wanting to savor the pleasure of feeling him move inside me. "What?"

"Baby – "

"Don't call me that!"

"Slow down. There's no rush."

I open my eyes to see that he's gritting his teeth. He's clearly on edge, and I don't like the way he's looking at me, like he's on the verge of confessing something I don't want to hear.

I tighten my sex on him, squeezing him hard, and he cries out as his orgasm hits him fast and hard. He comes with a hoarse cry, his expression tight, as if he's in pain. I don't bother to get myself off, because I can't stay here another minute. I've got to get out of here before he says something that will ruin everything... before he says something he can't take back, something we can't pretend away.

I push him off of me and roll off the sofa, leaving him in stunned silence, watching me as I pull on my clothes. While he deals with the condom, I let myself out of the room and shut the door behind me, then make a run for it, seeking the solace of my bedroom.

After a quick trip to the bathroom to clean up, I strip off my clothes and crawl between my sheets, hugging the spare pillow to me. My throat is painfully tight, and I can feel scalding tears on my cheeks. I'm shaking, and I feel like I've been put through a ringer.

"Shit!" It was supposed to be a hook-up, that's it! Nothing more! I never expected to feel like this. But now there's a giant, aching hole in my chest. I press my face into my pillow to catch the tears that won't stop. I don't want to feel anything, damn it!

I'm so wrapped up in my own emotional meltdown that I don't hear Jonah slip into my room. The only warning I get is the shock of his hot body sliding into bed behind me, his arms coming around me as he pulls me against his chest.

"Jesus, Lia," he says, holding me close. His lips are in my hair as he alternately kisses and nuzzles the back of my head, sending shivers coursing through me. "You want to tell me what the hell all that was about?"

↝ 21

I realize numbly that he's wearing sweat pants, while I'm butt naked. But at the moment, I really don't care. His arms feel so good around me, I turn to him and press my nose against his chest and breathe in deeply, loving the warm, male scent of him. I just want to close my eyes and enjoy the moment. And for a little while, I can pretend I'm not some fucked up girl who's incapable of trusting a guy.

"I'm not just some random fuck, you know," he says without heat, as he brushes my hair back from my face. "I won't let you trivialize what we did. Why did you run out on me? You couldn't get out of there fast enough."

"What are you complaining about? You got off."

He chuckles. "If getting off was all I was interested in, I could have done that alone upstairs in my room."

I try to pull away, but he holds me tight. "Well, that's all I'm offering," I say.

"That's not enough," he says. "I want more. I don't want a quick fuck in the dark. I want you."

"You had me."

"No, I didn't." He comes up on his elbows, looming over me. "I want you, Lia. Not just a fuck. I can get that anywhere."

His gaze drifts down to my lips, and my mouth goes dry.

"Why me?" I say, as my heart thunders in my chest.

He shrugs. "The heart wants what it wants, right? All I know is that when I look at you, my entire body sits up and takes notice. It's everything about you – your strength, your fearlessness, your beauty, hell, even your snarky attitude turns me on. I watch you go after people twice your size and I'm like, *Damn! Look at her.*"

I shake my head, chuckling. The man is nuts.

"Are you blushing?" he says, smiling. "You are. You're blushing!"

"I am not!" I half-heartedly shove him, but he doesn't budge.

He grins. "Lia, we both know you could break my balls in a heartbeat if you wanted to. But you haven't. Why is that?"

"Don't tempt me," I growl, trying to buck him off me.

"I think it's because you don't want to hurt me."

"Like I said, don't tempt me, Locke. I'm *this close* to tossing your ass across the room."

He leans down and brushes the tip of his nose against mine. It's an unexpected, gentle move, and it throws me off balance. My traitorous tongue comes out to wet my lips, as if it has a mind of its own.

"I know you can," he whispers, his lips just inches above mine. "But the thing is, I don't think you want to." He runs the tip of his index finger down the bridge of my nose. "I watched you drop those two guys at McIntyre Security without a second thought. You didn't hesitate for one second."

Slowly, Jonah skims his lips along my jawline, then down the curve of my throat to my pulse point, where he plants a deep kiss. I feel a soft fluttering in my belly and an aching heat between my legs. My body is so primed to come, right on the edge, and he's turning me into a wreck.

He breathes my name against my throat as he kisses my pulse, which I'm ashamed to admit is racing. "Make love *with me* this time."

The yearning in his eyes is palpable. He leans over me, and his hands grasp mine and press them to the mattress, one on either side of my head. He waits for an answer, as patient as always, while my heart is galloping in my chest and I'm drowning in need. He doesn't play fair.

I know what he wants, of course. It's not just sex – he wants a connection. He wants all that emotional crap – the very thing I've taught myself to live without. But I can't do the emotion thing. I did it once, and it nearly killed me. I can't go through that again. And with a celebrity who's always in the spotlight? Impossible!

I shake my head, sorrow gutting me. "I can't." My voice is little more than a hoarse whisper. "I can't give you what you want. You're wasting your time with me."

For a moment, he can't hide his disappointment. Then his expression hardens. "Why are you so afraid? Somebody really did a number on you, didn't they? I'd sure like to know who."

"Forget it. It doesn't matter."

"Of course it matters." He quickly switches gears. "You gave me one hell of a lot of pleasure tonight, and you got nothing. Now it's my turn to reciprocate."

He rolls on top of me, and I squirm beneath him, half-heartedly trying to buck him off. But he weighs a ton, and he's not easily dislodged. I feel his erection pressing against me, and my belly clenches with need. "You don't need to."

"But I want to. You had your mouth on me. What makes you think I don't want the same thing?"

Oh, my God, the thought of him going down on me is both thrilling and absolutely terrifying. I've never let any guy do that to me. "No, Jonah. We can't." It's been a long day, and I'm hardly fresh as a daisy. At least he had the luxury of showering earlier. "We just had sex, and I haven't showered."

"That's okay," he says. "I want to taste *you*, not your body wash."

"Jonah... no. Seriously, no."

He pouts. Honest to God, his lips turn down in a stupid, sexy frown, and he pouts like a little boy. "Please?"

"You're completely nuts, you know that?"

He grins triumphantly. "Is that a yes?"

I buck against him again, this time causing his erection to press against the apex of my thighs. The thick length of him feels so good, and I want him inside me again. I want to savor the feel of him, just this once.

I roll my eyes. "All right, fine. Just make it quick. I don't have all night."

Jonah chuckles. "Wow, you're such a romantic." He rolls off me and pulls the sheet away from my naked body, and I shiver in the cool air. His eyes widen as he looks his fill.

He still has his sweat pants on, which definitely puts me at a distinct disadvantage. I reach for the waistband. "Take these off."

"Not quite yet," he says, sliding down the bed and spreading my legs open. He's certainly not wasting any time.

"Jonah – "

"Shh."

I cover my eyes with one hand. Honestly, I'm not sure I'm ready for this.

After settling his broad shoulders between my thighs, he pries the lips of my sex open and studies me. Good God, I can't believe I'm letting him do this. To my utter horror, my thighs start shaking.

"Relax, Lia."

"That's easy for you to say."

"No one's ever gone down on you before, have they?" he says, sounding genuinely surprised and more than a little pleased.

"Oh, shut up and get it over with."

When his tongue flicks my clitoris, I cry out, my body bowing off the mattress. It feels shocking – shockingly good, shockingly intimate. I'm definitely not ready for this.

Jonah pins my thighs with his forearms and uses his fingers to hold me open. He gets serious, then, his tongue tormenting my clit with single-minded determination, pushing me right to the edge.

"Jonah!" Before I know it, I'm thrashing in his hold, gasping for breath as my heart hammers in my chest.

The blunt tip of a finger rims my opening, gliding easily through the wetness, and then it sinks inside me, stroking me deep with expert precision. His double assault leaves me mindless, and I writhe on the bed, alternately whimpering like an idiot and moaning like a banshee. His tongue is relentless as it teases and torments my clit, sending me spiraling upward into a devastating orgasm. At the same time, his finger rubbing inside me lights me up like the 4th of July. I don't think I've ever screamed so loud before. And I don't even want to contemplate the odds that someone might have heard me.

He gently teases my clit as I come down from the high, my nerves overwrought and exquisitely sensitive. My hands are in his hair, gripping him tightly one moment and then petting him the next. I don't think I've ever had such an explosive, toe-curling orgasm in my life.

Jonah surges up, wiping his beard and mouth on the sheet, then reaches inside his sweats pocket to pull out a condom packet. He frantically tears open the packet with his teeth, then shoves down his sweats and quickly rolls the condom onto his erection. Damn, he's hard again already.

He crawls between my trembling thighs and looms over me, leaning down to kiss me. It's shocking to smell myself, warm and earthy, on him. He grabs one of my legs and brings it up over his thigh and holds me wide open as he settles himself in place. He guides himself to my soft, wet core and presses in, slowly but steadily. My hands grip his biceps, and I gasp as he fills me once more. But I have a feeling this time will be different.

"Okay?" he says.

I nod, not trusting myself to speak. I feel overwrought, emotionally and physically. I'm definitely out of my comfort zone. Right now, he's the strong one, not me. He's the one taking no prisoners tonight. I have no choice but to... trust him, and that's not easy for me to do.

"Shh, it's okay," he murmurs as he lowers his mouth to mine, his lips nudging mine open to deepen our kiss. His tongue makes love to mine, mimicking the thrust and withdrawal of his cock. When my hands slip down to grip his buttocks, and my short nails bite into the twin globes, he groans raggedly. As he rocks into me with a slow and steady rhythm, I lose myself in him, just this once, savoring the heat and strength of him. Pleasure swells inside me as he strokes my insides, and I let him take me to a place I've never been before.

Just as he tenses in my arms and throws his head back to cry out, I'm caught by a second orgasm that I never saw coming. My shocked cries join his as we strain together.

* * *

Sometime later, I surface in the darkness to find myself plastered against Jonah. His arms are around me, and my head is lying on his shoulder. Our legs are entwined. I've never slept with a lover before. It feels... good.

"You okay?" His voice is low and rough.

"Yeah. What time is it?"

"A little after three."

I groan. "Why are you still awake?"

I feel his shoulder lift as he shrugs. "It's a miracle I have you naked in my arms, Lia. I'm going to enjoy the opportunity while I can. Go back to sleep, tiger."

"*Tiger*? Are you kidding me?" I don't know if I should be amused or offended.

"When I called you *baby* last night, you yelled at me. I figured if I called you *pumpkin*, you'd knee me in the balls."

"True," I say, and then I yawn.

He tightens his hold on me. "So tiger it is. Go back to sleep."

"Don't tell me what to do." And that's the last I remember, because my body is warm and satiated, and my eyelids weigh a ton. There's no way I can keep them open. I'll just have to kick him out of my bed in the morning.

22

When I awake again, it's light outside, and the digital clock by my bed reads nine-thirty. I never sleep this late. I'm lying beside Jonah, who's pressed up against my back, his arm a dead weight around my waist. My backside is toasty warm cradled against his body, and I have to admit I like it. I smile when I feel his erection nudge me. Even in his sleep, he's got sex on his mind.

Carefully, I extricate myself from his hold and head to my bathroom for a much needed shower. After dressing, I see I have a text message from Beth. It's an SOS.

Can I see you today? PLEASE? I really need to talk to you. Lunch maybe?

I'm surprised by how good it feels to see her reaching out to me like this. I was afraid we'd drift apart now that I'm assigned to guard someone else.

I text her back:

Sure. I'll arrange for back up. When and where?

Can you come to Clancy's later this morning?

I glance at Jonah, who's still out cold, then text her back:

You got it. See you soon.

Then I text Shane, telling him I need someone to fill in for me for a few hours so I can see Beth. He replies shortly afterward to let me know that Miguel will be at the rental house at eleven.

I leave a note for Jonah on my pillow: *Be back later this afternoon. Miguel Rodriquez is filling in for me. You'll like him. He's chill. Behave yourself.*

At eleven-thirty, I'm walking into Clancy's Bookshop, looking for its new manager. I make a quick round of the first floor of the store, but I don't see Beth. I also don't see Sam anywhere, but that's not a surprise. He's wherever she is. I do find the assistant manager, Erin O'Connor, arranging some hardcover books on a table. If I can't find Beth, Erin's the next best thing.

Erin smiles at me, flashing a pair of dimples. This girl really is too cute for her own good, with her soft round face and chin-length brown hair clipped back on one side with a barrette. She reminds me of a doll, with her porcelain complexion, freckles, and big blue eyes.

"Hey, Irish," I say. "Where's your boss?"

"Oh, hey, Lia," Erin says. "Beth's upstairs in her office. She's been holed up there all morning."

"Is something wrong?"

Erin frowns. "I guess you could say that. You'd better ask her."

"Thanks."

I race up the ornate, curved staircase to the second floor and head down the hallway that leads to the administrative offices. When I reach Beth's office I rap twice on her door, then walk in. Beth's seated at her desk, looking pale – I mean, more pale than usual. Even from across the room I can see the faint shadows under her eyes. Something's definitely wrong. Sam's lounging on a sofa with his scuffed leather boots propped up on a small coffee table, doing something pointless on his phone.

"By all means, red, make yourself useful," I tell him as I walk in.

"Thanks, shorty, I will." He doesn't even bother to look up from his phone.

I park my butt on the corner of Beth's desk. "What's wrong, Princess? Talk to me."

She looks up at me, swallowing hard, and then her eyes dart cautiously in Sam's direction.

"All right, cowboy," I tell him. "This is girl talk. Get lost."

"I can do girl talk," he says, winking at me. Then he looks at Beth, all seriousness now. "You want me to bug out, sweetie?"

She nods. "If you don't mind. I need to talk to Lia for a bit. Why don't you go down to the cafe and get something to eat? It's almost lunch time."

Sam jumps to his feet. "Evac time," he says, eyeing Beth speculatively. "You're sure?"

Beth nods. "Yes. I'll be fine."

"Take your time, red," I say. "I'm taking Beth out for lunch."

Sam nods, pocketing his phone. "You girls try to stay out of trouble."

I make a face at him. "Funny."

* * *

Beth and I walk three blocks to our favorite little coffee shop just off N. Michigan Avenue.

"Sam's gay, isn't he?" I say.

She smiles and nods. "He's not real open about it, so don't tell anyone. But yeah, he is. The whole *don't-ask-don't-tell* thing was still in effect when he was in the military."

"I never picked up on it before today. But he definitely set my gay-dar off back there."

Beth chuckles. "I think it means he feels comfortable around you now. He trusts you."

We reach our destination, a local coffee and sandwich shop owned by Gina Capelli, the younger sister of Peter Capelli. Much younger sister, that is. While Peter's pushing forty, Gina's in her late twenties. I guess the hospitality biz runs in the family. Gina's coffee shop could give Starbucks a run for its money with all their fancy coffee drinks, plus they serve great food and they have a kick-ass bakery. Plus, Gina's really cool, even if she is one of those high-brow Capellis.

We claim an available table in the corner of the cafe near a window overlooking the crowded sidewalk. The atmosphere is welcoming and cozy, and the tables are filling up quickly with both tourists and locals taking their lunch breaks. It's easy to tell the tourists apart from the locals. The wide-eyed tourists gaze out the windows at the bustling cityscape, trying to take it all in, while the locals have their noses buried in their phones and tablets. The whole place has a vintage feel to it, with the dark wood floors burnished to a warm glow. The dark wood tables are antiques with mismatched wooden chairs, and the windows are covered with lacey white curtains.

Almost as soon as we're seated, Gina stops by with glasses of ice water.

"Hi, Beth. Hi, Lia," she says, smiling as she hands us menus. She looks at me. "Peter said you were at Renaldo's last night with Makayla Hendricks and Jonah Locke. Are you really bodyguarding for Jonah Locke?"

I nod, taking one of the menus from her. "Yeah. Someone has to do it."

She shakes her head. "That guy is drop-dead gorgeous. Do you two know what you want, or do you need a moment?"

We each end up ordering the special, half a sandwich and a bowl of soup, along with an iced coffee drink. It's early fall now, so pumpkin spice is all the rage.

"She sure doesn't act like an heiress to a huge ass fortune," I say, as Gina walks away to place our orders.

Gina and her brother each inherited an ungodly amount of money from their paternal grandmother a few years ago, but you'd never know it by looking at Gina. She's dressed in jeans and a cream lace peasant top, and her shoulder-length chestnut hair is up in a ponytail. She could be hobnobbing with the rich and famous anywhere in the freaking world, but instead she chooses to run a quaint little coffee shop downtown Chicago.

Beth fiddles nervously with the little dessert menu on the table, flipping through the laminated cards picturing cupcakes, cookies, brownies, and pumpkin bread. My trouble radar goes off loud and clear.

"All right, Princess, spill it. What's wrong?"

She looks at me with teary eyes.

"Beth. Tell me."

She shakes her head dismissively. "It's not important, just forget it."

I snort in a very unladylike manner. "You wouldn't have sent out an SOS if it wasn't important. Now talk."

She takes a deep breath as she fiddles nervously with her empty straw wrapper. "All right, but you have to promise not to tell Shane."

I'm not about to make any such promise. "Continue."

"It's about the wedding."

That takes me by surprise. "What about it? Have you come to your senses finally? Are you dumping my brother's sorry ass?"

She looks shocked. "Of course not!" She starts to say something, then hesitates and covers her face with her hands, puffing out a loud breath.

"I'm not a mind reader, Beth. Spit it out."

She drops her hands. "This is not about Shane. Well, sort of it is."

I roll my eyes. "I knew it! What has my asshat brother done this time?"

"He left all the decisions about the wedding to me, and he gave me carte blanche. He said I could plan whatever I want. I know he was just trying to be helpful, but it's not working out that way. He hired a professional wedding planner to help me. Her name is Monica, and she's very nice and all, but... well, everything just keeps escalating. Shane has so many friends and business associates, and you McIntyres have a freakishly huge extended family. My God, I've never known a family with so many aunts and uncles and cousins! My family's tiny in comparison – just Mom and Tyler – and Gabrielle, of course, and I wanted to invite Sam and Mack and Erin. Anyway, now the guest list is nearly three hundred people. Shane said that's fine, but I can't stand up in front of three hundred people!"

"Beth, stop! For crying out loud, take a breath."

Beth is flushed, and she clasps her hands on the table in an attempt to still their shaking. When I start laughing, she scowls at me.

"This isn't funny, Lia! I'm scared to death. I just want to cancel the whole thing. I want to be married to Shane more than anything in the world, but don't want to *get married*. If that makes any sense. Can't we just bypass all the getting-married part and fast forward to the married part?"

A server brings our food and coffees to the table.

"Eat," I say, "before you pass out. Yes, it makes perfect sense." I bite into my sandwich – a grilled chicken and pesto panini – and groan. God, the food here is good.

Beth's food sits untouched. She looks utterly miserable, so I take pity on her. "Beth, there's an easy solution. Elope."

"What?"

"You heard me. Elope. Get married at the courthouse. Or run off somewhere and do it." I shrug. "Problem solved. You're married, but without all the hoopla."

She looks stricken. "I can't do that!"

"Eat your food. And why the hell not?"

"Because Shane would be crushed. He's so excited about this wedding. The dress, the tux, the wedding party, the catering, the reception. He asks me about it all the time. I can't just tell him we're tossing it all out the window and eloping."

I shake my head, amazed at how clueless this girl can be sometimes. For such a smart girl who's getting straight A's in her graduate MBA program at U. of Chicago, Beth can be a little dense at times. "He's doing all this for *you*, knucklehead. He probably assumes you want this big fairy tale wedding, and he wants to make sure you get it. Trust me, Beth, Shane couldn't care less about how you two get married. You could marry him in a back alley, for all he cares. He just wants to be married to you. He won't care one bit how it happens."

Her eyes widen. "Are you sure?"

I give her my *duh* face. "Yeah, I'm sure. Look, just cancel all the wedding plans and elope. Would you like that?"

Her expression brightens and she gives me a killer smile. "Oh, God, yes, I'd love that. We could have a small reception afterwards, with just our immediate family and close friends. Your family and mine, and Cooper, Sam, Mack, Erin, Gabrielle, Miguel, Peter. And your parents! We'll wait until they're home from Italy. They'll be home by Christmas, right?" She looks hopefully at me. "Do you really think he'd be okay with this? No big church wedding? No big reception? Just something small and private? Are you sure?"

These two really need to work on their communication skills. She could have just asked him and saved herself a lot of grief. "Yeah, I'm sure. He wants to be your husband. He doesn't give a flying fuck how it happens."

"Sorry, I couldn't help overhearing," Gina says as she returns to our table to set down a little dessert plate filled with an assortment of cookies and brownies. "I'd be happy to host a wedding reception for you, Beth, as our gift, mine and Peter's. We could hold it wherever you like. Here, or at Renaldo's, or any place you choose. I can cater anything you'd like, and I promise you a kick-ass wedding cake."

Beth smiles radiantly. "Thank you, Gina. That sounds wonderful."

"It's our pleasure," she says. "And lunch is on the house today. Consider it an engagement present."

While Beth and Gina are bonding over reception plans, my phone vibrates with an incoming message. Thinking Jonah might be trying to reach me, I check it. It's not from Jonah, though. It's from Miguel. That can't be good.

You might want to get back here. All hell's breaking loose on your boy.

Shit! I look at Beth, ready to apologize for ditching her.

Beth looks like the weight of the world has been lifted off her shoulders. "You have to go, don't you?"

I nod. "Yeah. Sounds like there's trouble back at the house."

She reaches for her purse. "Then let's go."

I feel a pang in my chest as I realize just how much I miss Beth. I miss seeing her every day. We hurry back to Clancy's so I can turn her over to the watchful eyes of Sam, who's loitering near the front entrance, watching for her.

"It's about time!" Sam says, as we reach the front doors. "I was about to put out an APB."

"Ha, funny," I tell him. When Beth gives me a tight squeeze, I whisper in her ear. "Elope, got it? No worries, no pressure. Tell him tonight, all right?"

She nods. "I will. I promise."

23

I make it back to the rental house in record time. The second I hop out of my Jeep, I can hear the ruckus coming from inside the house. Numerous voices, all shouting, and it's impossible to make out what they're griping about. Miguel wasn't kidding. All hell is breaking loose.

As I approach the back door, the security guard steps back to let me pass. "They've been goin' at it for nearly an hour," he says, shaking his head.

I stalk through the kitchen – right past a silent Esperanza – and head for the source of the commotion, the dining room.

My eyes immediately light on Jonah, who's seated at the dining room table, a half-eaten breakfast sitting on the table in front of him, long abandoned. Miguel is leaning against the wall behind Jonah, his arms crossed over his chest and a disgusted look on his face.

I nod at Miguel. He comes away from the wall and marches right past me, slowing down only long enough to bump fists with me. "Thanks for the heads-up," I tell him.

Miguel nods. "Anytime. They're all yours." And then he's out the door.

Dwight's on his feet, directly across the table from Jonah, leaning toward Jonah with his hands planted on the table top. Dwight's doing most of the shouting. Makayla, the other one who's yelling, is pacing the room in a pair of gold fuck-me heels, a red mini-skirt, and a transparent, white silk halter top. Her nipples are rouged a deep dark red – I can tell because she's not wearing a bra. *Really?* Dressed like a hooker at one o'clock in the afternoon?

The rest of the band is seated around the table, warily eyeing the bickering grown-ups like little kids watching their parents having an argument.

I smack my hand on the table, and everyone jumps. "What the hell's going on?"

All eyes turn to me, accompanied by a variety of expressions. Dwight looks irritated at my arrival, Makayla pissed off. The boys seem to perk up at the addition of a new variable in this clusterfuck. Jonah looks relieved.

Dwight lifts a dismissive hand in my direction. "This doesn't concern you, Lia. Go to your room."

I plant my arms across my chest and glare at the king of the douchebags. "Excuse me? Did you just tell me to go to my room? Seriously, dude, you are not the boss of me."

Jonah chuckles and Makayla steps forward, towering over me in her pointy-toed, witchy shoes. "This is none of your business, Lia," she says. "So just butt out."

I return her icy stare. "Does it have anything to do with Jonah?"

"Of course it does!"

"Then it *is* my business." I turn to Jonah. "What the hell's going on?"

Jonah leans back casually in his chair. "Dwight wants me to sign on to an additional North American tour starting next month. We just toured the U.S. and Canada last winter and spring. We're not supposed to tour again for another year."

"Do you want to go on tour again?"

"No."

"Okay, then don't do it. Simple."

Dwight glowers my way. "Lia, this is none of your fucking business."

"Yeah, Lia," Makayla says. "It's none of your fucking business." She grabs my arm and tries to pull me out of the room. "Can I talk to you?"

"No, you cannot." I pull my arm free. "Why are you even here? Who invited you?"

"I did," Dwight says. "She's part of this discussion."

Then it dawns on me what this is about, and I look at Jonah for confirmation. "He wants you to tour *with Makayla*?"

Jonah nods, looking less than enthused.

I start laughing – I can't help myself. "I guess Dwight's not been paying attention."

"Lia, just get out," Dwight says, pointing toward the kitchen. "Your services are no longer needed."

Fed up, I skirt the table and grab hold of Jonah's T-shirt. "Can I see you in the hall please?"

Jonah follows me out into the hallway, and I close the door behind us – maybe a little harder than necessary – effectively shutting out the noise.

"Do you want to tour with Makayla?"

He rolls his eyes at me. "Have *you* been paying attention?"

"All right then. Do you have anything important scheduled between now and the performance Friday night?"

"No."

"Good. Go pack a bag. Pack light, and be quick about it. We're leaving."

Jonah takes the stairs two at a time and disappears from sight. I head to my room and pack my own bags, and I'm back at the foot of the staircase just as he reappears with a gray duffle bag thrown over his shoulder and an ancient brown guitar case in his hand.

"Let's go." I push him down the hallway toward the door that leads directly into the kitchen. "We'll be gone before they even know it."

"Where are we going?" He seems more curious than concerned.

"Away from here."

Esperanza is standing at the kitchen counter cutting up potatoes as we pass through on our way to the back door. Her elegantly-shaped, dark eyebrows rise in surprise, but she doesn't say a word.

"If Dwight asks, tell him I'll have Jonah back Friday afternoon in plenty of time for the show."

She nods, not missing a beat as we slip out the back door.

* * *

"Where *are* we going?" Jonah says, as I drive the Jeep through the gates and out onto the street.

"Away from here."

"Care to be a little bit more specific?"

"Nope."

As soon as we hit the highway heading north, I hit a speed dial number on my phone and Jake answers.

"Hey, sis. What's up?" he says.

"I need to borrow the cabin for a couple of days."

"Sure, help yourself. Everything okay?"

"Yeah, everything's fine. We just need a break from Crazytown."

Jake chuckles.

"Let Shane know, will ya?" I say. "Tell him I'll have Jonah back in time for Friday's performance."

Jake laughs. "Why aren't you telling him this yourself?"

"Because he'll yell at me, that's why."

"All right. I'll see you Friday. Have Jonah at Rowdy's by four o'clock for a sound check and dress rehearsal."

"Will do. You'll be there?"

"Yep. I'm handling security."

Once I hang up the phone, Jonah looks at me. "A cabin?"

"It's an old fishing cabin just outside of Harbor Springs, out in the middle of nowhere. We can hide out there until Friday."

I can't help noticing that Jonah looks a little haggard, and there are shadows beneath his eyes. "How much sleep did you get last night?"

He shrugs, looking away. "Three or four hours maybe, early this morning."

"Then lie back and get some sleep. We have a two-hour drive ahead of us. You might as well make the most of it."

Jonah reclines his seat and leans back, closing his eyes. "Wake me when we get there."

* * *

Surprisingly, Jonah does fall asleep. I'm pretty sure he suffers from some kind of sleeping disorder. A lot of things make more sense now... like why I often hear him putzing around upstairs late at night and why I've never seen him come down for breakfast with everyone else. The poor guy's probably just getting to sleep when we're getting up. At first I thought it was just his lifestyle – the whole rocker thing, staying up late, partying, crashing all day. But now I know it's not that at all.

I stick earbuds in so I can listen to music as I'm driving and not disturb sleeping beauty. Listening to music while I'm driving keeps me alert and frosty.

We've got a full tank of gas, so it's smooth sailing up the highway to our destination, no need to make any stops. We'll stock up on supplies once we get there. It's a rough old fishing cabin set on thirty acres of woods, with a quarter mile of private shoreline right on Lake Michigan. The only amenities are a small private dock, a couple of canoes and a four-seater fishing boat moored under a canopy. When we were young, my dad used to bring us kids up there during summers, before the guys all went off to do their own things, most of them in the military. Eventually, Jake bought the place from our dad, and he continued coming up here pretty regularly by himself. He still does. I think it's his escape to get away from... things.

I pull off the highway at a nondescript exit and head east on a two-lane road that looks like it goes nowhere. It's a short drive through heavily wooded countryside that leads to Harbor Springs, population less than two thousand. Harbor Springs is a die-hard fishing town with more rental cabins than actual residents.

In the center of town, if you can call it that, there's a small grocery store, a gas station, a tackle-and-bait shop, an all-night diner, a barbecue joint, a bar, and a few other businesses. All that takes up three city blocks. That's about it. After that, there's nothing but the occasional one-story, white clapboard house with peeling paint and huge yards. And then there are all the rental cabins along the shoreline and a few charter fishing boat businesses located at the public docks.

This place is perfect for our needs. I just want to get Jonah away from the noise and the crowds and the demands on his time. I especially want to get him away from Dwight and Makayla – those two are trying to suck the life right out of him, and he's too damn nice to push back.

It pisses me off – Dwight doesn't give a fuck about what Jonah wants or needs. He's out for whatever he can get for himself. He's just using Jonah to further his own career and line his pockets. And as for Makayla – she just wants Jonah back, probably because he's a trophy boyfriend. She doesn't really care about him, or she wouldn't treat him the way she does.

* * *

Once we're in the town limits, I slow down to negotiate the narrow, brick-paved lanes. Jonah stirs from his nap and raises his seat, glancing around at the quaint throwback to a previous century.

"We're here?" he says.

His voice is rough from sleep, and the sound of it does something to my insides. Unbidden memories fill my head. I have half-formed memories of him whispering in my ear in the dead of night. There's a fluttering deep in my belly that feels suspiciously like butterflies. Ruthlessly, I shove the sensation aside.

"Yeah, we're here." I pull into the little parking lot behind the grocery store. "First things first. We'll need some groceries."

We grab just the basics that we'll need – beer, coffee, milk, eggs, bread, deli meat and cheese for sandwiches, and chips. We grab a few toiletries, just in case. Then we're back on the road. A half mile down Main Street, I turn off onto a single-lane gravel road that leads out to Jake's place on the outskirts of the little town.

"Let's drop off our stuff, then head into town," I say. I know he didn't get a chance to eat his breakfast. "We'll get you something to eat in town, then I'll give you the grand tour."

* * *

Jake's log cabin sits deep in the woods, in the middle of a clearing. It's a modest cabin, just one story, with a covered porch across the front. There are the two requisite wooden rocking chairs on the porch, along with a creaky old swing. The only sounds out here are the wind whistling through the trees and the ceaseless chatter of birds. It's all very tranquil and picturesque. Just what we need.

It's October now, so the leaves are changing into vibrant yellows, oranges, and reds, and the temperatures are pleasantly cool. The ground is littered with fallen leaves that crunch beneath our feet as we walk across the gravel drive to the front porch.

The old porch creaks and groans beneath our feet. Looking quite out of place, there's an electronic control panel next to the front door. I punch in a passcode. There's a faint click as the security system disengages the front door locks. I push the door open and step inside the sparsely furnished living room, Jonah following me in. On the wall just inside is another electronic panel – this one showing a schematic of the entire cabin.

"What's that?" Jonah says.

"Infrared scanners. They detect any heat signatures bigger than a mouse. It's to check for squatters."

The scanner looks quiet – there are no flashing indicators.

"I guess we're safe then, except maybe from mice," Jonah says, the corners of his lips turning up.

The cabin is bare bones. There's just this front room on the left side of the cabin, with a little kitchen behind it, as well as a fitness

room not much bigger than a closet. On the right are two small bedrooms with a tiny shared bathroom between them.

We carry in the groceries and put them away, then go back out to
the Jeep to get our bags and Jonah's guitar.

"Take your pick," I tell Jonah, pointing to the two bedrooms.

He heads toward the back bedroom, and I dump my stuff in the
front bedroom. Each bedroom has a double bed, a nightstand with
a lamp, a small dresser, and two windows. There are also doors that
connect each bedroom into the shared bathroom. The cabin's quite
cozy, and by cozy, I mean it's small.

After dumping my stuff and putting my gun safe under the bed, I
head to Jonah's bedroom. I sit on his bed and watch him hang his few
items of clothing in the closet. I know he's used to five-star accom-
modations. This is zero-stars. "Sorry, it's certainly not the Hyatt."

"It's fine," he says, closing the closet door. "It reminds me of my
grandpa's fishing cabin. I used to spend summers there with my
grandparents."

I can't tell if that's a good memory for him, or a bad one. "Shall we
head into town to get you a bite to eat?"

"Yes. I'm starving."

24

There was a time, a really bad, dark time, when Jake practically lived up here. I'd ride up with my dad, or with Shane or Jamie, to visit him and we'd try to talk Jake into coming back home. Usually he wouldn't. And half the time he was drunk on his ass.

I was just a little kid then, barely ten years old, and I didn't understand why Jake stayed here so often, all by himself, looking like a miserable shadow of himself. Shane always told me not to worry, that Jake would be okay. But I never understood why he was so unhappy. I figured it had something to do with his girlfriend dumping him at the last minute to get married to another guy. That had to suck.

Whenever anyone mentioned Annie's name, Jake would fly off

the handle and start throwing things. Or worse, he'd get drunk and punch holes in the walls. Even then, at the age of ten, I knew it was a shitty thing his girlfriend had done to him. How could a girl just up and marry some other guy when she was engaged to another? And why did Jake even care? Surely he could find another girlfriend. What was so special about Annie anyway? She wasn't even that pretty.

Jake was never the same again after she did that. Even today, he dates occasionally, but it's never anything serious. I can't help wondering if he's still pining for that quiet, mousey girl he almost married.

If he is, he's an idiot.

* * *

It's only a ten-minute ride into town. Already, I can feel the mood lightening in the Jeep. Jonah seems relaxed, happy even, as he turns on the radio. There's only one radio station we can pick up clearly out here without a satellite, and it plays oldies from the 60s and 70s.

"What's your favorite music, Lia?"

"Hip-hop and rap."

He chuckles, and I'm not sure if he's making fun of me or not. "Who do you listen to?"

"Pitbull, Flo Rida, Eminem. Pretty much anyone with a good beat. What about you?"

"I grew up in Detroit, so it was Mo-town all the way, Marvin Gaye, Aretha Franklin. Later I discovered rock and roll, The Rolling Stones and Aerosmith."

"We're not far from Detroit now, you know," I say. "It's just across Lake Michigan."

"Yeah, but it might as well be a million miles away."

"Do you get back there often?"

He shakes his head. "Not if I can help it. I'll go back if my mom needs something, but otherwise I stay the hell away. There are a lot of bad memories for me back there. She and my brother come visit me in LA a couple times a year. My little brother's a sophomore at the University of Michigan."

"Are you close to your mom?"

Jonah shrugs, but doesn't say anything.

"No? Yes? Maybe?"

"It's complicated."

"Your dad?"

"I have no idea where he is. No one's heard from him in a decade."

I can tell from his tone of voice that this is not something he wants to talk about. It's hard for me to relate. My family's really close. Our parents have been living abroad in Europe for the past year – a retirement gift to themselves – so we haven't seen them in a long time, but we're all really close.

"Not everyone grows up with hugs and kisses, Lia."

There's a wealth of pain in that one statement, and just like that, I realize I know *nothing* about Jonah Locke. Suddenly there's a gnawing, hollow pain in my chest, and I feel like an ass. "I'm sorry."

He shakes his head. "You have nothing to be sorry for. Don't worry about it."

* * *

I park in front of the quaint little diner in town, and we walk inside. The restaurant looks like a throw-back to the 1950's. There's a long row of booths with white Formica table tops and red vinyl benches, matching tables in the center of the room, and a row of red-vinyl barstools in front of a long counter. A middle-aged woman with a blond bee-hive hairdo welcomes us and leads us to an empty booth.

"What can I get you two to drink?" she asks as she hands us laminated menus that have seen better days.

"I'll have a Coke," I say.

"Same for me," Jonah says, opening his menu.

While our server goes off to fill our drink orders, we scan our menus. It's typical diner fare, the same food they've been serving for well over fifty years... burgers, fries, chicken tenders, hot dogs, deli sandwiches, shakes and three different kinds of pie.

I study Jonah as he peruses his menu. I can't help wondering if he regrets telling me as much as he did, even with that one rather cryptic statement about his family. I realize now just how close-lipped he's been with me about his past – and who he is.

"So it's just you, your mom, and your brother?"

He looks up from underneath his dark lashes. "Yeah." Then he goes back to looking at his menu.

"Does your brother play music?"

"No."

"Your mom?"

"No."

"Did your dad?"

His lips tighten in a flat line. "What's with all the questions?"

"Nothing. I guess I'm just curious about your family."

He frowns. "My dad was in a band years ago, back in the sixties. They never made anything of it. Just a bunch of guys singing in seedy, rundown bars."

"I guess you inherited your musical talent from him." I'm trying to make small talk here, something I'm not good at. I'm trying to get him to open up, but it's not going well. He obviously doesn't like talking about his family, but his dad in particular seems to be a sore spot with him.

When he looks at me with hard eyes, I feel like I've been punched in the gut.

I glare back at him. "What? What did I say?"

"I don't want to talk about my dad," he says.

"Yeah, I figured that much."

Jonah orders a burger, fries and a Coke. I've already had lunch, so I'm not that hungry, but I do indulge in a chocolate shake. Jonah's quiet as we wait for our food, his gaze focused on the foot traffic on the sidewalk outside the diner. Other than a few pick-up trucks driving past the diner, the street traffic is pretty nonexistent.

Finally, he meets my gaze. "I'm sorry. I just don't like to talk about him."

I nod. "It's okay. There are things I don't like to talk about too."

He nods. "In the end, he was a drunk and a bully. He used to beat my mom and my little brother."

Whoa. I wasn't expecting that. "He beat them, but not you?"

Jonah shakes his head. "I was bigger than my dad. He hit me once, and I hit him right back. After that, he was afraid of me."

"What did you mean when you said *in the end?*"

"He wasn't always a monster. I have good memories of him when I was little. It wasn't until after he lost his job and started drinking that things got bad. It was all downhill from there. He died from alcohol poisoning about five years ago."

Our waitress brings our food, and we eat in silence. Occasionally I glance up and catch Jonah watching me, and it's making me feel self-conscious. I think he might say more about his family, but he doesn't.

When our waitress comes to the table with the check, she hands it to him. I reach out to take it from him, but he holds it out of my reach.

"I've got it," he says, pulling out his wallet. He hands the woman cash. "Keep the change."

She regards the money in her hand and gives him a big smile. "Thanks, honey."

As soon as she's out of earshot, I say, "You're my client, Jonah. You shouldn't be paying my bill. It's not like this is a date."

He shakes his head. "Don't take offense at this, because you're the best bodyguard I've ever had, but you're fired."

"You can't fire me."

"Yes, I can. I just did. I guess that makes us just two people on a road trip together. Friends then, right? And as your friend, I can treat you to a shake."

"You're an idiot."

Jonah stands and holds out his hand to me. "Friends can go for a walk, can't they? Come with me. There's something I want to do."

I shake my head in dismay as I follow him out of the diner. I don't know what he's up to, but it can't be good.

25

We stroll down the sidewalk – all three blocks of it – past a little grocery, a florist shop, a used bookstore, a tattoo parlor, and an auto parts store. When we reach the end of the tiny little business district, Jonah takes my hand and leads me across the street.

Two guys on motorcycles, wearing black leather jackets and dark helmets, come speeding down the street, swerving around us as one of them yells, "Get out of the way, tourists!"

"Punks," Jonah says, laughing as we reach the opposite sidewalk.

He's still got hold of my hand, and when I try to pull free, he tightens his hold and smiles at me. "Come, there's something I want to do," he says.

It feels odd holding his hand – I'm just not used to it. No one's ever held my hand since I was a little kid. His hand is so much bigger than mine, solid and warm. And I have no idea what the gesture means to him.

We walk a couple blocks back the other way until we come to a busker on the sidewalk standing outside a clothing resale shop. He's a big, burly man with unkempt shaggy brown hair and a full, bushy beard, dressed in a pair of worn overalls and a red plaid shirt. He's playing a beat-up old guitar and singing a classic Bob Seger song – *Still the Same* – from the '70s. His empty guitar case lies open on the sidewalk in front of him, filled with coins and wrinkled dollar bills, courtesy of the good-sized crowd that has gathered to listen to him perform. His voice is as gruff as he looks, perfect for a Bob Seger song.

Jonah squeezes my hand and smiles as he watches the man perform. This is what Jonah loves, music for the sake of music. Playing just for the pleasure of it, and not for money or fame. Just for the love of lyrics and melodies.

The street performer does a double-take when he catches sight of Jonah, his eyes widening in disbelief, and I can tell the old man recognizes him. The busker nods at Jonah, and Jonah nods back, smiling. After he finishes his song, the old guy props his guitar against the front window of the shop and comes toward Jonah, offering his big hand for a shake. Jonah readily clasps the old guy's hand.

"Do you know this guy?" I hiss at Jonah.

"No."

"No, ma'am," the guy says, pumping Jonah's hand with both of his. "But I sure do recognize him." He turns his attention to Jonah. "Name's Bill Harper, son. It's a pleasure to meet you."

The folks who'd been standing around listening to Bill Harper play are blatantly eavesdropping on their conversation.

"Thank you, sir," Jonah says. "That's a fine guitar you have there. It's a Martin, isn't it?"

"You bet. It's the most precious possession I have in this world. Care to give it a try?"

"You don't mind?"

"Of course not. We musicians have to stick together." Bill picks up his guitar and hands it to Jonah, who slings the strap over his neck and grips the guitar familiarly before he begins strumming a few chords.

The crowd eyes Jonah surreptitiously, trying not to be too obvious as they watch him.

"I'd be honored if you'd play us a song, son," Bill says, pointing at the spot where he'd been standing.

Jonah looks at me and I shrug. He looks happy and relaxed, more so than I've ever seen him. A few more people join the crowd on the sidewalk, wondering what's going on.

Jonah starts strumming the guitar, and I recognize the chords. It's one of the band's earliest hits, a well-recognizable ballad. As soon as he starts singing, I see recognition lighting up the faces of the people in the crowd, and they move in closer to get a better look at the man they've likely heard on the radio countless times.

Bill opens a second guitar case and pulls out a guitar, and then he joins in with Jonah, adding some rhythm to complement Jonah's melody and offering a little vocal harmony as he accompanies Jonah. They perform two more of Jonah's songs, and the crowd on the sidewalk grows steadily. It's a well-behaved crowd of mostly adults, respectful and simply enjoying the impromptu show, nothing like the screaming hordes of girls that camp outside his house.

Jonah and Bill hit it off great, and they segway into performing some top hits from the 70s, including a couple of Rolling Stones hits and a classic Neil Young song. I smile when people throw wads of money into the guitar case. I suspect some of the people watching don't even know who Jonah is. Dressed in his ripped jeans and ratty old T-shirt, he could easily pass for a panhandler.

It's a pleasure watching Jonah enjoy himself for once, as if all the stress of the world has fallen away from his shoulders. This is what he loves – music, for its own sake.

Finally, despite several calls for an encore, Jonah hands the Martin back to Bill and shakes the older man's hand. "Thank you, sir. It was a pleasure."

"The pleasure was all mine, son."

Jonah's smiling from ear to ear when he makes his way through the small crowd to my side. Strangers are patting him on the back and thanking him for the impromptu show.

"God, that was great!" he says when he reaches me. He's breathing hard from the exertion of performing, his body putting off waves of heat. He wraps his arms around me and squeezes me in a bear hug. Hesitantly, I slip my arms around his waist and hug him back.

"I've never seen you this happy," I say, the side of my face pressed against the front of his T-shirt. I can feel his heart pounding with adrenalin.

He pulls back, smiling like a little kid who was just given the keys to the candy store. "That was awesome."

"You should play incognito more often."

He nods, but his smile falls. "I wish I could."

"Of course you can. You can do whatever the hell you want."

He gives me a half-smile, but I know it's fake.

He takes my hand again. "Let's go check out the bar. Do you play pool, tiger?"

I roll my eyes at him. "Of course I do." There isn't a game or a sport that my brothers haven't tortured me with.

"Why am I not surprised?"

* * *

The sun's going down now, and the neon lights are starting to flicker on, lighting up the front of the bar – *Lucky's*. Jonah opens the heavy wooden door, and we walk into a dimly lit honky-tonk filled with the sounds of country music coming from the juke box, the smell of beer and fried food, and the crack of pool cues striking balls and sending them careening around the billiard tables.

Jonah takes my hand and leads me to the bar. I recognize the middle-aged man behind the bar drying glasses with a white cloth. He's the owner of the place. I think his name is Hal.

I'm not sure, but I suspect Jonah and I are on a date. Or at least Jonah thinks we're on a date. The jury's still out on how I feel about it. Part of me likes the novelty of it, but if he expects me to suddenly become the docile little girlfriend, he's got another think coming.

The bartender nods at Jonah, then glances my way and does a double-take. "Well, I'll be damned! Lia McIntyre!" A big grin splits his round, craggy face. "Are you even old enough to be in my joint, young lady?"

"Yeah, I am. Hi, Hal."

Hal scans the bar, as if looking for someone. "Are your brothers here?"

"No, it's just me. And Jonah. We're staying at Jake's cabin for a couple nights. Thought we'd come check the place out."

Hal eyes Jonah critically. "You'd better behave yourself, young man," he says, wagging a finger in Jonah's face. "I know those brothers of hers quite well. If you take one step out of line, buddy, you'll be sorry."

Jonah chuckles. "Thanks for the warning. I'll keep that in mind."

We order two draft beers and go find an empty table near the pool tables. We finish off our beers, and one of the servers brings us fresh bottles, courtesy of Hal, she says. I pass on the second bottle, after all I'm technically on duty, but Jonah doesn't hesitate. As he drinks his second beer, we eye the pool tables, and when one opens up, Jonah hops up to claim it.

"What'll we play for?" Jonah says, racking up the balls. "We've got to have some stakes."

"How about... the loser cooks breakfast tomorrow?"

"Cook breakfast? No." Shaking his head, he comes around to my side of the pool table and cages me against the mahogany table with his arms. His lips graze my ear, sending a shiver down my spine. "Surely you can do better than that. How about... the loser gives the winner a full body massage? Naked. Tonight."

I roll my eyes at him, fighting a grin. He's in a fine mood tonight, and I realize just how much I enjoy simply being with him. We have more than a professional relationship. We have something akin to... friendship. Maybe it's more like a friendship with benefits, after all we've already been naked together.

"Let me get this straight," I say, trying not to smile. "If I win, you get to put your hands on *my* naked body. And if you win, I have to put my hands on *your* naked body. Either way, somebody's going to end up naked. This sounds like a win-win situation for you."

He taps the tip of my nose with his index finger and grins. "Precisely. I'm diabolically clever that way."

I laugh. I don't know if I can resist a playful Jonah. And, I think he might be just a tad tipsy. He's only had the one meal today, and he's on his third beer now. Maybe it's time for some more food. I flag down our server and ask for a couple of appetizers.

We play our game – Jonah wins the break after a coin toss – and all the while, I'm trying to get him to eat something.

He plays pretty good pool, but he's had a little too much to drink tonight to beat me. Still, I'm undecided if I want to win, or if I want him to win. Do I want to give or receive a naked, full-body massage? More importantly, I have to decide if I can even bring myself to play this game, because I've already fucked him once, and that's my limit. Actually, twice if you count both times. I've already broken my own rule. If I sleep with him again, I'll be in unchartered territory.

Not long into our game, it's obvious who's going to win. I couldn't throw this match even if I tried – I could never play pool *that* badly. It wouldn't be ethical, and I can't shame the McIntyre name that way. So I trounce him easily, and he's elated, because he thinks I'm going to run my hands all over his naked body tonight. I have only myself to blame.

"I'll tell you what," I say. "Let's go for the best two games out of three. Winner gets to decide who touches what, if anything."

That definitely catches his attention, but he's too tipsy to realize it's a losing hand for him. "Deal!"

"One caveat..."

He frowns. "What?"

"You have to eat some more and drink some coffee first. You're having a little too much fun right now. It wouldn't be a fair competition."

He reluctantly agrees and orders a pot of black coffee.

* * *

As we're sitting there drinking coffee and eating hot wings, a guy dressed in black leather pants and jacket walks up to our table and grins down at me. I recognize him as one of the bikers who nearly ran us down in the street earlier in the evening. He's got longish blond hair and a long, scraggly beard. There's a red-and-white bandana tied around his neck.

"You're not bad for a girl," he says to me, nodding at the pool table. "I was watchin' you all play."

"And you're not so tough without your motorcycle."

His eyes widen, and then he starts laughing. "Holy shit, was that you?"

"Yeah, it was."

He smiles at me, undeterred. "I watched you playin' pool, sweetheart. You're pretty good. You been playin' long?"

"Since I was old enough to see over the side of the table, so yeah."

"Then how about a little match, babe? Just you and me."

Jonah's watching our exchange with a great deal of interest.

"First of all," I say, "I'm not your *babe*."

"You could be, if you play your cards right."

Oh, my god, seriously? "No thanks, pal. Not interested."

He gives me a smug grin. "Why don't you quit wasting your time on this pretty boy here and upgrade to a real man?"

I can't help laughing. This punk has nothing on Jonah, and he's too stupid to even realize it. "Like I said, not interested."

This whole time, Jonah's just been sitting there with a smirk on his face, watching the conversation unfold. I look at him. "What are you smiling about?"

He shrugs. "I figure it's only a matter of time before you hand this guy his ass. Frankly, I'm looking forward to it."

"You wanna say that to my face?" blondie says, scowling at Jonah. "I could wipe the floor with your face."

"I'd like to see you try," Jonah says, chuckling.

Blondie turns beet red, and he looks like he's about to blow a gasket. "What, you think I can't do it? I could whip your ass with one arm tied behind my back!"

"Oh, no, it's not that," Jonah says, grinning. "It's just that if you even try, she'll wipe the floor with your face."

"Not helping," I say, glaring at Jonah. "Cut it out. I don't want any trouble here."

I turn to blondie, who's sputtering in outrage, hoping to distract him and win a hundred bucks in the process. "How about a wager?" I say, pulling my wallet out of my back pocket and withdrawing a crisp hundred dollar bill, which I slap down on our table. "A hundred bucks says I'll beat you, straight up 8-ball."

"You're on, babe!"

"Don't call me *babe*. Do you wanna rack or break?"

"I'll rack, cause when you miss on the break, I'll run the table."

Yeah, good luck with that, pal.

26

B londie lays a hundred dollar bill on top of mine, then sets his beer bottle down on *our* table and proceeds to rack the balls. I grab my cue stick and chalk up.

Since blondie racked the balls, I break, sending the cue ball hard into the formation of colorful balls. The balls scatter across the green felt surface of the table like cockroaches skittering away at the first light of day.

I manage to pocket the solid blue ball, so it's solids for me. I take another shot, then another, and I've pocketed three of my balls. Blondie looks disgruntled as he scowls at me.

"You didn't really think she could play, did you?" Jonah says, grinning smugly at my competitor. Jonah's hovering next to the pool table, and I don't think it's a coincidence that he manages to keep himself positioned between me and blondie.

"You shut the fuck up, pretty boy," blondie says, pointing at Jonah.

I miss my next shot, so it's blondie's turn. He tries for the red stripe into the corner pocket and misses, but just barely. Ha! The balls are well placed, and here's my chance to run the table. I sink three more of my solid colored balls, and I could probably drop the seventh in the corner pocket, but blondie looks like he's in danger of having a stroke, and I don't want any trouble, so I forfeit my last shot to give him another shot at winning.

He manages to sink two balls on his next turn, but he bungles the third shot. I sink my last ball, then the 8-ball, and the game's over. It took less than ten minutes.

"Good game," I tell him, giving him a respectful nod. *And thanks for the hundred bucks.*

As I reach for the money, he slaps his big, sweaty paw on top of my hand. "Not so fast, babe. Let's go for best two out of three," he growls.

Jonah's eyes narrow as he takes a few steps toward Blondie. I shake my head, signaling him to back off. Like I said, I don't want any trouble here. My brothers come to this bar when they're staying at the cabin. I don't want to make waves unnecessarily.

"Sure," I say to blondie. "Two out of three. Rack or break?"

He grabs the rack and sets up the balls. "You break."

"Fine." I shoot the cue ball, hitting the formation spot on, sending the balls crashing with a loud crack. The 8-ball shoots across the table, following an unobstructed path to the far corner pocket. It's sheer luck that it goes straight into the pocket, a swift and clean shot. I've never managed to sink the 8-ball on a break. Game over! I just wish my brothers could have been here to see this.

Blondie, who'd brought his beer bottle up to his lips, chokes on his brew. "What the fuck!"

I smile apologetically. "That was a lucky shot."

"No, it wasn't!" Blondie slams his beer down on the edge of the pool table, splashing liquid on the felt. "You cunt! You're a ringer! You're a God-damned fucking ringer!"

Jonah lunges toward Blondie, who cracks his pool cue on the edge of the table, snapping it in two, holding Jonah back with one of the jagged ends. He points the other jagged end at me. "You fucking bitch!"

I scoff. "I'm no ringer, asshole. You just can't take being beaten by a girl."

Blondie swings the broken stick at my face, just barely missing me as I jump back. That little prick nearly cut me! I'm done with playing nice. He swings at me again, and I catch the stick and jerk it out of his grasp. I throw the stick behind me, out of his reach. "Walk away," I tell him, pointing toward the exit. "While you still can."

"Fuck you!" He charges around the corner of the table to face me, his hands balled up into fists and his face beet red. "You don't tell me what to do, bitch!"

He reaches for my arm, but I've had enough of this douchebag. It's time to end it. But before I can touch him, Jonah comes barreling past me like a locomotive, crashing into blondie and sending the pair of them right to the floor. Jonah lands on top of blondie, rises his fist and slams it into blondie's face. Blondie's head snaps back and hits the wooden floor with a loud thud.

Well, shit. I can envision all sorts of lawsuits directed at Jonah. "Jonah, stop!"

But Jonah's just getting warmed up. He hauls back his right arm and drives his fist into blondie's face, once more, then again.

"Jonah, that's enough!" I intercept Jonah's fist mid-blow and hold it firm, catching his attention. "I said stop!"

Jonah looks affronted. "He tried to hurt you!"

I smile. "Tried, yes. Succeeded, no. Big difference. Now, get up."

Hal comes over to us, drying his hands on a less than pristine white dishcloth. "You two had better go," he says, looking at me. "I'm gonna have to call 9-1-1."

Great. That's all I need... for Jonah to get arrested for assault and battery while on my watch. "Come on, *tiger*," I say, urging him to his feet. "The party's over. Let's go."

Once on his feet, Jonah sways into me, and I catch him. He's still not quite sober. The coffee didn't help as much as I'd hoped.

Now there's another biker, an older guy, kneeling on the floor beside Blondie, shaking him. "Neal, wake up, man! Neal!"

At least now I know his real name. That'll come in handy when the court summons arrives.

* * *

I walk Jonah out to the Jeep, making sure he doesn't fall on his ass as he climbs inside the vehicle. Yeah, he's definitely a little worse for wear, thanks to the alcohol.

"Are *you* all right, Lia?" he asks.

"I'm fine. Are you all right?" I pick up his right hand and look at his battered knuckles, which are already discolored and swollen. There's blood on his hand, too, but I can't tell if it's Jonah's blood or blondie's – Neal's. Neal, the guy who will sue Jonah for a fortune if he gets wind of who his assailant is.

"I'm fine." He groans as he leans his head back in his seat and closes his eyes. "I am a little dizzy, though. Probably shouldn't have had that last beer."

"You don't say." I latch his seatbelt and lock his door, then walk around to the driver's side and climb in. I waste no time hightailing it out of there before someone starts asking questions. Technically, Neal started it, and Jonah was only defending my honor. As there were plenty of witnesses in the bar to testify to that, I doubt the local cops will charge Jonah with anything. But still, Jonah doesn't need the publicity.

We're barely a block from the bar when the sheriff's car passes us, lights flashing. In my rearview mirror, I watch as the vehicle pulls up to the front of the bar. Great.

* * *

"Sit down, before you fall down," I say, guiding Jonah to his bed.

He drops down on his ass and falls back on the mattress, groaning. He's absolutely wiped, from the pressures of his life, the stress of tonight, and a poor food-to-alcohol ratio for the day.

I pull off his boots and drop them on the floor. "Can you take it from here?"

"I gotta take a piss," he says, rolling to his side and then pushing himself up and off the bed. "Wait here."

"Don't worry, I'm not coming into the john with you."

He chuckles. "That's not what I meant. I meant wait here in my room for me to come back. Don't leave."

After a few minutes, I hear the water running in the bathroom, and a moment later he comes out. He walks right up to me, swaying a little on his feet.

"Get in bed, Jonah. You need sleep, badly."

He shakes his head. "What I need is *you*."

He envelopes me in his arms and holds me against his chest, his arms wrapped tightly around me, practically smothering me. Standing this close to him, I can smell him, his scent. The hint of a man's cologne, and a little sweat. And he's radiating heat like a furnace which, surprisingly, makes me want to latch onto him. But sadly, that's not part of the plan.

I walk him backward until his legs hit the side of the bed, then I gently maneuver him flat onto his back. "You need sleep."

He glances at this watch. "It's too early. I can't sleep yet. You know that."

"Why not, Jonah? You're clearly exhausted. Just relax and let yourself go to sleep."

He closes his eyes and shakes his head. He takes hold of my upper arms and tries to pull me onto the bed with him. "Lie down with me, Lia. Please. Just for a little while."

I'm finding it damn hard to resist him when he's like this. "Jonah

_ "

"Please. Just until I fall asleep."

He's manipulating me, but frankly, right now I don't care. Half of his hair has come loose from his ponytail, and he looks like a disheveled dark angel.

I know this is a really bad idea. "All right. Give me a minute." I run to my room and grab my toiletries bag, then spend a few minutes in the bathroom getting ready for bed. When I return to his darkened bedroom, I climb into bed with him, and he turns us on our sides, spooning behind me. My pulse speeds up, and I'm vibrating like a live wire.

"Just rest a while, that's all," he says, lightly stroking my arm as if trying to gentle a wild animal.

His arm snakes around my waist, and he tucks me into him. The warmth of his body is seductive, and I feel his lips in my hair. I can also feel a very impressive erection nudging my butt cheeks.

"Shh, just relax," he says. "Don't move. I'm dizzy and I might puke."

"Oh, that's a lovely thought."

"Shh, don't jinx me."

He chuckles, his breath ruffling the hair at the nape of my neck, sending tingles along my frayed nerves and making me shiver. "Shh. Don't think, don't talk, just let me hold you. Don't be afraid, Lia. I'll stay awake to protect you. I won't let him touch you. I won't ever let him touch you."

Protect me? From whom? At first, I think he means blondie – I mean Neal. But then I'm not so sure.

"Protect me from whom, Jonah?"

His breathing slows and deepens, and I suspect he's on the verge of passing out. "Hmm?"

"Who are you going to protect me from?"

"Shh, you're making the room spin. No talking."

It's well past midnight, and we've both had a long day. I'm so comfortable lying here with him that it's making me drowsy. I could easily fall asleep like this.

* * *

I must have dozed off for a while. When I stir, it's still dark outside. I roll over onto my back and look at Jonah, who's wide awake, staring at the ceiling. I can just barely make out his face in the moonlight filtering through the curtains.

"You're awake," I whisper. Although it's silly to whisper since we're the only ones here.

"Yeah. I guess old habits are hard to break."

He sounds a lot more alert now. It looks like the alcohol has run its course. But the guy needs sleep, badly. He has a performance coming up in less than 48 hours, and he needs his rest if he's going to perform in front of a crowd, even a small one. I figure if anything can knock him out, it's a really good orgasm. And if I'm going to be honest with myself, I could use one too. I woke up feeling... needy.

I unfasten my jeans and push them and my underwear off. I can tell myself I'm doing this solely for his benefit, like it's a public service or something. That way I don't have to examine my feelings too closely.

"What are you doing?" He sounds part suspicious, part amused.

"Nothing." I sit up and pull off my T-shirt and bra and toss them onto the armchair across the room.

His eyes widen in the semidarkness. Now that I'm naked and have his full attention, he stops asking stupid questions. I kneel on the bed and begin to undress him, starting with unfastening his jeans.

"Lia – "

"Shut up and go with the flow. Sit up."

He obeys, probably because he's in shock, and I strip off everything below the belt. Then I straddle his hips and pull his T-shirt up over his head and toss it aside, leaving him as butt naked as I am. We're just two naked people sharing a bed, that's all.

"Don't read anything into this, Jonah. I'm just doing you a favor." Maybe if I keep telling myself that, I'll start to believe it myself.

He's grinning at me like a fool, and he shivers when I run my hands along his muscular shoulders and down his arms, my fingers following the firm curves of his well-shaped biceps. He has strong arms thanks to his guitar playing, which is a huge turn-on for me. I get off on arm porn, especially when tats are involved. Even in the darkness, I can make out the interlocking shapes and lines of the dark tattoos snaking down his arms.

I kiss his sternum, then run my tongue down his torso, over ridges of muscle down to his belly button. He flinches when I swirl the tip of my tongue around the rim of the little indentation, and I suspect he might be ticklish there. But I keep going, following the happy trail that leads to his beautiful cock rooted in a nest of dark hair. His length rises long and thick from its base, defying gravity as it lifts into the air, almost as if it's searching for something. The broad head of his cock is a deep ruddy hue, blatantly advertising his arousal, and the thought of that blunt knob pushing inside me makes my stomach quiver.

God, I want to make him come completely undone. I want to make him shout the roof off. I lower my head and suck the broad head of his cock into my mouth, twirling my tongue around the tip, taking a moment to tease the sensitive skin beneath the rim. I can already taste his pre-come.

He gasps, threading his fingers into my hair. "What are you doing, Lia?"

I lift my head just long enough to ask, snaring his gaze. "Is that a trick question?" I had assumed he'd want this, but maybe I'm wrong. "Do you want me to stop?"

He growls low in his throat. "No, I don't want you to stop. I just thought you didn't want – "

That's all the green light I need. I draw him deeply into my mouth until the head of his cock hits the back of my throat.

"God, Lia!"

I proceed to torment the hell out of him, sucking and licking and drawing him deeply into my throat. My intention is to bring him right to the edge and keep him there as long as he can take it. He lays back on the bed and blindly fists the sheets, holding on for dear life as he groans helplessly.

He's close, really close, but I'm not ready for this to end, so I release his cock with a loud, wet sound, and his hands come up to cup my face.

"You amaze me," he says.

He reaches for the lamp on the nightstand beside the bed and switches on the light. It's just a nightlight, so it hardly puts out any light. But it's enough light to send me straight into panic mode.

"Turn it off!" My pulse jumps into my throat, and it's all I can do to keep from lunging across the bed and ripping the power cord right out of the wall.

"Lia, I want to see you."

"No! I told you, no lights. Turn it off." I'm holding on to my panic, trying not to let it overwhelm me. I'm sure he thinks I'm nuts, that it's some neurotic quirk of mine, and maybe he's right. But I really don't give a flying fuck right now. It's this way, or no way.

"All right," he says, sounding resigned as he switches off the light. His hands come to rest at my waist, and he slides them up my sides to my breasts, which feel full and tender. His big palms cup my breasts, as his thumbs sweep up to brush my nipples, making them pucker instantly. I shudder in response, as intense pleasure shoots from my breasts down to my sex.

Jonah reaches down between my legs and touches me, his fingers slipping through my wet folds. "Please tell me I can have you," he says, his voice rough with need.

Reality intrudes with a vengeance. "Shit! Do you have condoms?"

He tips his head toward his duffle bag on the armchair. "Ribbed, for your pleasure."

I smack him on the shoulder as I scramble off the bed and unzip his duffle bag. Inside, I find an unopened box of extra large condoms. An entire box. "You're an optimistic man."

I think he shrugs, but it's difficult to tell in the dark. "It never hurts to be prepared." He sounds awfully pleased with himself.

~~~~

∽ **27**

I roll a condom onto his thick erection, and damn, if that extra large condom doesn't fit him perfectly. *Show off.*

Sliding in beside him, I urge him down over me, then grab hold of his ass and pull him close, savoring the feel of his hard length pressed against my heat. His erection nudges blindly between my legs, eager to be inside me. And I'm more than ready for him. I take hold of him and direct him to my opening.

He lowers his mouth, touching his lips to mine, just a light glancing of his flesh over mine, and a shiver ripples through me. He chuckles at my reaction, then deepens the kiss, his warm lips melding with mine. We kiss like that, just a gentle melding of lips for several long, languid moments. In the back of my mind, I realize this isn't just fucking. This is something different, something more.

Something I've never experienced before... or even wanted. When his tongue slips into my mouth, searching and seeking, I sigh, our breaths mingling.

Jonah lifts his head and gazes into my eyes, and there's more emotion there than I'm prepared to deal with. "Lia – "

"Don't! Don't say a word. Just shut up and kiss me." I pull his mouth back down to mine and offer him my tongue as a distraction. It works. He greedily accepts, drawing it into his mouth and sucking on it.

I feel a connection between his sucking and the hot, aching place between my legs. My hips start moving on their own, and as I clench down hard on my sex, the pleasure is exquisite. He's the best kisser I've ever had. His mouth makes love to mine, stroking and licking and sucking until I can barely breathe. Just kissing with him is better than a lot of sex I've had.

He sinks slowly into me, the girth of him stretching me. The feeling of fullness takes my breath away, and I revel in it. My body gradually softens as it opens for him, and I take a deep breath as he seats himself fully.

He lets out a low groan. "My God, you feel so good."

I latch onto his mouth, kissing him hotly as I start to move beneath him. He withdraws almost to the tip, then sinks back inside me, slow inch by slow inch.

I gasp when he hits my cervix. "Jonah!"

He chuckles a little breathlessly. "You're trying to kill me, aren't you?"

He starts moving, slowly at first, in long, fluid strokes, his hot length dragging along my sensitive tissues. As he gradually picks up speed, pleasure sinks into me, a sweet gliding warmth that ratchets up my pulse. Before long, I'm panting like a marathoner, and we've hardly even started.

Jonah's eyes are at half mast, and he looks lost in pleasure. I smile, happy that I'm able to give him that. He's so selfless, he doesn't ask for much. It's about time somebody gave to him, without thought of receiving anything in return. I want to give him pleasure. I want to drive him wild. I lift my hips to meet his thrusts, taking him in as deeply as I can.

His eyes look almost black in the darkness. "I could stay inside you forever," he says.

He rocks his hips into mine, apparently in no hurry. He must be angling himself just right, because very soon I feel a sweet sensation swelling deep inside me. God, the man knows what he's doing.

"Right there!" I gasp. "Oh, God, don't stop. Right there!"

He maintains his angle, and I realize he's determined to make me come. So much for my idea of wearing him out with a mind-blowing orgasm. It's more like he's going to blow my mind instead. Sure enough, I feel my orgasm building, wave after wave of sensation sweeping through me. My orgasm strikes hard, lighting me up inside like a Christmas tree. I cry out as my body clenches down tightly on his cock. He starts moving in earnest now, fast, long strokes, and his climax is fast on the heels of mine. He barely lasts more than a couple minutes. He throws his head back, the tendons in his throat pulled taut as he grimaces with pleasure. "God!"

I can still feel the residual tremors from my orgasm sweeping through my body, warming me and turning my muscles to putty. Suddenly I feel exhausted, and I can only hope he does too.

We lay there for a moment, still fully joined, our hearts pounding in unison. My body is throbbing with pleasure, as is his. I know, because I can feel it. He rolls us on our sides to take his weight off of me and brushes my hair back from my face.

"That wasn't so bad, was it?" he says.

I roll my eyes. "It was all right."

He makes a mock face of indignation. "Just all right?" Then he smiles and kisses the tip of my nose. "Be right back."

Jonah disposes of the condom in the bathroom. As soon as he returns to bed, it's my turn in the bathroom as I clean up. I'm torn between going to my own room to sleep for the rest of the night or staying here with him. The truth is, I hate the thought of leaving him right now. My body's still reeling from post-coital hormones and bliss, and I just want to feel his big, warm body wrapped around mine. I'm still trying to make up my mind when he appears in the bathroom doorway.

"You're coming back to bed, aren't you?"

I nod, unable to resist his hopeful expression. He doesn't want to be alone tonight, and frankly neither do I.

Back in bed, he spoons with me, his arm around my waist, drawing me back against his chest. We lie that way for a long time, silent, relaxed, both of us lost in our own thoughts.

His hand comes up to gently cover my left breast. "Why does the light have to be off when we have sex?"

My heart starts hammering, and I think he can feel it.

His voice is a low murmur in my ear. "It's okay. I just need to understand."

There's no explanation I can give without telling him what happened, and I can't do that. Talking about it just brings the pain and the horror back again, the humiliation. My God, if he knew, if he ever saw that video, I'd die. "I can't talk about it."

"Don't you trust me?"

"I do trust you. But I can't talk about it. Please don't ask me to."

He sighs heavily. "I'd never hurt you, Lia. Surely you know that."

I don't respond, because there's nothing I can say. I don't think he'd ever hurt me intentionally – he's not a cruel person. But he can't make promises like that. Even people who love each other hurt one another sometimes.

He kisses the back of my head and tightens his arm around my waist. "It's late. Go to sleep."

"You too." After all, that was my objective. To help him get to sleep.

"I will."

Somehow I fear sleep is the last thing on his mind.

* * *

When I awake, the sun is up, and Jonah is fast asleep. I extricate myself from his iron-clad hold and slip quietly out of bed, not wanting to wake him. After a quick stop in the bathroom, I return to my room to get dressed. Then I head for the kitchen to make coffee and check my messages.

Shane, Jake, and Beth all left me messages last night, mainly just checking on us. I text them all back to let them know we're fine.

Dwight has sent me several text messages over the past few hours.

Lia, where the hell is he? Bring him back to the house ASAP.

Lia, god dammit! I need to speak to him. He's not answering his phone. Have him call me.

If you don't bring him back here within the hour, I'm calling the cops to report him as a missing person.

You're fired. I'm calling Shane to cancel our contract with McIntyre Security.

I take great pleasure in sending him back one text:

I'm fired? Good. Now leave me alone. I'll have him back in time for the performance. Stop whining.

I even have a few texts from Makayla, who apparently got my number from Dwight.

How's Jonah? I'm so worried about him.

He's the love of my life, and I'm not giving up on him. We are destined to be together. He'll realize that and come back to me.

Tell him I love him and I'll see him soon.

I block Makayla.

After turning off the security system, I take a mug of black coffee and my phone out to the front porch and sit on the swing, enjoying the tranquility. It's mid-morning, and I figure Jonah's had only a few hours of sleep. I'll let him sleep as long as he needs to.

I read for a while, then decide to walk in the woods just around the cabin. I have my phone with me, and I leave a note for him on the kitchen table in case he wakes up and wonders where the hell I am.

Jonah and I each have our own secrets. I suspect there's a reason he has trouble sleeping, and I'm afraid it's not a pretty one. I can't stop thinking about the comments he made when he was half out of his mind, about staying up all night and keeping me safe – *I won't let him touch you.* For some reason, I don't think he was talking about the biker.

Around noon, the Harbor Springs sheriff pulls up to the front of the cabin. I've been expecting him – I'm surprised it took this long. I walk down the porch steps and meet the him half way.

His name tag says SHERIFF JAMES MITCHELL. He seems young for a sheriff, in his early thirties I'd guess. Average height, trim build, with sandy blond hair, blue eyes, and wire-framed glasses. He takes off his hat and smiles. "Lia McIntyre, right?"

I nod. "That's right."

"Sheriff Mitchell. What brings you to Harbor Springs?"

I cross my arms over my chest, wondering where this is going. I have to assume he's here because of what happened at *Lucky's* last night. "Just a short visit. This is my brother's cabin. I'm visiting with a friend."

"I've played poker many a time with your brother Jake, and with Shane." He takes a small notepad and pen out of his shirt pocket. "I heard you were involved in an altercation last night at *Lucky's*."

"You could say that. Some guy accused me of cheating at pool and started manhandling me. My friend took offense at his behavior and asked him to stop."

Sheriff Mitchell grins. "*Asked* him?"

"Yeah. With his fist. It was a fair fight."

The sheriff jots down a few things. "Is your friend around? Can I talk to him?"

"He's asleep."

"At this hour?"

"He's not a morning person."

"I see. What's his name?"

"Jonah."

The sheriff makes another notation on his little notepad. "Has Jonah got a last name?"

"Are you charging him with something?"

"No. At least not yet. The guy your friend beat unconscious last night is named Neal Barker. Barker claims Jonah attacked him without provocation. Barker's considering assault and battery charges."

Shit! That's the last thing Jonah needs. "Look, blondie tried to assault me with a broken pool cue. I'd hardly call that without provocation. Jonah was just defending me. There were a dozen witnesses in the bar that night, including the owner, and any of them can vouch for Jonah's actions."

Mitchell nods. "I've spoken to a few of them already last night and this morning, and their reports support what you just said – that Neal tried to hit you with the pool cue."

"Then maybe *I* should press charges against him."

The cabin screen door opens on squeaky hinges and bangs shut, and the sheriff and I both turn to see Jonah coming down the porch steps. He's dressed in jeans, a plain white tee, and boots. His hair is pulled up haphazardly into a man-bun, and his eyes are on me. He looks sexy as hell. "Lia? What's going on?"

"Sheriff Mitchell just stopped by to say hello. Apparently, he's a family friend."

Jonah eyes the sheriff, not fooled for a second. "Is that right, Sheriff?"

Mitchell smiles politely as he shakes his head. "No. Well, yes, I guess I qualify as a family friend. But I'm here now on official business. I'm following up on assault and battery charges."

"He had it coming. He could have hurt Lia badly."

"That's what I've been told. Do you have a last name, Jonah?"

Jonah's expression hardens. "Locke."

Mitchell's eyes widen, and I wonder if it's because he realizes who Jonah is. "I see. Welcome to Harbor Springs, Mr. Locke."

"Thanks. So, now what?"

Mitchell makes another note on his little pad, then he tucks the pad and pen back into his uniform shirt pocket. "Nothing. Based on the witness statements, and my conversation with Lia, I don't think charges are warranted. If something changes, I'll let you know."

Jonah nods, extending his hand to the sheriff. The two men shake, and I see a lot of unspoken man-communication going on. Give me a break.

The sheriff heads for his patrol car. "I hope you have a nice stay, Mr. Locke. Sorry for any trouble you might have experienced. Barker and his buddies can get a little out of hand sometimes."

～ 28

S ince it's past noon, we make sandwiches, grab a bag of chips and two cold beers and head out to the front porch to enjoy our food.

"So, what do you want to do today?" I ask Jonah, as we eat sitting on the porch swing. "We have the whole rest of the day to ourselves. Do you want to go back into town?"

He gives me crooked smile. "I think I had enough fun in town last night to last me a while. Maybe we could go back to the diner tonight for dinner. How about exploring around here for a while?"

"Sure. We could hike down to the falls. Jake's property butts up to a state park with a creek and waterfall. It's an easy trail through the woods."

After cleaning up our lunch mess, we prepare for our hike. It's only two miles to the falls, not too strenuous as the path is pretty level and well marked. I'm geared up with a satellite phone and my gun, just in case. Cell service out here is spotty as hell, especially deep in the woods and down by the falls. Jonah loads a backpack with water bottles and snacks in case we get hungry.

I take the lead, since I know the terrain well. Jonah walks behind me, and we hike in comfortable silence. I get the feeling Jonah's a little lost in his thoughts, and a few times I hear him humming the melody he's been working on at the recording studio.

Before long, we arrive at our destination, Cross Creek. It's a beautiful, peaceful spot, where a pretty good-sized creek falls vertically a hundred feet into a large pool. We have the place all to ourselves.

I climb up onto a massive boulder that overlooks the falls. It's sunny, and the stone's surface is delightfully warm. Jonah climbs up beside me, and we sit up here and enjoy the scenery.

My belly's full from lunch and the sun is warm on my skin, and after a while, I start to feel drowsy. Jonah's sitting behind me, and I can't resist leaning back against him. He responds by putting his arms around me. I'm pretty sure we're flirting with boyfriend-girlfriend territory, and I find it unsettling. I'm not used to being so touchy-feely and taking comfort from other people. But at the moment, I like it and I'm loathe to give it up.

Jonah kisses the top of my head. "Thanks for suggesting this. I used to hike and camp a lot when I was a kid. I haven't done it in years, and I just now realize how much I miss it."

The only sounds we hear are the running water and the sounds of birds in the trees. It's the antithesis of what tomorrow's concert will be like. Honestly, I'm not looking forward to it. It's sure to be loud and chaotic. And I hate that he's going to sing a duet with Makayla. It's not that I'm jealous or anything – I'm not. It's just that I know he doesn't want to encourage her.

There's a question I've been wanting to ask him, and it feels like this is the right place to open this can of worms. "Jonah?"

He sets his chin gently on the top of my head and tightens his arms around me. "Hmm?"

"Are you happy?"

I look back to see his response, and he frowns, as if he's surprised by the question.

"I'm happy sitting here with you."

"That's not what I mean. I mean, are you happy with your life? With your career?"

"I love writing songs. I love playing music and singing."

"You didn't answer my question. I asked you if you were *happy* living the life you're living. There's a difference."

He releases me and leans back, and I suddenly feel bereft. For a second I think he's going to get down off the boulder. He doesn't, but there's a some distance between us now that wasn't there before. I shouldn't have pushed him.

"Sure, I'm happy," he finally says. "I'm fronting one of the most popular bands in the country right now. I'm making money hand over fist. What's there not to be happy about?"

"You still haven't answered my question."

"I don't know what you want me to say."

"How about the truth? Do you wake up every day excited about your life? Do you wake up happy and itching to be *you* – Jonah Locke, rock star extraordinaire?"

He lets out a heavy sigh. "No."

"I didn't think so."

His arms come back around me and he pulls me against him so that I'm nestled between his thighs. "I'm not an ungrateful bastard, you know. I know I have it good. A lot of guys would kill to be in my position."

"I know. But it's just not for you, is it? The music, yes, the writing and performing, yes, I get that. But not the rest of it. Not the management and the scheming and the plotting and the publicity. Not the paparazzi and the mindlessly screaming girls who camp outside your home twenty-four-seven, pretending they're in love with you when they know absolutely nothing about you."

"God, I hate all that."

His whispered response was so quiet I almost missed it. "Why is that so hard for you to admit?"

He shrugs. "Because it's a huge responsibility."

I scoff. "What is? Being famous?"

He tightens his arms around me, almost angrily. "Yes. Do you know how many people's livelihoods I'm responsible for? Not just the guys, but Dwight, Ruben, Esperanza, the roadies, the bus drivers. I'm talking at least twenty people. Twenty people whose paychecks fall on my shoulders. If I walk away from it, they all lose their jobs."

"Jonah, they can find other jobs. You can't allow yourself to be a slave to this industry if it's making you unhappy. Just leave."

"I can't do that."

"Why not?"

He shakes his head. "You have no idea how bad it was for us after my dad lost his job. The auto plants were closing left and right – he couldn't find a job anywhere. My mom ended up working two minimum wage jobs just to keep a roof over our heads and put food on the table. It still wasn't enough. My little brother outgrew his clothes faster than we could replace them. And I can't tell you how many nights we went to bed hungry. Now I'm rolling in dough – I can't just walk away from that."

"Of course you can. I've spent this whole week with you, Jonah, and I've seen your spending habits. They're practically nonexistent. That means you're socking money away for a rainy day. I imagine you already have enough in the bank to live comfortably for the rest of your life, don't you? And maybe for your kids to as well. Am I right?"

Reluctantly, he nods.

"Then quit. Just walk away. The contract with your music label is up for renewal soon. Don't renew it."

"That's crazy."

"I'm serious! You don't have to do this if you don't want to."

He pulls away and hops down to the ground, walking away from me and toward the water. "You don't get it, Lia."

I slide down off the rock and follow him. "Yes, I do! You work so hard taking care of everyone but yourself. Why won't you take care of yourself for a change?"

He doesn't answer me. And the scary thing is, I realize I want to do it. I want to take care of him. And that scares the hell out of me.

* * *

Our privacy is soon interrupted by the arrival of a young couple with three rambunctious Labrador Retrievers off-leash. The dogs are playing in the creek, jumping and splashing as they chase sticks. Our tranquility is over.

Jonah stands at the top of the waterfall, looking over the drop and staring at the water where it churns in a frothy pool below us. He's alone in his head right now, distant and preoccupied.

"Let's head back," I say.

He nods and grabs the backpack.

I lead the way back to the cabin, but Jonah falls back farther and farther behind. Occasionally I glance back at him, to make sure he's still with me – that's how quiet he's being – and he seems completely lost in thought. I feel bad, because I'm the one who drove him there, but I think the question needed to be asked. I don't think he's ever really confronted his feelings on the matter. Maybe I overstepped my bounds, I don't know. But... I care about him. The realization throws me. I do care about him. I feel protective of him. He's too nice for his own good, and somebody's got to watch out for him.

I stop and turn back to face him, crossing my arms over my chest as I watch him approach. His gaze is on the path, and he hasn't even noticed I've stopped walking until he practically runs into me.

"Sorry," he says, coming to an abrupt halt just seconds before he runs me over. He frowns. "Is there a problem?"

"Yeah, there is." I reach out and clutch a handful of his T-shirt and pull him close. "I'm sorry if I upset you. That wasn't my intention."

He shrugs off my apology. "It's all right. Don't worry about it."

"No, I shouldn't have pushed you like that. I'm sorry." And then, to my own utter amazement, I go up on my toes and kiss him.

Surprised, he freezes for a split second, then his arms come around me and he hauls me against his chest. His mouth comes down on mine, and he deepens the kiss with a swift and sudden hunger.

"I just want you to be happy," I murmur against his lips.

"Then kiss me. That would make me very happy."

I laugh. "You know what I mean."

His hand slips down to my breast, molding itself to me, squeezing me gently through my clothing. He looks down at me and grins. "How about we go back to the cabin and I'll make *you* happy?"

I've already violated my one-time-only rule with him. And of course I've violated the I-don't-sleep-with-clients rule. The problem is, I don't know how to get off this slippery slope. Or, maybe I don't want to get off. I've never felt so grounded as I do when I'm with him. I've never felt so at peace with myself. He makes me feel safe. He makes me feel... happy.

His expression turns serious, and he leans down and kisses me gently. "Come on, tiger. Let's go home." Then he takes my hand and leads me in the direction of the cabin, and for once, I'm at a complete loss for words. He's taking me over bit by bit, and for some reason, I seem to like it.

As we step into the cabin clearing, we stop dead in our tracks to stare at the silver Jaguar parked next to my Jeep.

"Shit!" I say. We're busted.

"Do you recognize the car?"

"It's Shane's."

A moment later I notice Shane and Beth seated together on the front porch swing, his arm stretched across the back of the seat.

"Lia!" Beth jumps up and runs to meet me, giving me a big hug.

"Hey, you," I say, hugging her back. But my eyes are on my brother as I try to gauge his mood.

Shane walks into the yard to meet us. He shakes hands with Jonah, then he turns to me, his hands on his hips. He's dressed casually, in jeans and a white button-down shirt and black leather jacket. "So, what's this I hear about a bar brawl?" he says, eying me.

"How did you find out?"

"Mitch called me."

Mitch? Ah, Sheriff Mitchell, that rat. "It was nothing. We handled it."

"*We* handled it?" Shane shifts his attention to Jonah. "If it weren't for Sheriff Mitchell, Neal Barker might have already pressed assault and battery charges against Jonah."

"It was self-defense," I argue. "That prick came after me with a broken pool cue! Jonah was simply defending my honor."

Shane gives me a withering look. "Why didn't *you* handle it? You know better than to let a client get involved in a physical altercation."

Jonah looks indignant. "Come on, Shane! I wasn't going to just sit there and let that asshole try to hurt Lia!"

Shane shakes his head at Jonah. "Lia can handle herself against one slightly inebriated biker, right? She didn't need your help."

"I hope you didn't drive all this way just to yell at me," I say. "You could have done that over the phone."

"No, we're staying, at least for dinner," Shane says. "Beth wanted to see the cabin."

"We packed an overnight bag, just in case we were invited to stay the night," Beth says, looking hopeful. She slips her arm around Shane's waist.

"Of course you can stay," I tell her.

"The cabin only has two bedrooms, sweetheart," Shane says.

Beth looks up at him, determined. "Couldn't we sleep on the sofa or in sleeping bags on the floor? It'll be fun."

I glance at Jonah, who nods as if reading my mind. "You can have the front bedroom," I say. "Jonah and I will share the back bedroom."

Shane's eyebrow lifts at my not-so-subtle reveal. "All right," he says, refraining from voicing any judgments. "Thanks." He kisses the top of Beth's head. "I'll bring in our bag."

Beth gives me a radiant smile as she eyes me and Jonah speculatively, and I know she's chomping at the bit for details. She links her arm through mine and leads me inside the cabin. Jonah hangs back to wait for Shane.

"Oh, my God, you two are together!" Beth squeals, once we're inside and away from prying ears.

"Well, I wouldn't say that, exactly."

"But you're sharing a bedroom."

I shrug. "We slept together last night. I guess sharing a bed tonight isn't such a big deal, that's all."

"Lia, I saw the way he was looking at you outside. He never took his eyes off you once. He's crazy about you!"

I peer out the front window and see Jonah and Shane deep in conversation out in the yard. "It's complicated. Anyway, you know I don't do relationships."

"It sounds like you've already broken your own rules. And it sounds like you will again tonight."

I shrug. "I'm just bending them a little, that's all."

Beth smiles at me. "You really like him, don't you?"

"Maybe. But that doesn't change anything."

"Lia, come on! Maybe Jonah's the one. You never know. You've got to give him a chance."

Before I can respond, the cabin door opens and in walks Jonah carrying an overnight bag. "I'll just put this in the front bedroom," he says to Beth. Then he looks at me. "Your brother wants to see you. Outside."

Crap. "Okay. Thanks."

I find Shane leaning against the side of his car, looking relaxed with his arms crossed. But looks can be deceiving.

I join him, leaning against the car beside him. "Okay, talk."

"So, you and Jonah?"

I shrug. "We hooked up. It's not a big deal."

He doesn't look convinced. In fact, he looks a tad worried. "I'm not going to lecture you on getting involved with a client, because you know the risks. I just want to know you're okay."

"I'm fine."

"Jonah's a good guy, Lia, but he lives under a spotlight. That's not exactly your thing."

"It's not his thing either." I step away from the car and turn to face my brother. "I feel safe with him, okay? I've never felt that way about a guy before. I trust him, so I'm willing to break a few rules."

The corner of Shane's mouth lifts in a begrudging smile. "As long as you know what you're getting into."

"Relax! I'm not getting into anything."

"I'm pretty sure you're already in it up to your neck. Just be careful, kid." Shane pulls me into his arms and hugs me tightly. A lump forms in my throat. In a lot of ways, Jonah reminds me of Shane. They both look out for the people they care about. That's what Jonah was trying to do at the bar when he smacked down Neal Barker. He was taking care of me, when it's supposed to be the other way around. I'm supposed to take care of him.

Shane kisses the top of my head. "How about some dinner? It's after six, and Beth missed lunch. What do you say we head into town?"

"Sounds good." I take a few steps toward the cabin, then pause to look back. "Why did you assign me to be Jonah's bodyguard in the first place? I was already assigned as Beth's driver. Why the change? Why not assign someone else?"

"Because I'd gotten to know him a little, and he seemed like a genuinely nice guy. And, I saw the way he looked at you."

I frown. "How?"

"Let's just say I know the feeling."

29

On the drive into town, I can't help feeling uneasy. I don't know if it's because I'm worried about Jonah running into Barker again, or the fact that the four of us look an awful lot like a double-date – Jonah and I up front, Shane and Beth in the back seat. And going by the grin on Beth's face as her gaze meets mine in the rearview mirror, that fact hasn't been lost on her either.

I park on a side street, and we walk two blocks to the diner. Unlike the last time we came, tonight it's packed, the line spilling out the door. I'm not keen on waiting an hour jsut to get seated. "So, now what?"

Jonah glances down the street toward the bar. "We could go to Lucky's."

"Do they have good food?" Beth says.

Shane nods, wrapping his arm around Beth and pulling her close. "They do. And apparently rowdy customers too," he says, giving me an accusatory look.

"Hey, I didn't start it! Blondie did." I start down the street toward the bar.

"Who's blondie?" Shane says, following behind me with Beth.

I can hear Jonah chuckling. "That's Lia's nickname for Neal Barker, the guy I hit."

We head into the bar, and although the place is hopping, there are still a handful of tables available. We grab an empty table for four near the stage, and a server brings us glasses of ice water and menus. Shane hands a menu to Beth. I have to admit, they do make a cute couple.

"So, Jonah, are you excited about the concert tomorrow night?" Beth says, picking up her glass of water.

"Yeah, sure," he says. But he hardly sounds enthused.

"Makayla Hendricks is going to join you on stage, isn't she? That'll be exciting."

"That's the plan." But his voice is flat.

Jonah looks at me, and our gazes lock for a moment, and there isn't any need for words. I know what he's thinking. He's dreading the thought of performing with Makayla. Plus, Dwight will undoubtedly make sure the Internet is plastered with photos and videos of their sweet reunion.

"Well, look who's back! And you brought friends."

The four of us glance up at Hal Burke, who's standing beside our table dressed in a less-than-pristine white apron over jeans and a blue-and-black flannel shirt.

"You gonna bust up my place again, Lia?" Hal says, grinning good naturedly.

"Not if I can help it."

Hal reaches out to clasp hands with Shane. "Good to see you, man. How's it going?"

"I can't complain," Shane says. "Hal, I'd like you to meet Beth Jamison, my fiancée."

Hal's eyes widen as they move appreciatively over Beth. "Shane McIntyre is tying the knot? Whoa. I'll bet that news broke a lot of hearts back in The Windy City. Chicago's number one bachelor is off the market."

Hal gives Beth a genuine smile. "It's a pleasure to meet you, young lady. And as for *this one...*" Hal points at me and gives me the evil eye. "This one's trouble. She got one of my cue sticks broken last night and caused a brawl."

"It wasn't my fault."

"Just try not to get in any trouble tonight, okay?" Hal says. "I've already met my quota of police reports for the week."

"Ha!" I smirk at him. "Funny."

Hal takes our food and drink orders and heads back to the bar.

There are a number of couples on the dance floor in front of the old wooden stage, dancing to songs playing on the juke box. When the opening notes of John Legend's *All of Me* start to play, Beth's eyes light up and she smiles hopefully at Shane.

Shane runs a hand through his short brown hair and groans. "Do I have to?"

"Yes," she says, squeezing his forearm. "Please? I love this song."

Shane shakes his head in resignation. "All right, but just one. Excuse us, please."

Beth jumps up and heads for the dance floor, Shane following her closely. There's a small silver disco ball hanging over the dancers, casting sparkling light over the couples. Shane sweeps Beth into his arms and they have eyes only for each other, and it's sickeningly sweet. Despite his initial grumbling about having to dance, he looks quite content having her in his arms. One romantic slow song quickly melds into three.

"They make a great couple," Jonah says, watching them.

"They're a little too sweet for my taste. I never thought I'd see my big brother wrapped around a woman's little finger, but he's totally pussy whipped. She says jump, and he asks how high."

"They seem happy."

"They'd better be. They're getting married."

"Really?"

"Yeah. Although Beth's so stressed out about all the preparations and the growing guest list that she wants to elope."

"Why don't they?"

"She's too worried about what other people will think. I told her to forget all that and just do it. I love Beth to death, but she needs to grow a backbone and quit worrying so much about other people's feelings."

Jonah leans toward me and drapes his arm along the back of my chair. "Do *you* want to dance?"

"What, me?"

He glances around the table. "I don't see anyone else sitting at this table, so yeah, you."

"I don't dance, sorry."

"Ever?"

"Not if I can help it, no."

"Will you make an exception this one time? Cause I'd really like to dance with you."

"You're crazy."

He shakes his head. "Oh, come on. Just once. How about it?"

I'm thinking the guy's got to be crazy – hell, I'm a terrible dancer – but those steely dark eyes look awfully earnest. I'm just about to give in and make a damn fool of myself when the song ends and a popular country song starts up. As the dancers on the floor arrange themselves into line dance formation, Shane steers Beth back to our table.

"Oh, come on! It'll be fun!" Beth says, grinning at Shane as she tries to pull him back to the dance floor.

"Sorry, but I draw the line at line dancing, sweetheart," Shane says, maneuvering Beth to her chair.

Our food and beers arrive soon after, so there's no more talk of dancing. We eat burgers and fries and onion rings and barbecued pulled pork and hot wings, and sip ice cold beers in chilled bottles. Beth, who's not a big fan of alcohol, has a strawberry daiquiri.

Hal hurries back to our table and points an accusing finger at Jonah. "The girls tending bar tell me you're a famous singer. Is that true?"

Jonah shrugs. "Well, that's debatable. But yes, sometimes I sing."

"Would you do a couple of numbers on my stage tonight? I have a band coming in at nine to play live music, but they're just local boys. You, on the other hand... the girls showed me one of your music videos on her phone – it has like a hundred and sixty-five million views. You're famous! If you perform a few songs tonight, your beers are on the house."

I have to bite my lip to keep from laughing. I don't think Jonah's worried about the cost of a few beers. But the chance to play a small venue like this... I have a feeling it's right up his alley.

"You can borrow a guitar from the band," Hal says, pointing toward the stage where four guys are unloading their instruments.

Jonah glances back at the stage. "Sure. I'd be happy to do a few numbers. As long as Lia's doesn't mind." Then he turns to me. "Do you mind?"

Oh, my God. We really are on a date, aren't we? "Of course I don't mind. Go for it."

He stands, then catches me by surprise when he leans down to kiss me. "I won't be long."

As Jonah heads toward the stage, accompanied by Hal, Shane heads to the bar to order refills on our drinks.

Beth smiles at me from across the table. "Oh, my God, he's crazy about you."

I shake my head. "No, he's not. He's just confused."

Beth takes a sip of her bright pink drink and grins at me. "Lia has a boyfriend."

I watch Jonah as he makes friends with the four band members on stage. They obviously know who he is because they're crowding around him, shaking his hand and talking animatedly. I can't make out what they're saying, but Jonah looks like he's enjoying himself.

"Hey, gorgeous, can I buy you a drink?"

Some guy drops down into one of the empty seats at our table, eyeing Beth like she's on his dessert menu. He's young, in his early twenties, with sandy blond hair and blue eyes, wearing blue jeans and a red and blue plaid shirt.

Beth's gaze pivots to me, her wide eyes speaking volumes.

"Get lost, buddy," I say, glaring at him. "She's not interested."

"I'm not talking to you, sweet stuff," the idiot says, tossing me an arrogant grin. Then he turns back to Beth. "Hey, babe, looks like you could use a refill on your drink. Is that a daiquiri? Can I get you another one?"

Beth looks down at her glass, which she's gripping with both hands. "No, I – no. Thank you."

"Come on, babe," he says, scooting his chair closer to her and laying his arm along the back of her chair. "Just one drink. Let's get acquainted."

She sits forward, trying to put some space between herself and the guy's arm. Just as I'm about to get up and physically remove him from our vicinity, Shane beats me to it.

"Get up. Now."

The idiot looks up to find Shane standing directly behind him, hands fisted, looking like he wants to throttle the guy. Beth gazes at Shane with relief.

"Hey, buddy, mind your own business, will ya?" the idiot shoots back to Shane, sealing his own fate. "I saw her first."

⁓ 30

Beth's unwanted admirer shoots out of his chair, his right arm jacked up behind his back, squawking his fool head off. Shane slams him face-down on our table and presses down, pinning him fast with his hand around the back of the guy's neck. "Either walk out the door right now, or I'll break your arm. Your choice."

Hal comes running over from the bar, holding a baseball bat in his big hand. "What the hell's going on?"

"This asswipe was hitting on Beth," I say. "He wouldn't take no for an answer."

Hal lowers the bat and frowns at the guy whose face is planted on our table top. "You certainly picked the wrong girl to harass, Clyde. I'd do what this fella says, if I were you."

The idiot – Clyde – hyperventilates in between grunts of pain as Shane ratchets his arm up even higher. I can tell from the angle of the guy's arm that his joints are being strained to the max, and something's close to snapping.

"All right, I'll go!" Clyde cries. "I'll go!"

Shane releases Clyde's arm and hauls him upright, then marches him toward the door. Shane says something to Clyde, and Clyde's head bobs up and down repeatedly in agreement. Then Shane opens the door and shoves Clyde outside. When he returns to our table, Hal's hovering over Beth, apologizing repeatedly.

Shane sits in the chair close to Beth and takes her hands in his. "You all right, sweetheart?"

She nods, but I can see she's shaking. Her anxiety is getting the best of her.

Shane picks up one of her hands and kisses her knuckles. "Do you want to leave, honey?"

She shakes her head. "No. I want to watch Jonah perform. I'm fine now. Really."

Shane frowns, and I know he wants to take her back to the cabin. He reaches out to touch her face, his expression etched with concern. He lowers his voice. "Are you sure?"

"I'm okay." She takes hold of his hand and squeezes it. "I'm fine now. He startled me, that's all."

Shane cups his free hand around the back of Beth's head and leans in to kiss her. She responds, practically melting into him.

Watching them together makes my heart ache. They're so in tune with each other. I can't imagine having that for myself. I'll admit I want it, but I just don't think it's possible. For one thing, I'm a pain in the ass – just ask my family. But more importantly, I have trouble in the trust department. I trusted Logan, and look how that turned out. Granted I was an idiot back then. Logan was one of the most popular boys in my high school, and for some stupid reason, I equated that with integrity. I was dead wrong, and I paid the price for my naiveté. I'm sure as hell not going to let someone get close enough to betray me again. I'd rather be alone than suffer another gut-wrenching betrayal.

"Hey, is everything all right?"

I glance up to see Jonah standing behind my chair. "Yeah. Shane had to go into protective boyfriend mode to save Beth from a slightly-inebriated admirer, but we're good now."

Jonah looks very much at home with a guitar in his hands, the strap slung over his broad shoulders. I can't help noticing how drool-worthy he looks with his short, scruffy beard and his unruly hair pulled back in a bun. I also can't help noticing the fact that almost every female gaze in this joint is glued to his fine ass. He looks hot as hell in ripped jeans and an old T-shirt. It's like high school all over again, and this time Jonah's the most popular boy in the school. Hell, he may be the most popular boy in the entire country right now.

"Are you okay with this?" I say, nodding at the guitar. "Performing tonight?"

"Sure." He grins, and I can tell he really means it. He's calm and relaxed, and his eyes are lit with excitement. "The guys in the band are really great. They know my stuff, and they're going to play backup."

"Ladies and gentlemen! If I could have your attention!" Hal stands in front of the microphone on stage, brandishing a bottle of beer in his hand. "We've got a special treat tonight. Jonah Locke is in the house, and he's generously agreed to play a few songs for us."

The audience erupts in boisterous applause, and all eyes turn to Jonah.

Jonah reaches down with both hands to squeeze my shoulders. "I'll be back. Save my seat." And then he jogs back to the stage to join his impromptu back-up band.

"Break a leg, tiger!" I yell after him, and half the women in the room give me the evil eye.

After taking center stage, Jonah drags his microphone stand into position and does a quick sound check. "I'd like to thank Hal for giving me the opportunity to play for you tonight. I'd also like to thank Eclectic Fusion for joining me on stage."

More applause, as Jonah starts strumming his guitar. He plays just a few plaintive chords at first, as if he's getting a feel for the instrument. He adjusts the microphone at bit, and someone lowers the lights in the bar. A hush falls over the room, and a spotlight shines down on Jonah, drawing every eye in the place to center stage. I can't take my eyes off of him, and I catch myself holding my breath with anticipation. He looks magnificent up on that stage, his arm muscles and tendons flexing as he plays the guitar. His fingers are long and confident on the neck of the guitar as he effortlessly picks out the chords. He seems happy and completely in his element.

I realize I've never seen him like this before. At least not in person. I've seen him perform on TV award shows and in music videos on YouTube, and since I became his bodyguard I've seen him up close and personal when people are pulling him in a myriad of directions. But I've never seen him look this happy, this content. This is where he belongs, on a small stage, in a small, intimate venue like this, playing on his own terms. Playing for the love of the music, and not for photographers or publicity or riches. The man's already got more money than he knows what to do with. He certainly doesn't need more of it. He needs the freedom to be who he is, not who Dwight or his record label want him to be.

When he leans into the mic and begins to sing, his low, rough voice resonates throughout the space, giving me goosebumps. His gaze meets mine and he smiles, and my belly does a somersault. A shiver courses through me, making me want things I shouldn't.

Beth leans close and whispers in my ear. "You lucky girl."

"What are you talking about?"

"I'm not blind, Lia. I see the way he looks at you. And the way you look at him."

"You're crazy. We're just friends." But the truth is, I don't know what we are. We've had sex, yes, and it was good. *Really good.* And yeah, I broke my rule – two rules – for him. And I don't want to be anywhere else but here, *with him.* I like being by his side, I like protecting him, but that's because it's my job. "He's just a job, Beth. Don't read anything more into it."

She chuckles. "Keep telling yourself that."

When the guys from the band join in with Jonah, adding the drums, bass, a keyboard and another guitar, they sound great, like they've been playing together for years.

The audience is hanging on every word he sings, and I hear more than a few people singing quietly along with him. A lock of hair falls forward, brushing the side of his face, and I want to reach out and touch that unruly lock of hair, wrap it around my finger. *Possessive much?*

A break comes in the lyrics, and Jonah plays a riff off the melody, and the audience applauds. I see a lot of phones up in the air, as folks snap pictures left and right. Some of them are even recording the performance on their phones, and I'm sure it will end up on You-Tube before the night's out. Dwight will be pissed when he finds out about the impromptu performance, especially since he's not making any money from it.

In the middle of the second song, I start scanning the room out of habit. I'm looking for anything, or rather anyone, out of place – anything that could pose a threat to Jonah. I spot Neal Barker and his buddy seated at a table for two against the back wall of the room. They're sitting in the shadows and their small table is littered with a number of empty beer bottles and shot glasses. Barker, clearly in the process of getting drunk, is glaring daggers at Jonah.

Barker looks pretty rough, with a huge shiner for a right eye and abrasions on his forehead and right cheek. But what concerns me most is the icy hatred in his eyes as he follows Jonah's every move on the stage.

For the rest of the performance, I keep one eye on Jonah and the other on Barker. Fortunately, Barker and his friend maintain a low profile. It's not a good sign, though, when their server brings them another tray of shot glasses. Alcohol makes people do crazy things.

Beth leans toward me. "Is something wrong?"

I smile at her and shake my head, then turn to watch the stage. But I can't help glancing back at Barker again. He's really pissing off the little hairs on the back of my neck. I swear to God, if he tries to go after Jonah, I will flatten him.

As if my very thoughts summoned him, Barker looks my way and our gazes lock. He raises a shot glass to me and gives me an arrogant salute before downing the amber liquid.

Jonah's third and final number comes to an end, and I feel bad because I've only been half-listening. The crowd jumps to their feet and hoots and hollers as they applaud.

Jonah grabs the mic, smiling and a little breathless. "Thank you all very much, and have a great evening! Thanks, Hal!"

Jonah waves at the crowd, then pulls the guitar strap over his head and hands the guitar to one of the band members. After shaking the hands of his impromptu back-up band, Jonah jumps down from the stage and jogs across the room to our table. He heads right for me, an infectious grin on his face, and I can't help jumping up to meet him.

He swings me up into his arms, holding me tight. "That was incredible," he says against the side of my head. "I haven't had that much fun performing in a long time."

He sets me down and cradles my face in his hands. His gaze locks with mine, as if he's searching for something, and then he leans down and kisses me right there in front of everyone in the freaking bar.

I can hear the speculative murmurs all around us, along with the flashes of a dozen cell phone cameras capturing the image. "Dwight's definitely not going to be happy," I say.

"Why?" he says.

"Because he wants to maintain the illusion that you and Makayla are still together. These pics, which you know are going to end up on social media, prove otherwise."

"Well, fuck Dwight, and fuck Makayla." Jonah laughs as he pulls me close and whispers in my ear, "Let's go home."

I have a strong suspicion I'm the one who's about to get fucked, and the thought sends a shiver down my spine. I turn to catch Beth's eye, and she's beaming at me, with a smug *I-told-you-so* expression on her face. Shane's expression gives away nothing, and I can only imagine the lecture he's going to give me later.

Hal tears up our tab for the night, so our dinners and drinks are on the house. He shakes hands with Shane and with Jonah, and he extracts a promise from Jonah to come back and perform again sometime.

Just as we're walking out of the bar, I glance at Barker's table, only to find it empty.

Well, fuck.

℮ **31**

I half expect we'll get jumped outside the bar, but the sidewalk is empty for a block in each direction. As we walk the four blocks back to where I parked the Jeep, I'm on high alert for an ambush. I'm expecting Barker to waylay us at any moment. That much anger and resentment, combined with that much alcohol, is a recipe for disaster.

Shane and Beth walk ahead of us, Shane with his arm around Beth to keep her warm as the wind has really picked up and it's chilly outside. It looks like we're in for a storm tonight. It's dark and the shops are closed. There are a few street lights on, but that still leaves plenty of dark spaces, and the alleys between each block are shrouded in darkness. Barker could be anywhere. I'm itching to pull my handgun out of my ankle holster, but I don't want to worry Jonah or

Beth if I don't have to.

Shane's got the front covered as Jonah and I take up the rear. At one point, Shane glances back at me, his eyes narrowing. He knows alert mode when he sees it. I just shrug at him as I scan the area and come up with nothing. There's no sign of Barker when we reach the Jeep, so I relax a bit. If Barker was going to try to jump us, he most likely would have done it out on the street.

It's a quick drive back to the cabin. It's just starting to rain now, and everyone is tired. I can tell Shane's eager to get Beth to bed, because as soon as we're parked, he whisks her out of the Jeep and up the front steps. And if I'm honest with myself, I'm eager to get to my bed too. But not because I'm sleepy. All I can think about is putting my hands on Jonah's naked body. I want him. I need to feel that powerful body surging into me, filling me. Having him once wasn't enough. Twice wasn't enough. I'm starting to think I'll never get enough of him. Already I can feel my body heating, my arousal growing with the knowledge that we'll be alone in just a few minutes.

"You okay?" Jonah says, turning toward me in his seat. "You've been awfully quiet since we left the bar."

I keep my eyes looking forward, staring at the cabin rather than looking at him, afraid I'll give too much away – like how much I want to jump his bones. "Just tired. It's been a long day."

I'm not sure what he was expecting me to say, but he frowns as if disappointed.

The wind is whistling loudly through the trees now and buffeting the Jeep, heralding the impending arrival of a thunderstorm. I see a bright flash of lightning off in the distance, high over the treetops, and hear the accompanying crack of thunder on its heels.

Jonah opens his door. "We'd better get inside before the rain starts."

He walks around to the driver's side and opens my door. "So, what did you think?"

I step outside and close the door behind me, leaning against it. "About what?"

"The show. Tonight was the first time you've seen me perform live."

I feel the sting of the first few drops of rain on my face. "It wasn't bad."

He laughs. "It wasn't bad?"

I try not to smile, but it's a lost cause. My grin gives me away. "All right, I thought you were amazing. But I didn't think I should tell you, because your ego is big enough as it is." *Not true.*

He pulls me into his arms, and I can feel his erection pressing against the front of his jeans. "I loved having you in the audience tonight. Thank you for being there."

"You don't have to thank me. It's not like I had a choice. I was just – "

He stops me with a hot and hungry kiss, which revs me up even more. There's an ache blossoming inside me, and I feel flushed all over, breathless.

"Don't you dare say you were just doing your job," he says. Then his expression grows serious, and he looks so damn vulnerable. "I'm not just a job to you, am I?"

The doubt on his face makes my heart hurt. I always used to

think of myself as brave, fearless in the face of danger. Now I know it's total bullshit, because I'm afraid to tell Jonah how I feel. Hell, I can't even admit it to myself. "Jonah."

He leans down and presses his forehead to mine. His hands come up to cradle my face, and he kisses me gently, almost reverently, and the vice grip on my heart tightens.

"Lia, I – "

We both freeze at the telltale snick of a switchblade being released. I whip my head to the side just as Neal Barker presses the razor-sharp tip of a serrated hunting knife against Jonah's jugular. A bright red bead of blood wells up beneath the tip of the knife as Barker presses it into Jonah's skin. Jonah grunts with pain, but otherwise remains still.

"Don't move, you motherfucker!" Barker hisses at Jonah. His breath is saturated with alcohol. The man's clearly drunk, and his hand is shaking, which doesn't bode well for Jonah. "If either of you moves, I'll cut his throat! I guarantee you he'll bleed out before anyone can get out here to save his ass."

I can't breathe, and for a moment it feels like time has stopped. In the split second that it takes my heart to make its next beat, I weigh the odds, my response options, and the likely outcome. It'll take too long to pull my gun from my ankle holster, so it'll have to be hand-to-hand.

I shove Jonah to the ground with my right hand, out of the reach of the knife, then bring both hands up to trap Barker's wrist. I step into him, twisting my body and pivoting as I snap Barker's wrist back at a 120-degree angle. Barker screams as I apply pressure to his broken wrist, driving it back at an even more unnatural angle. Half-stunned from hitting the ground so hard, Jonah scrambles to his feet.

"Stay back!" I yell at Jonah.

"You fucking bitch!" Barker wails.

"I haven't even started, asshole!" I increase the pressure on his median nerve until he loses all sensation in his hand and the knife falls harmlessly to the ground with a thud. I kick the knife away, then twist Barker's wrist up behind his back. He drops to his knees, keening in an eerie, high-pitched wail. I shove him face down onto the ground, then follow him down, pinning both arms behind his back and planting a knee into his kidneys to pin him to the ground like a bug. Grabbing a zip tie from the pocket of my cargo pants, I secure his wrists behind his back, then finally draw my handgun and shove the muzzle into the base of his skull.

"I dare you to move," I growl at him. "All I need is an excuse to blow your head off."

The front porch light comes on, bathing us in the yellow light of an incandescent bulb. Shane steps out onto the porch, his hair mussed, wearing nothing but his unfastened jeans and an irritated expression. It's pretty obvious we interrupted something. His gaze goes immediately to Jonah. "You okay, buddy?"

"I'm fine," Jonah snaps, apparently irritated but uninjured.

"Oh, I'm sorry," I shout at Shane over the sound of the approaching storm. "Did we interrupt something important?"

"Funny, Lia." He holds up the sat phone. "Mitch is on his way."

～ 32

While we wait for the sheriff, I have to listen to Barker alternately whimpering, cursing, threatening me, and puking. Mitchell arrives about ten minutes later to take Barker into custody. With the guy's wrist broken as badly as it is, the sheriff doesn't even bother with handcuffs. After taking Jonah's statement and mine, he arrests Barker for aggravated assault and battery with a deadly weapon. Those charges will most definitely land him in jail for quite a while. Then Mitchell loads Barker into the back of his cruiser and sets off for the nearest hospital to take care of the guy's wrist, which is hanging at an odd angle and turning all sorts of pretty colors.

Shane heads back to bed, most likely to resume whatever it was we interrupted. I walk over to Jonah, who's looking at me with a sullen expression.

I have no idea what his problem is. "What?"

"I suppose you're the type who runs *into* burning buildings, too."

"Yeah, so? Somebody's got to do it. It might as well be me."

He shakes his head as he looms over me. "Barker had a fucking *knife*, Lia. He could have hurt you. You should have let me handle him."

"Oh, my God, are you serious? Have you been paying attention? He was here to *hurt* you, and it's my job to protect you. Don't expect me to sit back on my ass while you play the big he-man and handle the big scary thug. It's not going to happen."

"That guy was nearly twice your size!"

"Yeah, and I disarmed him in four seconds. Did you notice that part?"

It's raining pretty hard now, and we run inside the cabin. Jonah stalks off to the back bedroom, and I lock up for the night and set the alarm system. No more surprises for us tonight. The rain's really coming down in sheets now, and lightning lights up the night sky. There's something pleasantly cozy about being locked up inside a snug cabin when all hell's breaking loose outside.

I head to the back bedroom and find Jonah standing at one of the windows, staring out at the rain. When I close the door behind me, he turns to face me. "Look, I know you're trained in all sorts of martial arts, but God, Lia, it scared the shit out of me watching you go up against Barker alone. If something had happened to you – "

"If something had happened to me, it would have been my own damn fault for being too slow. Jonah, I can handle a rookie punk like Barker with one hand tied behind my back. Honestly. There was nothing to worry about." I grab a pair of shorts and a tank top to sleep in from my duffle bag and head into the bathroom to get ready for bed.

The entire time I'm using the facilities and brushing my teeth, my mind replays the evening's events, over and over. I'm pissed that Barker got the drop on us. He must have found out where we were staying, and he must have left a few minutes before we did and parked his vehicle in the woods nearby. When there was no sign of Barker out on the street back in town, I thought we were in the clear, but I was obviously wrong. I dropped my fucking guard too soon, and Jonah nearly got hurt because of it.

When I open the bathroom door, Jonah's standing right there with his arms braced on the door frame overhead, his biceps straining the fabric of his T-shirt. I love the black ink on his arms, those intricate and interlocking shapes and lines. I could spend hours just studying his tats, tracing them with my finger. Tasting them with my tongue.

Then my gaze goes to the dried spot of blood on his throat, which reminds me of how close he came to serious injury, or even death. If Barker had managed to really cut him.... An image of him bleeding out in my arms hits me hard. Shit! I'm pissed at myself for lowering my guard, and like an ass, I take it out on Jonah. "Now what!"

He lowers his hands in a defensive posture. "Whoa. Just waiting for my turn in the bathroom."

I push past Jonah and walk into the bedroom, while he disappears into the bathroom. I'm agitated, too restless to lie down or even contemplate trying to sleep. Antsy, I stalk over to the window and scan the rear yard, half expecting to see more assholes preparing to ambush us. Sometimes it's hard for me to dial down the adrenalin after an incident.

I hear the toilet flush and then water running in the bathroom. This is a bad idea. I shouldn't be sharing a room with him tonight. I'm still wound up and angry at myself for letting Barker get the drop on us, and I'm taking it out on Jonah, which isn't fair. Jonah's probably in a bit of shock still from what happened.

Before he returns to the room, I slip out, quietly closing the bedroom door behind me, and head to the living room where there's a perfectly good sofa I can sleep on. I grab a spare pillow and bedding from the front closet and start making up my bed.

Just as I'm spreading a sheet on the couch, Jonah slips his arms around my waist and draws me back against him. I look back at him, scowling, and notice he's wearing nothing but a pair of black boxer briefs.

"Sleep with me, Lia."

"No." My heart is pounding. This is definitely new territory for me, and I feel like we're at some kind of crossroads. I've already broken my own rule – twice. I can justify that to myself, but if I go to bed with him *again*, then I can't keep lying to myself. I want him. I want to *be* with him.

"Please," he says, his voice low and gentle.

His body heat and scent are enveloping me, and I feel my knees going weak. I want to fall back into his arms, and that scares the daylights out of me. "No." *But God, I want to.*

"We need to talk," he says, and then he sweeps me up into his arms and carries me back to the bedroom. I contemplate making him put me down, but in the end I don't. I guess I'm too selfish. He sits me on the bed and stands facing me, his hands on his hips.

"Talk about what?" I say, mulishly crossing my arms over my chest.

"About you and me." He leans forward, his face practically in mine. "About *us*."

Seeing him standing there in just his boxers is quite a distraction, and I have to fight the urge to reach out and touch him. "There is no *us*." *Liar.*

"That's bullshit, Lia!"

He said that loud enough to shake the rafters, and I swear I hear Shane chuckling in the other bedroom.

Jonah must have heard him too, because he glances in the direction of the other bedroom, then back at me. "Sorry," he whispers, and I laugh.

He leans forward again and I fall back onto the mattress as he looms over me. He nuzzles the side of my neck, giving me warm, open mouthed kisses, and I can't help giggling because it tickles.

He raises his head and grins. "You were magnificent tonight, by the way," he says, gazing down at me with a combination of lust and adoration. "I'm sorry I was an ass about it. I should have just said *thank you*."

"Just doing my – "

He presses a finger to my lips. "Don't say it. Let me keep my illusion, please."

"What illusion?"

"That you care about me."

"Jonah, of course I care about you."

"No, I mean *really* care about me. Like I'm a person to you, and not just a job. Like I'm a man you'd choose to be with – not the guy you're *paid* to be with."

The uncertainty in his eyes kills me. How can he even think that? Any woman would jump at the chance to be with him. That damn vice tightens even more around my heart, and I don't think I can take much more before my heart shatters into a million pieces. Hot tears prick my eyes, and I wipe them away angrily. "You can have anyone, Jonah. Why would you waste your time on someone as broken as I am?"

His expression falls. "You're not broken."

"Yes, I am." I push him back and rise to face him. "Of course I care about you," I hiss, angered by the pain that's swamping me, threatening to choke me. I hurt all over, every inch of me hurts, inside and out, and it's so reminiscent of *before*. Logan betrayed me, and it almost killed me. I'd never survive if Jonah did the same. Hot tears stream down my face, and that only pisses me off more.

Jonah reaches for me. "Lia – "

I back away, raising my hands up like shields. "I can't do this, Jonah. I can't do relationships. Fucking, fine. I have needs too. But this – the emotional stuff? No. I can't do this. I told you, I'm *broken*."

Jonah's arms fall to his sides and he looks gutted.

"And I sure as hell don't need your fucking pity!" I hiss at him, heading for the door.

Jonah snags me with his arms and hauls me back to the bed. He sits down and pulls me to stand between his legs, so we're face to face. "Talk to me, Lia. What the hell is going on in your thick skull? Why do you think you're broken?"

My jaw tightens so hard I'm afraid my teeth will crack. "Because I am!" I hiss. It's hard to argue quietly.

"That's ridiculous," he says, his tone perfectly even, as if we're discussing the weather.

I don't know how he can remain so calm when I feel sick and ashamed and weak. "You don't know what the fuck you're talking about!"

"Then explain it to me."

I try to pull away, but he holds onto my wrists.

"Explain, Lia," he growls, finally starting to lose his patience. "What the hell happened to make you think you're broken?"

"Fine!" The words pour out of me, scalding my throat. "My first and only boyfriend – in high school – God, I was so fucking stupid!" Tears sting my eyes. "I thought I loved him. I thought he loved me. But I was just a stupid kid, and I believed everything he said. That I was *special*. That it was *true love*. That we were *meant to be together*. But I was an idiot! He was playing me for what he could get. He – " I have to stop, because tears are clogging my throat, choking me, and I can't bear to cry in front of him.

Jonah squeezes my hands, whether to offer me support or to prevent me from running, I'm not sure. His jaw tightens. "How old were you?"

"Sixteen."

Jonah winces. "Shit." Then he takes a deep breath. "What happened? What did he do?"

I shake my head. "Never mind. I shouldn't have said anything." I can't go there with him. It's bad enough that I told Beth. I couldn't bear for Jonah to know about the video.

"I'm not giving up until you tell me, so you might as well get it over with. Just pull off that band-aid, right now. Rip it off, because we're not moving from this spot until you tell me. And if you refuse, I'll go beat down Shane's door and get it out of him. And don't think I'm bluffing, because I'll do it."

Jonah's not bluffing, I can tell. He's literally vibrating with suppressed aggression. "All right, fine! He betrayed me."

His eyes narrow, and I can tell he's digging in for the long haul. "How? Did he hurt you? Physically?" Jonah practically holds his breath as he waits for my answer.

"No."

"Emotionally then." Jonah releases one of my hands and scrubs his face with his hand. I know he's frustrated, but I can't tell him about the video. I'd never be able to get past the pity I'd see in his eyes. Already, I see sorrow there, and it's ripping me up inside. I can almost feel my heart tearing.

Rationally, I know he's not Logan. He couldn't be more different from Logan. While Logan was a cold-hearted bastard who never really cared about me, Jonah wears his heart on his sleeve, and he's grieving right along with me even though he doesn't even know the whole story. All he knows is that I'm hurting.

I don't deserve Jonah. I don't deserve this kind of unconditional –

what? *Love*? And then it hits me like a ton of bricks. Jonah *loves* me. And I don't deserve it.

Desperate to stop my brain from going down that rabbit hole, I pull free and cup his face with my shaking hands. His lips are so beautifully formed – no man should have such beautiful lips. I lick my own lips, because right now I want him. I want to stop thinking and I just want to feel him, inside me and out.

I lean into him and kiss him, catching the puff of warm air that escapes him on a gasp. I know he doesn't want to drop this discussion – he thinks he can outlast me. Ha! Silly man, no one is more stubborn than I am. I lay my hands on his bare shoulders and press him back onto the mattress, then climb up over him, straddling his hips and pressing my sex against his penis, which is already half-hard. "Can we please stop talking and have sex? I want you."

He groans. "Lia – baby."

"No talking. Just fuck me."

Jonah scowls at me, and I think I managed to actually piss him off. "This is not just fucking, and you know it."

"Well, whatever it is, shut up and do it, okay?"

℮ 33

To my surprise – and relief – he pulls me down and our mouths latch on to each other's, and we breathe each other in. I can taste his frustration, and I regret causing it, but there's nothing I can do to change my past. It is what it is, and I am who I am. There's no changing that.

"You're way overdressed," he says, trying to lighten the mood.

"What are you going to do about it?"

He grins. "Something I've been dying to do since the day I met you in Shane's office. I'm going to strip you naked, and then lick every inch of your body from head to toe." He reaches for the hem of my T-shirt, but then he hesitates.

I hate the look of uncertainty on his face. I hate knowing what put it there. Desperate to move past it, I reach for my shirt, but he brushes my fingers aside and gently pulls it off me himself and tosses it aside. He stares at my bare breasts with blatant hunger. When his hands come up to palm me, his thumbs brush my sensitive nipples and the aching pleasure makes me whimper. My nipples pucker up into tight little knots, and I shiver violently.

Feeling desperate for him, I start rocking my hips on his growing erection. I can feel the scorching heat of him even through the material of my shorts and his boxers.

"We've got to get these off," he says, reaching for the waistband of my shorts.

I scramble off the bed to remove my shorts and try not to freak out. I hate being exposed like this. Jonah removes his boxers and tosses them onto the chair, then lies back on the mattress and pulls me down beside him so that we're lying side by side. Kissing me, he rolls me onto my back and looms over me. He grips my chin and makes me look at him, all seriousness now. "It's not just fucking, and you know it," he says.

He slips his hand between my legs and groans when he encounters hot, wet flesh. His fingers slide easily through the wetness, spreading the silky moisture over my clitoris, which he begins teasing with light strokes that make me shiver. When he rubs his thumb on my clit in tiny little circles, the firm pressure makes me squirm.

Before long, I'm bucking my hips against his touch, seeking more. "Jonah, please."

He must know I'm close, because he reaches beneath his pillow and pulls out a condom packet and rips it open. He quickly sheaths himself, then settles his hips between my thighs, his cock in his hand as he directs himself toward my opening. I'm so wet and ready, my arousal coats him quickly and he sinks deep. We both groan as he fills me.

He starts to move, slowly at first, giving my body a chance to adjust to him. He glides in and out of me, his erection dragging deliciously along my sensitive flesh. He holds my gaze with his own, connecting us, refusing to let me hide from him. He finally sinks deep, then rolls us so that I'm on top.

Dark memories of me being on top before hit me hard, like a blow to the stomach, and I feel sick. I roll off Jonah, intent on scrambling off the bed in search of my clothes.

"Lia, wait! What's wrong?" He catches me and pulls me back onto the bed.

Rolling me onto my back, he rises up over me, shielding me under his body as if he's trying to protect me from the world. I look away, trying to block out the shame and the sick feelings swamping me.

"Lia, talk to me, damn it. Let me help you."

I look at him and I'm overwhelmed by the raw emotion in his face. No one has ever opened himself up to me like this. No one has ever asked me to do the same. I'm so desperate to take him up on his offer, I can barely breathe. But I'm afraid. I brush my thumb across his lips and he squeezes his eyes shut, but I'm not sure if it's from pleasure or pain.

When he opens his eyes, I smile at him, but I know it's a sad, broken smile. Time seems to have stopped, and all I can hear is the rain hitting the roof. Alone in this dark room, it's like we're the only two people in the world at the moment. Something unfurls inside me, and I make a decision I never thought I'd make. "When I was sixteen, I fell in love with a boy at school. His name was Logan."

Jonah says nothing. He's as still as a statue.

"Logan was a senior, the starting quarterback on the football team. He was a god on campus. All the guys wanted to be his buddy, and all the girls wanted to be his girlfriend. I was a sophomore, a nobody, and for some crazy reason, he wanted *me*. He started hanging out around my locker, and then he started walking me to my classes. He'd come to my table at lunch and ask if he could sit with me. I was blown away by his attention, and I fell crazy in love with him. Or so I thought."

"We'd been dating a few weeks when he invited me up to his bedroom one night. His parents were out for the evening, so we had the house to ourselves. One thing led to another, and we ended up in his bed. It was my first time, ever. I didn't know it at the time, but he videotaped it."

"I was on top, and I was scared, and it hurt. I was in way over my head. I tried so hard to act like I wasn't scared shitless, but in the end I cried like a baby. When I found out a few days later that he was two-timing me with another girl, I got angry and broke up with him. I made a scene in the cafeteria, embarrassing him in front of the other students. He retaliated by uploading the video to an amateur porn site on the Internet.

The video went viral. Millions of people watched me lose my virginity, watched me raw and vulnerable. I was devastated. Absolutely gutted. If it weren't for my family, I don't think I would have survived the humiliation. My brothers taught me how to channel my grief and rage through martial arts, and after I graduated from high school, I went to work for Shane."

Jonah swallows hard. "And now you're afraid to trust anyone."

I nod. "I won't let anyone hurt me again."

"Is that why you don't want the lights on?"

I nod. "So I can't be videotaped."

Jonah closes his eyes tightly, and when he opens them again, they're filled with pain. He brushes my hair back and tucks it behind my ear. "Lia McIntyre, have you ever considered the possibility that there's a guy out there – just a regular guy – who thinks you're the bomb? A guy who'd give his left nut just to be near you. Maybe a nice guy, one who would never, ever hurt you. Has that possibility ever crossed your mind?"

I smile. "You're hardly just a regular guy, Jonah. You have legions of fans following you everywhere you go, not to mention a crazy-ex-girlfriend who won't take no for an answer."

Jonah makes a show of scanning the small, sparsely furnished room. "Don't see any fans in here. No ex-girlfriends either. It's just you and me, tiger."

His smile fades. "Lia, you can't keep your life on hold forever because your first boyfriend was an asshole. You've got a lot of living ahead of you. And there are plenty of good guys out there who'd give *anything* to be with you, including yours truly. You're amazing. You're beautiful, funny, smart, and great at kicking ass. You're a very well-rounded woman."

"Well-rounded?" I laugh. "That hardly seems like a compliment."

"You're the full package, babe. So, how about giving me a chance to prove that not all men are assholes? I'm certainly not."

I brush back his hair. "No, you're not."

$\mathcal{e}$ 34

'm not prepared for this.

I He won't let me hide, and he won't let me pretend this is just another fuck. He hovers over me, studying my face, tracing the shape of my eyebrow with the tip of his finger.

"Get on with it, will you?" I say, pressing my hips against his in the hope of spurring things along. But no such luck. The man won't be hurried.

He smiles. "No. I'm going to savor this." His finger trails down my nose and then skips over to skim across my cheek. His voice drops as he turns serious. "I was scared earlier."

"When?"

"When Barker pulled that knife."

I scoff. "I wouldn't have let him hurt you. There was nothing to be afraid of."

He shakes his head and looks at me like I'm nuts. "I wasn't afraid for myself, Lia. I was afraid for you."

"I can take care of myself. You know that."

He shakes his head. "No one's invincible. When I saw that knife, all I could think about was the damage that thing could do to you."

It's weird – I'm not used to someone worrying about me. Even my brothers gave up worrying about me a long time ago. I reach up to cup his face, my thumbs stroking his short, soft beard. "My heart stopped when I saw the tip of that knife against your jugular. *That* was something to worry about. I didn't have much time to react. If he'd cut you – "

"But you did react. You probably saved my life."

I shrug it off. "It was nothing."

He chuckles. "At least you didn't say you were just doing your job. I think we're making progress." His expression darkens. "I don't ever want you in harm's way again," he says.

I smirk. "So, what are you going to do? Fire me?"

But he doesn't seem amused. "I think maybe I am."

"Technically, you can't fire me. Dwight hired McIntyre Security, not you."

"I'm serious. If something happened to you – "

I thread my fingers through his hair and pull his mouth down to mine to shut him up. But the resulting kiss is more than I bargained for. It's slow and sultry. His lips move over mine like warm velvet, caressing me, sucking and stroking. His kiss makes my entire body tingle, from my scalp to my nipples to my sex. After a long moment of exquisite torture, he nudges my mouth open and slips his tongue inside to stroke mine.

His arms are propped on the pillow, and his hands cradle my head. I feel cocooned, wrapped in his warmth and tantalizing scent. I've never experienced anything like this. His body, his touch, are simultaneously comforting and arousing, and I'm torn between wanting to jump him and melting into a puddle. When he sucks on my tongue, I feel an answering pull between my legs, and it makes me restless. My hips start moving as I rock against his pelvis, enticed by the feel of his thick erection. The dull ache between my legs quickly turns into a throb, and I push my sex against him, seeking the contact I need.

"All in due time," he says, lifting his hips from mine.

I growl at the loss of him. "Don't tease me!"

"I won't." He reaches down to cup me between my legs, and his thumb presses on my clit as his fingertips slide between my wet folds. I gasp when one long finger glides gently inside me, pushing through swollen flesh. His thumb circles my clitoris wickedly, ratcheting up my desire, sending waves of pleasure radiating outward from my core.

I can feel my orgasm looming, and just when I'm about there, he removes his fingers. "Jonah!"

"Relax. We're not rushing this." He moves down the bed and wedges his broad shoulders between my legs, opening me up.

"Jonah, don't."

"Why not?"

I squirm uncomfortably. "I need to shower for that."

"Oh, please. I'm going to make you come so hard, you won't be able to see straight, let alone think about showering."

And then he proceeds to make good on his promise, lashing my clit with his wickedly ruthless tongue, stroking and teasing and swirling it around that tiny bundle of nerves.

I'm squirming on the bed and biting my bottom lip in a futile attempt to keep quiet. "There are people in the next room, you know!" I hiss.

He lifts his mouth just long enough to say, "Then come quietly."

I lay my head back and close my eyes, resigned to this torture. He's determined to push me over the edge, and I'm needy and greedy enough to go right over. I'm helpless against the one-two punch of his tongue on my clit and his finger stroking inside me. He knows exactly what he's doing, finding that sweet spot and stroking me relentlessly. The pleasure is back with a vengeance, swelling inside me, rising like a wave ready to crash. He's right, damn it. I come hard, pressing a pillow against my face in a desperate attempt to muffle my cries.

Jonah surges up, removing the pillow so he can kiss me. He tastes like me, of course, earthy and warm and slightly salty. He reaches for a condom on the nightstand and rips the packet open with his teeth. He sits back on his haunches and rolls on the protection. My legs go around his hips, and he guides his erection to my opening.

"Put me inside you," he says, taking my hand and wrapping my fingers around his thick girth. When he dips his head to kiss me again, I can taste his hunger.

I lead him directly to the aching place between my legs, and once the head of his cock is wedged inside me, he gently presses forward, filling me one slow inch at a time. I'm so wet, so ready for him, he glides slowly inside me. The sensation of being filled is exquisite. "Jonah!"

"I know. I feel it too." He rocks himself inside me, not rushing things, just pressing forward inch by inch until he finally sinks that last little bit and he's hitting my cervix.

We both gasp.

He stays fully seated for a moment, his eyes closed as if he's savoring the moment. I can't resist squeezing my vaginal muscles around him.

He heaves a deep sigh. "God, that feels good."

"It would feel even better if you'd start moving."

He chuckles as he slowly pulls out of me, but not quite all the way. When he surges inside again, in a smooth, fluid motion, I gasp. I don't think I'll ever get used to the feeling of being filled so perfectly.

Jonah sets his own rhythm, surging in and out as he kisses me. My legs are wrapped around his waist, holding him close, and my hands stroke up and down his arms, exploring his muscles and reveling in his strength. His hair has come loose around his face, falling down in a curtain of dark mahogany silk. I run my fingers through it, brushing it back.

Jonah picks up the pace, stroking smoothly into me. I lift my hips to meet each thrust, wanting to drive him deeply inside me. I know I'm going to be sore tomorrow, but it will be worth it.

When he lowers his head to latch onto my left nipple, suckling and tugging gently, I feel a corresponding tug between my legs. He sucks at one nipple, laving and pulling on the sensitive tip, then switches to the other one and provides the same thorough treatment.

His movements are strong and fierce now, his mouth tormenting my breasts, when he reaches down and rubs my clitoris with the tip of his thumb. To my shock, I feel another orgasm looming... something I wouldn't have thought possible. But he's relentless as he torments my clit, and soon my hips are rocking into his as a tiny explosion rocks me for the second time in one night.

As Jonah explodes right along with me, he throws his head back, grimacing with intense pleasure. The tendons in his neck are taut, and his jaw is clenched tightly. He cries out, a deeply gutteral sound as he presses deep inside me, emptying himself in violent spurts.

Time stands still as we lie there, still entwined, simply enjoying the physical connection as well as the emotional.

When he eventually withdraws, he slips away to take care of the condom. I know I should go clean up, but I feel absolutely boneless and don't want to move a muscle. A moment later, he slips back into bed and presses his nakedness against my back, warming me. He tucks the sheet around us so that we're cocooned together in the dark. A light rain is still hitting the roof and the window panes.

"Do you think they heard us?" I whisper.

"Don't worry about it."

"That's easy for you to say. Your brother isn't in the other room."

Jonah chuckles. "Thank god. I'm pretty sure my little brother's still a virgin."

"I can't keep my eyes open," I admit, letting my lids drift shut. My sex is throbbing, a very telling reminder of what we just did. I don't want to think about it and what it might mean. I didn't just break my rules, I shattered them. There's no going back now.

"Go to sleep," he murmurs. He kisses the back of my head as his arm steals around my waist and tucks me close to him.

Exhaustion pulls me under quickly.

* * *

I awaken sometime in the night and lie quietly listening to the wind soughing through the trees outside our cabin. When I roll over to face Jonah, I'm surprised to find him wide awake, watching me.

I lay my hand on his chest, which is as warm as an oven. "What's wrong? Can't you sleep?"

He shakes his head. "Not yet."

I suspect Jonah has demons of his own. "You have a problem falling asleep, don't you?"

He shrugs. "I can't fall sleep until early morning. I guess I'm a night owl."

He yawns, and I know he's dead tired. We had a long day, with the hike to the falls and then his performance at Lucky's earlier this evening. I remember the nights at the house when I'd hear him prowling around upstairs in his attic suite.

"Why can't you sleep, Jonah?"

He looks at me, but doesn't answer.

"Is there a reason?" I say.

He nods.

"Are you going to tell me?"

"It's nothing you need to worry about, I promise."

"That's hardly fair. I spilled my ugly guts to you tonight. At least you could do the same."

He sighs heavily. "It's old history, Lia."

I shake my head. "Not if it's still affecting you."

"It's just an old habit I got into when I was a teen. Don't worry – "

I sit up and pull the sheet up to cover my breasts. "Now who's doing the bullshitting?"

He sighs and pulls me back down into his arms. "I told you before my dad lost his job working in an auto manufacturing plant. After that, he couldn't find any work in his field. He was devastated. He didn't know what to do. He had no college degree and no other marketable skills. He knew how to build the cars, and that was it. He grew more and more angry and depressed, and he turned to alcohol to deal with the pain. He spent every single evening in a drunken haze. And he was a mean drunk."

"But what does that have to do with your insomnia?"

He shakes his head. "It's not insomnia. It's self-preservation."

"What are you talking about?"

"My dad would come home late every night from the neighborhood bar, drunk as a skunk and pissed as hell. At first, he tried to take it out on me, but I was already as big as my dad by then, and I fought back. When he hit me, I hit him right back. Pretty soon he left me alone. But my little brother, who was only eleven at the time, wasn't so lucky. One night, while I was out with my friends, I came home around midnight to find my dad beating the shit out of my little brother."

"Where was your mom while this was happening?"

"At work. She worked two jobs, both first and second shift – plus all the overtime she could get, which meant she wasn't home very much. It wasn't her fault she was never home. I got in the habit of staying up all night to watch after my brother, until my dad eventually passed out after ranting and raving for a few hours. Only once he was out cold for the night could I allow myself to fall asleep on the floor of my brother's bedroom. I guess over time, it became a habit. I'm still anxious at night, and I can't sleep until it's nearly dawn."

"Is your dad still around?"

"No. When I finally told my mom what was happening, she kicked him out. They're still married, but she hasn't seen or heard from him in ten years."

"And your brother?"

"He's fine. He's a junior at University of Michigan."

I brush his hair back. "You can sleep now, Jonah. He can't hurt you anymore. He can't hurt anyone you love."

He smiles sadly. "I wish it was that easy."

ꙮ 35

My internal alarm clock wakes me at the usual time, six thirty. Jonah is fast sleep, pressed up against my back with his arm around me. I snuggle into him, wallowing in his delicious warmth. But as nice as this cuddlefest is, I have to pee really badly, and I need coffee. So I carefully extricate myself from his death grip and leave him to his much-needed sleep. Knowing him, he's probably only been asleep a few hours at best, and he needs all the rest he can get before tonight's performance.

After a quick stop in the bathroom, I'm refreshed and dressed in cargo pants and a T-shirt, and I head to the kitchen to make coffee. To my surprise, Shane has beat me to it. He's pouring two mugs of coffee.

I reach around him and grab one of the mugs. "I'll take that, thanks."

He gives me the evil eye, then pulls another mug out of the cupboard. "So, what's the plan for today?" he says.

I take a seat on one of the kitchen barstools. "I'll let him sleep as long as he needs. Then we'll head back."

"You know you're in violation of company policy, right? *No fraternizing with the clientele.*"

I scoff. "You're one to talk. You're *marrying* a client. Besides, it may be a moot point. I think he fired me last night. He's afraid I'll get hurt."

Shane smiles. "I told you he's a good guy. I can't fault him for wanting to protect my little sister."

I shrug, not liking where this conversation is going.

But Shane doesn't miss a thing. "Are you okay?"

"Sure. Why wouldn't I be?"

He gives me a wry look. "Lia, come on."

I wrap my hands around my hot mug and stare out the back door, desperately wanting this conversation to end. "I told you, I'm fine."

He doesn't look convinced. "Just make sure you have him at Rowdy's by four. They're going to do a sound check and a rehearsal before tonight's show."

"Yeah, I know." For some reason, I find the idea of going back to real life depressing. I wouldn't mind staying gone for a while longer, but I know Jonah has commitments he has to keep. At least while he's under his recording contract.

Shane is dressed in jeans and a navy crew-neck sweater. His hair is slightly damp, which means he's already showered. My brother's an early riser. Beth is not. "Beth still asleep?"

"She was when I left her. She wants to get back to the city this morning so she can go to work, so we'll be leaving soon."

We finish our coffee in silence, just the two of us. The peace and quiet is nice, and I'm relieved Shane's not pushing me on the subject of Jonah.

Eventually, he breaks his silence. "Did Barker hurt you last night?"

"No, he didn't touch me. I'm just pissed that he got the jump on us. I blame it on the storm. With all the wind and thunder, I didn't hear a thing until he was on us."

"Mitch texted me this morning. Barker was charged with assault and battery, and assault with a deadly weapon. He's scheduled for arraignment next week, but his attorney is saying he'll plead guilty. He's probably banking on a shorter sentence if he cooperates."

"I hope he rots in jail for a while."

"You handled it well." Shane washes out his mug, then sets it on the drying rack beside the sink and pours fresh coffee in another mug. "Let's see if I can lure Beth out of bed with this."

* * *

Shane heads toward the front bedroom to wake sleeping beauty, leaving me alone with my coffee and my thoughts. Now that I'm alone, I can afford to spend a few moments acknowledging the tenderness deep inside me – an undeniable reminder of what Jonah and I did last night. I squeeze my vaginal muscles and feel a definite twinge deep inside.

I honestly don't know what to do about Jonah. I've obliterated my own rules, which definitely blurs the lines between a convenient fuck and a... a what? *A relationship?* I trust Jonah. I really do. He's a good guy with a good heart – maybe too good. I trust him not to play callously with my feelings, but I'm not sure I trust myself to open up to him and hold up my end of the bargain. I don't even know if I'm capable of being in a relationship.

By the time I've finished my coffee, the door to the front bedroom opens, and Shane and Beth walk out. Beth is dressed for work in a skirt and blouse and sandals, her freshly-brushed hair hanging loose just past her shoulders. Shane's carrying their overnight bag.

"Hey, Lia," Beth says, blushing as she passes me on her way to the kitchen sink. "Did you sleep well last night?"

"Yes." I have a feeling she's not talking about sleep, though.

Shane carries their bag outside to his car, leaving us alone.

Beth comes up beside me and puts her arm around my shoulders, pulling me in for a hug. "I didn't realize you were such a screamer," she says.

"I am not!"

"Are too." She gives me an innocent smile and another squeeze. "I heard you, more than once."

I can feel my face burning. "Did Shane hear?"

"Did I hear what?"

I jump at the sound of Shane's voice right behind us. I hadn't heard him come in. Crap! Some things are just too mortifying to even contemplate. At least he has the courtesy to pretend he doesn't know what we're talking about.

"It's nothing, baby," Beth says, smiling at him. "Just girl talk." She squeezes me one last time. "I'll see you this evening at the show."

I can't seem to match her enthusiasm. "Yeah, I'll see you then."

It's seven-thirty when they leave. I figure I'll let Jonah sleep until noon or one o'clock. We'll have to leave shortly after that to make it back to the city on time. I have a second cup of coffee, then check my e-mails and texts on my phone. Then I read a little. Beth's got me hooked on these pornographic romance novels about vampire sex slaves.

After a while, though, I'm bored and need some physical activity, so I head to Jake's compact work-out room at the back of the cabin, right behind the kitchen. It's hardly bigger than a good-sized walk-in closet, but it will do.

* * *

Just as I'm wrapping up a three-mile run on the treadmill, I hear a noise behind me and turn to see Jonah standing inside the open doorway wearing nothing but a pair of cotton shorts. He looks... edible.

"Hey you," he says, his arms braced on the door frame above his head.

I nearly swoon from the arm porn. His damp hair is up in a messy man-bun, which he totally rocks. He looks like he's just begging to be fucked.

He comes into the room and wraps his arms around me, drawing me close. His skin is warm and damp from a shower, which means he smells good and I don't.

I gently push him back. "I just ran three miles, pal, and I'm a sweaty, stinky mess, so you might want to keep your distance. I need a shower. Badly."

"Let's take one together."

"You just took a shower. And besides, have you seen how small the shower stall is?"

He grins as he pulls me against him, wrapping me tightly in his arms. He leans down to kiss me, and I taste minty toothpaste. "Then we'll have to stand *real* close together," he says, nuzzling my neck.

The feel of his lips on my throat makes me shiver. But it's his thick erection pushing insistently into my belly that makes my knees go weak.

Swamped with pleasure, I struggle to keep my wits about me. "We have to leave soon, you know, to get you back in time."

He starts sucking on my neck, and I'm sure he's going to leave a mark.

"Then we'll just have to be quick about it. I'm not leaving until I put my soapy hands all over your body."

As he sweeps me up into his arms and carries me toward the bathroom, I get the feeling we're going to waste a lot of hot water.

∾ 36

J onah never fails to surprise me. The longer I know him, the more I see what a good person he is. He's nothing like I expected the front man of a popular rock band to be. Honestly, I don't know what I expected – a big ego? A demanding diva? A womanizer? But he's none of those things.

We are indeed crammed into the tiny shower stall. As the hot water sprays our naked bodies, Jonah turns me to face away from him and grabs my shampoo bottle. As he starts lathering my hair and massaging my scalp, I'm not sure which one of us is enjoying this more. His fingers feel incredible on my scalp, and I can feel the evidence of his pleasure poking me in the back. For a few moments, I allow myself to relax and lean back into him, letting him give me the most seductive hair washing I've ever had in my life.

"Close your eyes," he says. And when I do, he gently puts me under the spray to rinse my hair. When I come out from under the water, he grabs a towel and blots the water from my face.

"My turn." I motion with my index finger for him to trade places with me. It's a difficult logistical maneuver, but we manage it. We take turns with the soap, running our hands all over each other's body.

"I think you're enjoying this way too much," I say, and he just smiles, his eyes warm and glittering with undeniable heat.

He rinses me off, wraps me in a towel and carries me into our bedroom to lay me on the bed. He follows me down. Our bodies are damp, and I brush my nose against his bicep to breathe in the smell of his skin. The scent of his skin is the best aphrodisiac I've ever encountered. This is working for him, too, because his erection is nudging my crotch, seeking entrance.

Jonah reaches under his pillow and pulls out a strip of condom packets.

"You're certainly prepared," I say. "Were you a boy scout?"

He grins. "No. I'm just a very practical man." He rises up and sits back to roll on a condom. He pauses a moment, looking down at me, and runs his finger down my chest, following some invisible path between my breasts, down my belly, to the blond patch between my legs. His index finger sifts through my curls, then dips between my folds to touch my clit.

I buck my hips in protest. "Don't just tease me."

"I'm not teasing. I'm exploring." He scoots down the bed and opens my legs.

"Am I loud? Beth said she heard me last night."

He smiles. "Yes, you are."

"Well, shit."

He chuckles. "I don't mind. I like hearing you scream my name."
And then he proceeds to show me just how loud I can be.

* * *

We're packed up and ready to head back to Chicago at one o'clock.
Leaving this place is bittersweet. While I am excited about watching
his performance tonight, I wish we didn't have to leave. I've enjoyed
having him mostly to myself for a couple of days. I could get used to
this.

We'll arrive just in time to stop at the rental house so we can
change clothes and get to the pub in time for the rehearsal.

"Are you looking forward to the performance tonight?" I ask as
we're cruising down the interstate toward Chicago. We have clear
weather and the traffic's light, so it's easy driving.

"It's a small venue, which I much prefer over a stadium. But no,
I'm not really looking forward to it. I'll have to deal with Makayla,
and that never goes well. She sucks the fun right out of everything."

"Then tell her she's not invited. It's your concert. Un-invite her."

"It's not that easy. Dwight's using this performance as a public re-
lations event. He wants us seen together. He says it helps both our
careers."

"You mean it helps Dwight's career. What about what you want?"

"I don't think what I want really matters to Dwight. He's focused on the bottom line....profits."

"Jonah, your contract is up for renewal in two weeks. Don't renew it. Walk away."

He shakes his head. "I can't do that to the guys."

"Look, they're young, talented guys. They'll find new jobs quickly. So will Ruben and Esperanza. Give them all great severance packages and wish them luck. You can certainly afford it. I'm sure you have plenty of money stashed away in the bank."

"More than enough."

Jonah turns on the radio – I think he just wants to shut me up – and we listen to music for a while. I want him to think about what I said. I want him to envision living the kind of life he wants to live, not what he's gotten himself roped into.

Out of the blue, he turns off the radio and turns to face me. "When you've grown up in poverty, it's not easy to walk away from so much money. It feels... irresponsible."

I roll my eyes at him. "You're not irresponsible, Jonah. You're the most responsible rocker I've ever known."

"I'm probably the only rocker you've ever known. Have you ever gone to bed hungry? Have you ever had to listen to your little brother cry himself to sleep because his stomach hurts – because it's empty? Have you ever worn the same pair of jeans to high school every single day for a year because it's the only pair you've got?"

I frown. "No."

"Yes, now I have more money than I know what to do with, but that doesn't cancel out years of struggling just to scrape by."

* * *

When we arrive in Lincoln Park, I head straight to the rental house, and we have to inch our way through the crowd of fans to get through the gates. I park behind the house and we sit there for a few moments, saying nothing. This is the quiet before the storm. I suspect neither of us is looking forward to going inside and facing the music.

"You ready?" I ask him as I turn off the engine and pocket my keys.

He stares through the windshield at an ivy-covered brick wall. "As ready as I'll ever be."

I walk around to the back of the vehicle to get our stuff, and Jonah meets me there.

"I've got it," he says, taking our bags and his guitar case from the back of the Jeep.

We enter the house through the rear door, passing through the mud room into the kitchen – and right into the middle of a hornet's nest. Dwight is in the kitchen with Esperanza, and their conversation comes to an abrupt end when we step into the room.

Dwight slams his beer bottle down on the kitchen counter and stalks toward Jonah, trying to get in his face, which isn't easy as Jonah's so much taller. "Where the fuck have you been?" Dwight yells at Jonah.

Jonah sets our bags and his guitar case on the floor and props his hands on his hips. "We went on a little road trip. I told you we'd be back in time for the show."

"And you!" Dwight pivots toward me and shoves his skinny finger in my face. "I know you were behind this, Lia. You do nothing but cause trouble for him!"

Jonah bristles at the comment. "That's enough, Dwight."

Makayla breezes into the kitchen, sees Jonah and squeals as she runs to him. He catches her before she plows into him, and she uses the opportunity to wrap her arms around his waist.

"Jonah! Baby, I missed you so much. I was worried sick!" She has the gall to kiss him right on the mouth.

Jonah pushes her back and holds her at arm's length. "There was never any need to worry."

"You're fired!" Dwight says, jabbing his finger in my face as he crowds me. "Pack your stuff and get out. I'll have Shane send someone else to provide security for Jonah."

I've had just about enough from this guy. I get in his face, enjoying the way he blanches. "You can't fire me, asswipe."

"Oh, yes I can!" he blusters, turning a nice shade of red.

He tries to back away, but I follow him, keeping in his face. "No, you can't, because Jonah beat you to it. He fired me last night."

Dwight looks to Jonah for confirmation. "Is that right?"

Jonah shakes his head in disgust and picks up his duffle bag and guitar case. "I'm going upstairs to change." He looks at me. "Ready to go in thirty minutes?"

I nod. "You'd better believe it."

"I thought you fired her," Dwight says, looking confused.

"I did," Jonah says. "She's no longer my bodyguard."

"Then why are you leaving with her? I said I want her gone!"

Jonah grins. "Because she's my girlfriend, that's why."

"What!" Makayla's screech can probably be heard throughout the entire house. She puts her hands on Jonah's face. "Baby, no," she croons, practically petting him. Her hands slip down to his chest. "Don't do this. You can't give up on us."

"We're through, Makayla," he says, pointedly removing her hands.

Jonah nods at me, then sidesteps Makayla and heads for the hallway stairs.

She runs after him and grabs his arm. "Jonah, wait!" She digs her nails into his arm hard enough to leave marks. "Baby, don't do this."

I slip between them and apply pressure to a nerve in her wrist to make her release him. She glares at me as I push her back. "Leave him alone," I say.

She shoves me hard. "Get your hands off me, you bitch!"

She tries to go after him, but I block her way long enough to give him enough time to get upstairs to his suite. She bristles at my interference, but I don't give a fuck. She's toxic, and I don't want her anywhere near him. And yeah, maybe I'm a tad jealous of their shared past. After all, he was her boyfriend until just recently. And the thought of him choosing to go back to her makes me a little nuts.

With Jonah upstairs changing, I head to my room to change quickly into jeans and a black McIntyre Security T-shirt. I strap on my ankle holster and slip in my handgun. Then I run up the two flights of stairs to Jonah's suite. I knock on his door, and it opens almost immediately. He's standing there in ripped jeans and a pair of boots and nothing else. His hair is freshly brushed and put up in a bun. He's so edible, I'm at a loss for words.

"Almost ready," he says, walking to the closet to grab a faded

T-shirt and slip it on. There are two guitar cases laid out on his unmade bed.

"These are going?" I say, picking up one of the cases.

He nods and grabs the other one. "Let's get out of here, please."

The urgency in his voice makes me chuckle. He's no more a fan of this place than I am. At least where Dwight and Makayla are concerned. The others are okay.

When we return to the kitchen, Dwight and Makayla are gone, thank God. Esperanza is standing at the sink rinsing a few dishes.

"Hello, dears," she says in her gentle voice. "With all the commotion, I didn't get a chance to say hello earlier. How was your trip?"

"It was good, thanks," I say.

"Yeah, we had a great time," Jonah says. "It was far too short."

She smiles at me as she pats Jonah's shoulder. "I'm glad you had a good time. Jonah shoulders a lot of responsibility for such a young man. He needed a break."

37

It's a quick trip to Rowdy's, and we park in the rear parking lot off a side alley. Jonah grabs his guitar cases from the back of the Jeep and we head inside through the back door, passing a security checkpoint manned by McIntyre Security personnel. It's chaotic inside the bar, with security personnel and bar staff bustling about as they get ready for the guests to arrive.

I lead Jonah to the manager's office, which has been set up as a private lounge for the band members tonight. There are two McIntyre Security personnel standing guard outside the door and another guard standing at the next door down the hall, which leads to a room that has been set up for Makayla and her entourage.

The guards wave us in to the manager's office, and we find the rest of the band members seated on a pair of brown tweed couches.

There's a large cooler on the floor filled with ice, pop and beer bottles, and a buffet of hot food has been spread out on a long table covered with a white tablecloth.

"Hey, Jonah! Nice of you to join us!" Dylan cheers, holding up his beer bottle. Travis and Zeke follow suit, toasting Jonah's arrival.

"I thought we might have to go on without you tonight, dude," Zeke says.

Jonah sets his guitar cases on the floor. "I told you guys I'd be here."

"The food's awesome," Travis says. "Feed your face and then we'll go do a sound check and run through our sets."

After Jonah and I grab a quick bite to eat – we haven't eaten much all day – the band goes out to the stage to perform a sound check with Ruben. I stand off to the side of the stage, watching Jonah go about his business as he checks the sound on his mic and guitars.

Ruben sits at a console on the far side of the bar, operating the lighting and sound boards. I'm surprised by how much work it is to test the sound and adjust the levels and the positioning of speakers and lights.

Every once in a while, I catch Jonah watching me, and he smiles or winks at me when our gazes connect. I have to admit I spend a lot of time just watching him. I love the way he moves, the way he carries himself. And I can't help smiling as I watch him joking around on the stage with the guys. They do make a good team. I can see why Jonah would be reluctant to break them up.

Dylan's seated at his drum kit, making a lot of noise as goes through his drills. Jonah and Travis are showing off on their guitars, while Zeke accompanies them on his bass guitar. They act like a bunch of kids on stage, and the excitement is contagious.

"Lia!"

I turn to see Beth making a beeline toward me. Shane's following close behind her, dressed in a suit and tie. I guess he's on duty tonight too.

Beth looks amazing, as always, in a pale mocha baby-doll dress and brown leather ankle boots. She has several long strands of tiny pearls hanging around her neck and pearl drop earrings. Her hair is up in a style that's part sophisticated twist and part sex kitten. The effect is stunning – and the best part is, she has absolutely no idea of her own appeal.

"You look hot, princess," I tell her, fanning myself. "If you weren't already taken, I'd do you."

She blushes hotly and smacks me on the arm. "Stop that. I do not."

Shane's right behind her, and of course he heard our little exchange. He lays proprietary hands on her bare shoulders. "Sorry, but she's taken."

"We're opening the front doors at six o'clock," Beth says, "and the show starts at seven. We're giving out two drink tickets to each guest, and soft drinks and all the appetizers are free tonight. We also arranged for every guest to receive a free copy of Locke's newest CD and a T-shirt."

"Wow, that's pretty generous," I say.

She shrugs it off. "It's sort of a thank-you from me and Shane to our employees."

Shane eyes the stage and then scans the floor seating arrangements. "There's Jake," he says, noticing our brother standing by the front entrance speaking to a couple of the door security staff. "I need to speak to him for just a minute." Shane gives Beth's shoulders a light squeeze. "I'll just be a few minutes, sweetheart. Stay with Lia until I get back, okay?"

"Sure."

Shane leans down from behind to kiss the side of her neck. It's a lingering kiss that speaks volumes. I look away, not wanting to intrude on their private moment. Watching them together, seeing how happy they are, makes me wistful. I'm happy for them, and I'm also envious of their closeness. I've never before let myself get that close to anyone – not until Jonah.

Once Shane's out of hearing, Beth turns to me. "So, tell me all about you and Jonah."

I shake my head. "There's nothing to tell."

Beth frowns. "Oh, come on! I don't believe that for a minute."

I shrug. "So we hooked up a few times. You know I'm not the girl-friend type."

"I've seen the way you two look at each other, Lia. Trust me, that's not simply hooking up."

As if on cue, we both look across the stage at Jonah, who's strapping his guitar on for the rehearsal. As he's adjusting the fit, he glances over at me and smiles.

"I told you," she says, elbowing me. "He doesn't smile at anyone else like that. He's smitten with you."

Jonah looks at Ruben across the room and taps his mic. "Testing, one, two, three, testing."

There's a loud screech of feedback and everyone cringes.

"Sorry!" Ruben says, lifting an apologetic hand. "All right, try it again, Jonah."

Jonah does, and the sound is good this time.

"Okay, guys," Ruben says, waving at the stage. "Everything looks good here. You can start anytime."

The band starts off their rehearsal by playing their opening set to a rapt audience of a dozen bar employees and roadies in the audience. Throughout the first song, Ruben continues to adjust the stage lighting and the sound. The acoustics in the building sound great to me.

Shane rejoins us. "There's a line forming outside. Jake will start letting them in at six." He puts his arm around Beth's shoulders and pulls her close. "I've reserved a table for us in the front row," he says. "Why don't you join us, Lia?"

The band finishes their first set without mishap. The first set includes a lot of their previous and current hits. There's some discussion amongst the band about changing the order of a couple of songs, but nothing major. After a quick break, they play the second set, which features several of the songs from their new album. When the second set is done, one of the roadies runs off to notify Makayla that she's needed on the stage. I swear, it takes her twenty minutes to get her skinny ass out here, and I know she's just trying to be difficult.

Makayla comes out on the stage in a pair of skinny jeans, a red sequined halter top that shows more than it covers, and four-inch red fuck-me heels. Her hair is pulled up in a complicated do, with long curling tendrils hanging down to frame her oval face. I'll admit she looks gorgeous. Too bad her personality doesn't match her looks.

Dylan and the guys are only too happy to clear off the stage to take a break, and Jonah and Makayla perform their duet alone on stage. It's an acoustic number, with Jonah on guitar and Makayla prancing around him on stage. It's a hot, sexy number about a volatile couple – a guy and girl who fight and then make up, only to fight again and keep repeating the cycle. The irony isn't lost on me – it pretty much describes their former relationship. They sound perfect together, though, their voices blending beautifully. It's no wonder Dwight wants them together. They're an amazing music industry power couple.

At the end of their duet, when the lyrics are poignant and the melody haunting, Makayla presses up against Jonah's back, and when the song is over, she comes around in front of him to surprise him with a kiss. He steps away from her, but she's got her arms wrapped around him, and his hands are full of guitar, so he has difficulty separating from her.

I can't stand watching her fawn over him like this. There's plenty of security in the place, and I'm not particularly needed here at the moment. So I head back stage to make my escape – at least long enough to get my head on straight.

"Lia, wait!"

I hear him calling me, but I just want to be alone so I keep going, past the make-shift dressing room for the band. I pass Makayla's dressing room and the kitchen, which is bustling with employees gearing up for the night's event.

At the end of the hall is a metal door, and I punch through it and step out into the alley. The door closes behind me with a loud clang that reverberates down the alley that runs between two large brick buildings. Apparently, the door is an exit only, as there is no handle from the outside, no way to open it. Great!

I needed some fresh air – although the freshness of this alley is debatable as there are several ripe garbage dumpsters back here. I never wanted this. I never wanted to get so close to someone that I could feel pain like this. I'm jealous of a bimbo, and I hate it!

The door opens, and Beth pops her head outside. "Are you okay?"

I'm pacing like a caged tiger. "Do I look okay?"

She steps outside and releases the door, and it starts to swing shut.

"Don't let the door shut!" I warn her. "Or you can't get back in."

Just before the door closes, Shane pushes it open and steps outside, propping the door open with his foot. "Come back inside, sweetheart," he says to Beth. "It's cold out here, and you aren't wearing a jacket."

Beth looks torn. "But Lia – "

Jonah steps through the door, brushing past Shane, his eyes on me. Beth glances between the two of us, then reluctantly follows Shane back inside the building.

Jonah uses a discarded brick to prop the door open. Then he crosses his arms over his chest and stares at me for several long brooding moments, saying nothing. Damn, no man has a right to look so good. No wonder Makayla can't let him go.

I can tell he's mad at me, and I find that aggravating. "What?" I snap, hating how defensive I sound.

"Why did you walk out like that? She's doing it on purpose, you know. She's trying to get a rise out of you. Why do you let her?"

"She drives me crazy! And I can't stand to see her fawning all over you."

He shakes his head in dismay, and I see the beginnings of a smile. "Are you jealous? Seriously?"

"No. Of course not."

"Sure looks like it to me."

I know he's right, and I hate it. I don't want to care for him. I don't want to care for anyone! If I don't care, then it can't hurt me.

"I told Makayla to return to LA in the morning. She keeps crossing the line. You know I don't want anything more to do with her, so don't act like an idiot."

"Did you just call me an idiot?"

He grins. Of course he did. The bastard knows just how to get to me.

"Well, you're certainly acting like one." He steps forward and pulls me into his arms. I resist at first, but he tightens his hold. "Stop squirming and let me hold you."

I fight it for a moment, but his chest feels too good to ignore... solid and warm. The slightly musky scent of his perspiration makes me want to melt into him.

"See, that's not so hard, is it?" He presses his face to my hair. "You don't always have to be the strong one, you know. I can take care of you, too, if you'd let me."

"I don't need someone to take care of me." But the truth of my words is a bit undermined by the fact that my face is muffled against his T-shirt.

He leans down, getting right in my face. "I know you don't. You're the strongest person I know. But you can humor me once in a while, can't you?"

I can't help smiling. "Maybe once in a while."

His mouth drops to mine. It's a soft, gentle kiss to start, as if he's testing the waters. But when I respond with a moan, he deepens the kiss and slips his tongue into my mouth. His tongue stroking mine sets off a chain reaction of pleasure rippling through my body, stealing its way down to my core. I melt into him, my hips pressed to his, and he groans into my mouth.

I have butterflies in my belly. "How much time do we have before the show starts?"

He chuckles. "What did you have in mind?"

Dylan pops his head through the open doorway. "Shane told me you guys were out here. Dwight wants to see you, Jonah. In the band lounge. He said right now."

❧ 38

Jonah takes my hand and drags me along with him down the hall to the make-shift green room.

"What does he want?" I ask Dylan.

"I dunno," he replies. "But hurry, dude. The show starts in twenty minutes."

We find Dwight seated alone on one of the sofas in the manager's office. Zeke and Travis are seated on the other sofa, kicking back and watching videos on their phones.

"There you are, Jonah," Dwight says when we enter. He frowns at me. "Lia, this is a private business meeting for the band. No guests are allowed."

Jonah tightens his grip on my hand. "She's not a guest. She stays."

Dwight scowls. "Fine. Then keep her quiet, or she leaves." With a pleased grin on his face, Dwight turns his open laptop to face us. There's a document open on the screen. "I received your new contract offer from the label today, and it's full of good news. I successfully negotiated a 20% raise for all of you."

Jonah stiffens beside me and squeezes my hand hard enough to cut off the blood flow. He glances guiltily at the guys. "Dwight, we discussed this. I told you I'm not sure – "

"Don't be ridiculous, Jonah," Dwight says. "I went to bat for you to get this increase."

The smug expression on Dwight's face drives me nuts. "And how much of a raise did you give yourself, Dwight?"

Dwight's face turns red as he bristles. "That's none of your business, Lia. What part of *keep quiet* did you not understand?"

I release Jonah's hand and step forward, getting right into Dwight's weaselly face. "What's the matter, Dwight? Did I hit a nerve? Why don't you tell the guys how much of a raise you got?"

Jonah's remarkably calm as he checks his watch. "This isn't the time or place to discuss this right now, Dwight. We're going on stage in eighteen minutes."

I know Jonah feels guilty about even considering not renewing, and I hate that Dwight is putting him on the spot like this, especially in front of the guys.

Dwight shuts his laptop and shoots to his feet. "You can't walk away from a contract like this, Jonah! You'll be blacklisted in the industry."

The guys all look at Jonah, obviously taken aback.

"You don't want to renew our contract?" Dylan says, looking at

Jonah as if he'd just killed his puppy.

Travis and Zeke both look nervous, but they don't say anything.

Jonah rubs the back of his neck. "Guys…"

"Of course he's renewing," Dwight says, daring Jonah to contradict him.

Don't count on it, I think, but I refrain from saying it out loud because I don't want to freak out the guys right before they're supposed to be on stage. Dwight's timing is rotten.

"Guys, you have nothing to worry about, I promise," Jonah says.

One of the stage hands pokes his head into the room. "Guys? It's time."

Jonah offers Dylan his hand and pulls him up from the sofa. "There's nothing to worry about, all right? Let's go."

* * *

Jonah and the guys are standing behind the curtains, just waiting for their cue to walk on stage. Every seat in the house is filled, and the audience is buzzing with anticipation. The media outlets Dwight invited are all in place, with a dozen video cameras set up on tripods stationed around the room to capture the performance from every possible angle, including a couple overhead. Ruben and Dwight are seated at the control console opposite the stage. The room is filled with energy and excitement.

"Where will you be during the show?" Jonah asks.

"I was thinking I'd watch from back stage, right here." I'm not a fan of crowds.

"Would you mind sitting out front? I asked Shane to save you a seat at their table. Would you sit with them?" He leans down to press a quick kiss to my lips. "Please?"

I really don't want to be out front, but Jonah rarely ever asks for anything. "All right, fine. Just don't expect me to throw my panties up on stage or anything stupid like that, cause I'm not that kind of girl."

He grins. "Got it. No panties."

* * *

Beth saved the seat beside hers for me, and I sit down just as the lights dim in a five-minute warning. I glance around the table and see a few familiar faces: Sam, Erin and Mack from the bookstore, and of course Beth and Shane. Cooper's hovering around our table, but with me there, all the seats are taken. I offer to give him mine, but he declines.

There's a mad last-minute rush as guests who were mingling at the bar take their seats. The audience goes quiet in anticipation. A single spotlight shines down on center stage at the microphone stand.

Phil Peters, the owner of Rowdy's and a friend of Shane's, steps up to the mic and greets the audience. "Ladies and gentlemen, I have the distinct privilege of hosting Locke tonight. You'd have to be living under a rock to not know who this band is. Their hits have been dominating the charts all year, and they've been nominated for Best New Artist of the year at the American Music Awards and at the

MTV Music Video Awards. Sit back and enjoy the show, folks. Let's give it up for Locke!"

More spotlights light up the stage, and the audience roars with applause. First Dylan walks out from behind the curtain and takes his seat behind the drums. Then, Travis and Zeke walk out together to take their places, one on either side of the center mic. They pick up their guitars and strap them on just as Jonah walks out on stage and the hoots and hollers escalate to a deafening level.

Jonah smiles as he waves at the audience. When the applause finally starts to die down, he speaks into his mic as he straps on his guitar. "Ladies and gentlemen, thank you for coming tonight. I'd like to thank Shane McIntyre of McIntyre Security and Beth Jamison of Clancy's Bookshop for making this event possible tonight. And I'd like to thank Phil Peters for hosting us here at Rowdy's. I hope you all enjoy the show."

The lights dim for just a moment, then come back up. The audience renew their applause as Jonah kicks off the opening number with a quiet, "One, two, three, four."

I have a perfect front row seat with an unobstructed view of the band. My eyes are glued to Jonah, and for a change I can sit back and simply enjoy watching him perform and not have to be on guard every second. The building is crawling with security tonight.

I've seen Locke's music videos on YouTube a thousand times, and I know how good they are. Jonah's an amazing song writer, and he has an amazing voice. All of the guys sing backup, and their voices blend effortlessly together. Jonah's voice stands out, of course, with its perfect, deep resonance.

They start off with their newest hit, and the audience applauds, hollering and whistling to show their support. Jonah scans the front row tables and zeroes in on ours. His gaze locks on me, and I give him a discrete wave. He nods at me without missing a note.

They sound fantastic. I love watching Jonah on stage... watching those arm muscles flex as he plays the guitar. My eyes are drawn to his tattoos, which are sexy as hell. His T-shirt hugs his chest, and his jeans – worn and ripped – hang on his lean hips. The guy is sex-on-a-stick. It's no wonder all those fan-girls go nuts over him.

When they finish the first song, the crowd jumps to their feet and applauds thunderously, including me. I can't resist getting swept up in the excitement. Beth and Erin stand, too, and they're just as excited as I am.

The band continues the first set, singing one hit after another with some new material mixed in. Throughout the show, food and drinks appear at our table, courtesy of Rowdy's owner. I can't take my eyes off Jonah, and I often find him looking at me. I'm glad I agreed to sit in the audience. I can get my fill of ogling him without drawing any unwanted attention.

As the second set nears its end, I start to get queasy, as I know his duet with Makayla is coming up soon. It's the last number of the night, and I'm so not looking forward to it.

Sure enough, as the final song of the set wraps up, the guys take their bows and applause, then Dylan, Travis and Zeke exit the stage. Makayla sweeps out onto the stage, wearing tight black leather pants, a black leather halter top, and huge glitzy diamond earrings.

Jonah leans into the mic. "Ladies and gentlemen, Makayla

Hendricks."

Makayla waves, and the audience roars with applause loud enough to shake the rafters. Makayla beams from ear to ear. She's obviously in her element, on stage in front of an adoring crowd, and she's clearly enjoying the attention. Jonah starts strumming his guitar, playing a plaintive, simple melody, and they begin to sing.

I really don't want to see this. I lean over to Beth. "I'm going to the bathroom. I'll be back."

She grabs my hand. "Don't you dare leave!" she hisses.

The power couple on stage have the rapt attention of the audience, and the room is hushed as they sing their romantic duet. I hear a ringing in my ears, and my vision narrows to the two people on stage. I know it's just a performance, and I know he doesn't want her anymore, but a knot forms in my stomach as I watch them gazing at each other as they sing. It's a duet, I tell myself. Of course they're singing to each other. Of course they're supposed to look at each other. But I struggle. I've never felt jealously before, and I have to admit I don't like it. It makes me feel out of control.

As the song comes to a close, they're standing face to face on stage, with a single spotlight shining down on them. The crowd hushes as Jonah and Makayla gaze at each other as they sing the final refrain in perfect harmony, their faces only inches apart. My throat closes up and I stop breathing. The audience falls silent.

As the song ends, Makayla leans toward him with a smile on her face, with the obvious intention of kissing him. But he deftly turns his face to the side, giving her his cheek instead.

Jonah turns to the audience. "Ladies and gentlemen, let's hear it for Makayla Hendricks!"

The crowd goes crazy, screaming with approval, and Makayla – looking flustered at Jonah's swift dismissal – takes a reluctant bow and heads off stage.

Jonah's the only one left on the stage, and he waits patiently while the thunderous applause for Makayla dies down. I'm expecting him to say good night to the crowd and take his exit, too. But he just stands there, patiently waiting for the crowd's attention.

The spotlight dims a little, leaving him in a soft pool of light surrounded by a sea of darkness. He adjusts his guitar strap over his shoulder and leans into the microphone, all the while looking right at me. My heart starts pounding.

"I want to thank you all for coming here tonight," Jonah says. "I love playing small venues like this, where I can actually look out beyond the stage and see real people in the audience, and not just an ocean of impersonal bodies and lighters."

There are some quiet chuckles from the audience.

"Tonight marks a big turning point in my career – in my life. I'm retiring from the band after tonight."

There are numerous gasps in the audience and a quiet murmur at his announcement. I'm shocked myself. I had no idea he'd made up his mind and was ready to announce his plans.

"From now on, I'll just be Jonah Locke, a guy who writes songs and performs to small crowds once in a while. But first, I have one more song I want to sing on this stage tonight. This is a song I've been working on the last couple of days, written for a special someone who's in the audience tonight."

Jonah signals Ruben, and a second spotlight shines down on me, and I hear the shuffling of bodies and chairs as scores of people turn to look at me. My face heats up at the unwanted attention, but I still can't take my eyes off Jonah.

"I dedicate this song to someone very special to me, Lia McIntyre. It's called *I'll Catch You*." As soon as he begins picking out the melody, I recognize it as the song he's been working on.

I'm falling for a girl
With sunshine hair
And eyes that tear me apart
Fierce and lovely
She steals my heart
But she's just playing a part

Let me be there for you
Through your highs and your lows
Let me be there for you
I'll catch you when you fall

I'm falling for a girl
Who thinks she's broken
Because deep inside
Fierce and lovely
Is where the old wounds hide
But she can't see what I see

Let me be there for you

Through your highs and your lows
Let me be there for you
I'll catch you when you fall

You're always so strong
Let me be strong for you
Let me shoulder the weight of the world for once
Let me be there for you
Through your highs and your lows
Let me be there for you
I'll catch you when you fall

Let go of the past
The future is ours
You don't have to be the strong one
We can be strong for each other
Let me be there for you
Through your highs and your lows
Let me be there for you
I'll catch you when you fall

As he sings these beautiful lyrics – to me – my skin tingles from head to toe, and my mind is reeling. My vision dims and he's all I see. It's as if the rest of the room has fallen away, leaving just the two of us. The lyrics of this beautiful song take on a new significance, and I can't believe he's baring his soul to me like this, in front of over two hundred captivated people. I don't deserve this. I don't deserve him.

When the song comes to a gentle end, the audience remains hushed, as though hypnotized. It's so quiet in the bar we could hear a pin drop. Jonah sets his guitar down, propping it against his stool, then hops off the stage and comes right for me, pulling me out of my chair and taking me in his arms and kissing me in front of a captive audience.

I'm half laughing, half crying at his grand gesture, and glorying in the feel of his strong arms wrapped around me. For a moment, I can forget everything. Forget who I am, who he is, and just revel in this moment. I lose myself in the feeling of him pressed up against me, towering over me, wrapping me in his strength. The vice on my heart contracts once more, squeezing it painfully.

The lights come up, and the audience shoots to their feet, applauding wildly. The rest of the band come out from behind the stage to join us, along with Dwight, who's actually smiling for a change. Jonah keeps one arm around me as his bandmates slap him on the back. He keeps me at his side as he accepts all the well wishes and compliments for a great show. Beth is beaming at me, with tears in her eyes, and she steps forward to give me a hug. Even Shane looks pleased.

I honestly don't think I've ever been this happy in my life. I feel like, for the first time in a very long time, everything is right in my world. I have my family near me as well as the only man I've ever trusted, and I realize then that it's okay for me to love him. It's okay to trust, it's okay to let go of the past.

I look up into Jonah's face, and he leans down to kiss me. I return his stupid smile, at a complete loss for words. Blinking back tears, I shake my head at him. "You're crazy, you know that?"

Something catches Jonah's attention, and he looks past me just as Makayla walks up, holding out her phone, which she shoves in Jonah's face.

Jonah grabs the phone before she can hit him in the face with it. "Watch!" she says.

Jonah pales as he looks at the video playing on her phone. It's way too loud in the place to hear the audio, but it only takes me two seconds to recognize the video. It's me, six years ago, naked in broad daylight, straddling Logan Wintermeyer's hips as he thrusts hard up into me. There's a frightened, pained expression on my face, and my wan cheeks are wet with tears. Like an outsider, I stare at that girl, so young and so naive – it's a moment frozen in time, captured for all eternity, and destined to haunt her for the rest of her life.

In that split second, the bottom falls out of my world. My stomach heaves violently, and I know I'm going to be sick. Hot bile rises into my mouth, burning my throat and warning me of what's about to come. My worst nightmare has come true – I never wanted Jonah to see that video. But it's too late; the damage is done, and it can't ever be undone.

As soon as he realizes what he's looking at, Jonah grabs the phone from Makayla and shuts down the video, then shoves the phone in his back pocket. Makayla makes a grab for it, but he shoves her back so hard she topples on her spiked heels and falls hard to the floor.

"I told you it was her!" Makayla screams as she scrabbles to her feet. "She made a sex tape, Jonah! Are you seriously going to tell me you're in love with a porn star?"

✌ 39

M y mind is playing tricks on me, as my hearing fades in and out. I feel like I'm stuck on one of those amusement park rides that spins a million miles an hour, centrifugal force plastering the poor defenseless riders against the cage wall of the ride. I'm pinned there, frozen in time, stuck as this debacle plays out in front of me.

A furious Shane gives an abrupt hand signal, and two security guards grab Makayla and haul her backstage, despite all of her kicking and screaming. But it's too late. The damage is done.

Beth looks absolutely gutted, and her blue-green eyes glitter with tears. She reaches for me, but I pull back, shaking my head. I turn and head for the hallway that leads out the rear door of the building.

"Lia, wait!" Jonah shouts.

I can hear Jonah's boots thundering on the hardwood floor as he chases after me. But the crowd is in his way, and I'm fast. He can't catch me if I don't want him to, and I don't. I need to be alone. I can't be around anyone right now.

I bust out the rear door to the back alley just in time to empty my stomach on the pavement. I continue around the building to the parking lot where my Jeep is parked, and I'm pulling out of the parking lot just as Jonah comes into view.

I'm so blinded by tears, I can barely see to drive. Fresh ones appear just as soon as I brush the old ones away. My heart is thundering in my chest and there's a roaring in my ears. My phone rings nonstop, but I turn it off and shove it into my pocket.

By some miracle, I make it through the crowded Chicago streets and arrive back at my apartment building. I don't even remember parking, and before I know it, I'm riding up in the elevator to my apartment on the 46th floor. Once inside the relative safety of my apartment, I grab a brand new bottle of whisky out of a kitchen cupboard and collapse with it onto the sofa, sitting in the dark with only the moonlight coming through the glass balcony door for company.

Tears scald my cheeks as I sob like I haven't sobbed in years. It all comes back to me, like it just happened yesterday. I can't bare knowing that Jonah saw the video, even just a few seconds of it. The pain, the humiliation, the utter betrayal is burned into my brain. Millions of people saw that video when it first came out, and somehow Makayla got a copy of it. And God knows what she's done with it. I wouldn't be surprised if she's already posted it online. I don't know how she got it, but it doesn't really matter at this point. The damage is done.

I open the bottle of whisky and swallow a mouthful, choking on the fiery liquid as it burns a path down my throat. But I welcome the pain. I take another swig and another, bringing on a coughing fit. My stomach feels like it's on fire. I want to drink myself into oblivion so I can't feel another thing as long as I live.

Somewhere off in the distance, there's a steady pounding as heavy fists beat against a door. I wonder why someone doesn't answer it. The pounding is quickly followed by shouts and pleas, but still no one answers.

I swallow as much whisky as I can and let the poison burn a path to my belly. As my vision dims around the edges, I hear a crash and the sound of splintering wood. And then I hear nothing.

ꙮ 40

I'm floating in a fuzzy sea of darkness and pain, trying to block out all the voices and people around me. I recognize Beth's voice – the only feminine one of the bunch. The rest are Shane, Cooper, and ... and the one I can't face. *Jonah.* One of them pries the bottle of whisky out of my hand. One of them brushes the hair back from my hot, wet face.

Why won't they leave me alone? Why won't they let me drink myself to oblivion?

"Is she all right?" That's obviously *Beth*. "How much did she drink?"

"It looks like it's a new bottle, so she couldn't have drunk that much." *Shane.* "I think she just passed out. She'll be okay."

"Let's let her sleep it off." *Cooper.* "Poor kid."

"I'm carrying her to bed." *Jonah.*

Strong arms lift me off the sofa and carry me through the apartment, down the hallway toward my bedroom. I know from the scent alone that it's Jonah, but I don't open my eyes because I'm a fucking coward. He lowers me gently onto my bed, and my stomach churns violently. I roll over and vomit into the plastic trashcan beside my bed, wasting a lot of quality whisky.

The mattress dips as Jonah sits beside me and holds back my hair. "Are you okay?" he says, feeling my forehead.

I close my eyes and roll onto my back, groaning. I can't bring myself to look at him.

"I'll empty the trashcan," he says. He's back in a few moments, placing the rinsed out trashcan beside my bed, just in case, I'm sure. He presses a damp washcloth to my face and hands me a glass of water. "Here, rinse."

I rinse my mouth and spit into the trashcan. "Thanks," I mutter begrudgingly. Then I fall back onto the bed.

"Helluva night, huh?" he says, stroking my hair. When I don't answer, he continues. "So, did you like my song? In case it wasn't obvious enough, that was me declaring myself to you in front of the whole world. And I mean that literally because, trust me, the music video will be up on YouTube before morning."

My heart is pounding. I can't believe he's acting so damn casual, like nothing's wrong! He saw the video... well, he saw a few seconds of the video. It's one thing to know it exists, but it's something entirely different to actually see it. He saw me, naked, exposed, humiliated.

"You don't have to talk if you don't want to," he says, still playing with my hair. "It was quite a shock. I get that. Shane said he'll find out how Makayla got a copy of the video. He's pretty sure it came from Wintermeyer, and if he's right, then Wintermeyer violated a court order, and we might be able to press charges."

We? I can't stand his nonchalance, his easy acceptance. I open my eyes and glare at him. "What the fuck are you doing here?"

He looks affronted. "Where else would I be?"

"I don't know – maybe out signing autographs? I saw the fan-girls lined up and down the street outside Rowdy's tonight."

"You know I don't care about that." He frowns. "Who the hell are you, and what did you do with my Lia? Where's the kick-ass ninja I know and love?"

Love? He doesn't mean it. He can't, not after seeing that video.

He brushes his thumb over my cheek. "You never did say if you liked my song."

I look at him, trying to decide if he's crazy or just playing me. He must be crazy, because I honestly don't think he's playing me. He's too honest. I shrug. "It was fine."

He looks crestfallen. "It was *fine?* That's it? I'll have you know, I wrote that song in about two days, which is a record for me. I thought it turned out pretty well."

I elbow him. "Oh, shut up. Stop fishing for compliments. You know it was amazing."

He grins, but then he sobers. "Lia, honey, that video doesn't matter. It doesn't define you. All I saw was a young girl betrayed in a cruel, heartless way by an asshole. It's no reflection on you."

"It's a *sex tape!*"

He shakes his head. "No. It's a violation of your privacy, of your trust, but it isn't a sex tape. You need to let it go. No one can make you a victim without your consent, Lia. Please don't give it to them."

He has no idea how this has haunted me, eating away at me like a disease. It's impacted my life, my relationships, everything! How can he dismiss it so easily?

He reaches for my hand. "Do you know what went through my head when I saw the video?"

"What?"

"I thought, Damn, that girl is fierce."

I shake my head. "You just saw about two seconds of it."

"Baby, you've got to put that behind you and move on. You can't change the past, it's water under the bridge, but you're damn sure in control of your future. You taught me that."

I hear my apartment door close and realize the others left once they realized Jonah and I were talking, and I wasn't in danger of jumping out a window.

I reach for Jonah's hand. "Thank you."

He squeezes my hand. "For what?"

"For trying to make it all right."

"But it is all right. That tape isn't about you, Lia. It's about Logan Wintermeyer and what an ass he is."

Jonah pulls off his boots and climbs in bed with me, pulling me into his arms. I lay my head on his chest, my ear right over the steady beating of his heart.

He strokes my hair with gentle fingers. "We're not all asses, you know. Let me prove it to you." And then he starts singing the chorus of his new song again.

Let me be there for you
Through your highs and your lows
Let me be there for you
I'll catch you when you fall

His voice seeps into me, sinking deep beneath my skin and into my heart.

* * *

I must have fallen asleep to the sound of Jonah singing to me. When I awake, it's still dark outside my bedroom window. According to the digital clock on my nightstand, it's two-thirty in the morning. I'm lying in Jonah's arms, and he's propped up against my pillows, asleep. This is the earliest I've seen him fall asleep. He must have been as wiped out as I was.

We're both still dressed, and I'm uncomfortable. I've still got my gun holster strapped to my ankle, and I really need to put my gun away before I shoot myself with it. I extricate myself carefully from Jonah's arms and strip out of my clothes and stow my gun and holster. Then, after a quick trip to the bathroom, including a much needed teeth brushing, I crawl back into bed and coax Jonah into a more comfortable position.

"What time is it?" he says, squinting as he looks at my alarm clock.

"It's late. Or early. Depends on how you look at it."

He puts his hands on me, finding nothing but bare skin. "Good idea." He raises his hips and shoves his jeans and boxers off and tosses them to the floor. Then he sits up and pulls off his T-shirt and discards it. When he lies back down, I'm treated to the sight of his bare chest and those beautifully muscled and inked arms. His body is a work of art, and just looking at it makes me want him.

I keep rehashing what Jonah said earlier, about me not being a victim. The last thing I want to be is a victim, but that's exactly what I've been for the past six years. I did let that asshole Wintermeyer get the best of me, and that really pisses me off.

Making a monumental decision, I throw one leg over Jonah's hips and rise up to straddle him. I'm sure he can feel how badly I'm shaking.

At first he looks surprised, but then realization dawns. "Lia. You don't have to do this. You have nothing to prove."

I shake my head in disagreement. "You were right. I have to put it behind me. I'm done hiding." I reach over and turn on my bedside lamp, which bathes us both in soft, muted light. Then I grab a condom packet from the top drawer of my nightstand and toss it onto the bed beside Jonah.

His hands come up to cup my waist as he gazes with hot eyes at my breasts. "Are you trying to kill me?" he groans, reaching up to brush my nipples with his thumbs.

I laugh, my voice as tremulous as my limbs. "Maybe just a little."

I lean down and kiss his throat just below the edge of his soft beard. I can feel his pulse thundering beneath his skin. My lips drift down his throat and along his collar bone to his shoulder. "You were magnificent tonight, by the way," I tell him.

"Mmmhm," he mumbles, as my lips follow the curve of his bicep.

I can feel his erection lengthening between my legs. "No, really, you were." I bend down and flick his left nipple with the tip of my tongue, and he shudders. "I loved watching you sing." My tongue swirls around his nipple, and he bucks his hips up into me. "I loved watching you play the guitar." I move to his other nipple and show it some love too. "Watching your muscles flex as you play the guitar makes me hot."

When I suck his flat little nipple into my mouth, he cries out, "Lia!"

ᐧᑐ 41

I t's daylight outside my bedroom window when I awake with an ice cold lump of dread in my chest. I turn to Jonah, but the other side of my bed is empty. The sheets are cold, as is his pillow. For a moment, my heart stops beating. *He's gone.*

I sit up despite my pounding headache. "Jonah?" But there's no reply. I try again, my voice little more than a dry croak. "Jonah!"

He doesn't answer.

I frown. He's never up this early. My stomach turns over, and I know something's wrong.

Despite the dizziness dogging me, I crawl out of bed and check the bathroom. "Jonah?"

It's empty.

I head down the hallway to the living room and kitchen. Again, nothing.

"Jonah!"

It's not a big apartment. He would have heard me if he were here, and that means he's not.

There's a sick knot in my stomach, and it has nothing to do with my stupid hangover. *He's gone.* I shake my head in disbelief, because I can't imagine why he'd leave without telling me. That's just not like him.

Back in the bedroom, I grab my cargo pants off the floor and fish my phone out of the pocket. My hands are shaking as I bring him up in my contacts list and search for his location. The app begins a trace on his location, and a map of a downtown Chicago city block appears on the screen. I know that block well. I recognize the address where the little icon is pointing.

"Oh, fuck no!" I growl, frantically dragging on my clothes. "Oh, no no no!"

Grabbing my holster and gun, I race down to the parking garage and head to the law offices of Wintermeyer, Dawson, and Holmes, Attorneys at Law, where Logan works as an intern. "Shit!"

* * *

On my way to Logan's office, I speed dial Shane. "What's that idiot up to?"

Shane chuckles. "Good morning, sleepy head. Nice of you to join the land of the living. How's your head?"

"Never mind that. What the fuck is Jonah doing?" I remember Jonah telling me last night that Shane said he'd find out where Makayla got the video. Well, apparently he did find out, and he must have shared the information with Jonah.

"At the moment, he's about to depart Wintermeyer's office, on his way to the Cook County Jail. Jonah's been arrested for assault and battery for beating the ever-living shit out of Logan Wintermeyer."

"Oh, fuck."

"That's putting it mildly," Shane says. "Relax. I've already called Troy. We'll have him out on bail in no time."

"How did you know Jonah was there in the first place? I just woke up and found him gone without a clue."

"He called me early this morning to find out who gave Makayla the video."

"Let me guess – she got it from Logan."

"Yes. Logan sold her a copy of the video for fifty thousand dollars."

"And you told Jonah?" I'm incredulous. "Why did you tell him? He went off half-cocked and got himself arrested! He could have gotten hurt."

Shane sighs over the phone. "He had a right to know, Lia. He cares about you. And as for getting hurt, the jury's still out on that. He did bust his hand up pretty badly, though."

"How do you know?"

"Because I was there too, just to make sure things didn't get too far out of hand."

"And now he's on his way to jail. Gee, thanks, Shane."

* * *

As I walk into the Cook County police headquarters, Shane intercepts me in the hallway. He's in full CEO mode, dressed in a suit and tie.

"Relax," he says, laying his hand on my shoulder. He keeps pace with me as I head to the front desk. "Troy's in with him now, arranging for bail. Since Jonah has no prior arrests, the judge approved bail. They're letting him go on his own recognizance on the condition that he doesn't leave the city limits before the arraignment."

I barge up to the front desk. "Jonah Locke! Where the hell is he?"

The balding, paunch-bellied officer standing behind the desk smirks at me and points his fat finger at a row of metal folding chairs placed along one wall. "Cool your jets, and have a seat, sweetheart."

I step back, shaking my head. There's no way I'm sitting down. I'm far too agitated. I look at Shane. "Assault and battery? What the hell happened?"

"He walked into the lobby of Logan's dad's law office building and demanded to speak to Logan. When Logan came down to the lobby, Jonah hauled off and punched him in the face, knocking out Logan's two front teeth. Then Logan rushed him, and the two of them battled it out on the lobby floor."

"How bad is he hurt?" I'm almost afraid to hear the answer.

"He's a little worse for wear, but he'll survive. His hand might be broken."

I pace the hallway for what seems like an eternity, alternately wanting to strangle Shane for telling Jonah who gave Makayla the video, and Jonah for going after Logan in the first place. He's not really the vigilante type.

"Lia, sit down," Shane says, watching me. "Before you fall down. You look like shit."

I wipe my hand across my face. I barely had time to throw on some wrinkled clothes and brush my teeth. I know I look a mess, but I really don't care. I just want to see Jonah with my own eyes and make sure he's okay before I rip him a new one. "I take my eyes off Jonah for one minute, and he gets himself arrested!"

We must have been waiting at least an hour before Shane says, "Here they come."

I glance down the hallway and see Jonah walking toward us, escorted by Shane's attorney, Troy Spencer, who looks like he just rolled out of bed. Usually dressed impeccably in a suit and tie, Troy looks out of character in faded sweats, a hoodie, and a ratty old pair of sneakers.

"You couldn't dress for the part?" Shane says to his friend and lawyer, eyeing Troy's attire critically.

Troy scowls at him. "You got me out of bed early on a Saturday morning. You're lucky you got anything."

On my way here, I couldn't decide whether to kiss Jonah for his misguided heroics or kick his ass for being stupid. But now that I've gotten my first good look at him, all thoughts of ass kicking go by the wayside. He looks terrible! His hair is a tangled mess, half up in a ponytail and half down. There's dried blood on his bottom lip and chin, but the worst of it is, he's cradling his right hand which is covered in dried blood. Based on how carefully he's holding it, I figure it must be broken. The idiot doesn't even know how to throw a proper punch.

Jonah walks right up to me and wraps his good arm around me, pulling me close. He presses a kiss to my forehead, then lays his forehead against mine. He's shaking, and his bloodied hand is cradled protectively between us. He's definitely an artist, not a fighter.

"What the hell did you think you were doing?" I whisper.

He grunts with pain and steps back a bit, adjusting his hold on his hand. "Wintermeyer sold the video to Makayla."

"Yeah, I heard." I gently examine his injured hand, and he flinches. Two fingers are bent at an odd angle, clearly broken, and his knuckles are split open. "Your poor hand. We need to get you to the ER."

He nods. "I can't move these two fingers, and my hand hurts like a bitch."

I have to shake my head. "What were you thinking, Jonah? Logan could have really hurt you, and you're facing pretty serious charges."

"You should see the other guy," Jonah says, chuckling.

"So what's the word?" Shane asks Troy.

"Believe it or not, Wintermeyer dropped all charges," Troy says, sounding surprised. "He said it was just a *misunderstanding*. Jonah's free to go."

Surprised by this news, I glance sharply at Shane.

Shane gives me an enigmatic smile. "How fortunate."

"And I'm sure you had nothing to do with him dropping the charges," I say. I know my big brother. He takes care of his own, and I guess that includes Jonah now.

"It was easy," Shane says. "Logan's in contempt of a court order by selling a copy of the video to Makayla. He'll face some pretty serious charges of his own if he pursues charges against Jonah. I had no trouble persuading his father that they don't want to go down that path."

I happen to glance down the hallway just as Logan and his dad step out of a room, accompanied by a uniformed officer, and turn in our direction. I didn't know Logan was brought in too.

I shoot an inquiring look at Shane, and he smiles. "Logan was arrested for disorderly conduct and assault as well."

My heart is pounding in my chest as I look at Logan. He and his dad are both tall men, and Logan bears a strong resemblance to his father. They both have thick brown hair and brown eyes, tall imposing builds. I think his father played football in high school too. Still, it's easy to tell them apart, even from a distance, and not just because of his father's graying hair. Logan is the one with an eye swollen shut, bruises and lacerations on his face, and a split lip. It looks like Jonah held his own.

"Way to go, Jonah," I murmur.

Jonah turns to look behind him, snorting with derision as he sees Logan.

I realize this is the first time in years that I've seen Logan up close – the first time I've gotten a really good look at him since the trial back in high school. He's twenty-four now, an adult, but he doesn't look much different than he did in high school. He's filled out some, and he's a little heavier, and maybe not quite as muscular as he was when he was the football team's darling quarterback.

I stare Logan down as he approaches, and Jonah stiffens. When Logan's just an arm's length away, Jonah steps in front of him, blocking his path. The two men are eye-to-eye, of the same height. Jonah glares at Logan, his expression tense, his jaws clenched tightly. Jonah looks ready to throw down again, right here in the police station.

I grab Jonah's sleeve and pull him back. "Back off, tiger. You're in a police station. Not the right time or place."

"Hello, Lia," Logan says, looking at me. He looks surprised to see me, curious even. "It's... good to see you. You look great."

It's the first time I've heard his voice in nearly six years, and I find it rather anti-climactic. He's a little bloodied and battered, his white shirt soiled with blood and torn at the collar. This is the guy who ruined my life – or at least I thought he did. Now I'm not so sure. Seeing him in the flesh right now... I feel nothing. No anger, no sorrow, nothing.

"Excuse us," his father says gruffly, grabbing Logan's arm and marching him past us as they head to the lobby exit.

I can't help laughing. Logan was hauled off by his daddy, like a child being reprimanded for fighting in school. He's just a guy, just like any other – except this one happens to be an asshole. I shake my head.

Jonah looks at me. "Are you okay?"

"Yeah, I'm fine." And it's true. I thought if I ever saw him again, I'd be devastated, but I'm not. I take hold of Jonah's good hand. "Come on, tiger. Let's get you to the emergency room."

"Can we stop somewhere for breakfast first?" he says. "I'm starving."

42

I
t's mid-afternoon when we get back to my apartment after a trip
to the ER. His ring and middle fingers, both broken, were set, and
he's got a lovely blue fiberglass cast half-way up his forearm. He's
feeling pretty good now courtesy of some strong pain medication.
I lead him to the sofa and tuck him in beneath a fleece blanket. It's
been a long day, and he's exhausted.

"Do you need anything?" I ask him. "Something to drink? A potty
break?"

He shakes his head, chuckling. Then he grabs my hand and pulls
me down on the sofa beside him. "I just need you and a nap. Lie
down with me."

We rearrange ourselves comfortably on the sofa. He's lying behind me, spooning, with his good arm around my waist. He kisses

the back of my head, and I shiver.

He yawns. "I'm so tired, I could sleep for days."

But our brief respite is interrupted by the buzz of my apartment intercom, indicating a call from the front lobby.

"Are you expecting someone?" he says.

"Nope." All my friends and family already have access to this building. I have to extricate myself from his grasp to go answer the intercom. "Who is it?"

"Ms. McIntyre, there's a Dwight Peterson here in the lobby, asking to come up."

I don't know whom I was expecting, but it certainly wasn't him. "Well, fuck." I look at Jonah, and he sits up and shrugs.

"I guess you'd better send him up," I say.

When the knock comes, I'm tempted to ignore it. But this is something Jonah needs to deal with, so I reluctantly open the door.

Dwight pushes his way in, glaring at me. "Where the hell is he?"

Rolling my eyes, I point toward the sofa. I'm about at the end of my rope with this guy. I've tried to restrain myself around Dwight – as Shane asked me to – but it's getting difficult, especially since Jonah wants to make a clean break from him.

Dwight stalks over to Jonah, sees the cast and frowns. "What the hell did you do to your hand?"

"I broke two fingers," Jonah says, lifting the cast.

"Yeah, I can see that, wise-guy." Dwight crosses his arms. "How?"

I can't help the grin on my face. "He broke it on Logan Winter-meyer's face."

"Who the hell is that?" Dwight's eyes narrow as he puts two and two together. "Does this have anything to do with that sex tape?"

Jonah's jaw tightens. "It's not a sex tape, Dwight."

Dwight's face turns beet red as he points a finger at Jonah. "It's none of your damn business what Lia does. She can make a thousand sex tapes for all I care. You stay out of it."

Before I can even respond, Jonah's on his feet and in Dwight's face. He grabs hold of Dwight's pin-striped dress shirt and pulls him up close. "I swear to God, Dwight, if you say *sex tape* one more time, I'll gladly break my other hand on *your* face."

Dwight blanches as Jonah releases him with a small shove, sending him off balance. "Jonah, you have no idea the damage you're doing to your brand – "

"Fuck my brand!" Jonah yells. "If Wintermeyer does anything else to hurt Lia, he'll have to deal with me all over again."

Dwight's eyes widen. I don't think he's ever seen this aggressive side of Jonah. Frankly, I find it pretty hot. I should try to get him riled up more often.

"All right, look," Dwight says, raising his hands in an attempt to mollify Jonah. "I'll talk to the label execs. I'll tell them – "

"Dwight, I already told you – I don't care what the label thinks. I'm not renewing my contract."

Dwight pales. "Jonah, you can't be serious."

"I am dead serious. I told you, I'm done! I'm done with the record label, with LA, with all of it. I'm going it alone."

"You realize you're throwing away millions of dollars, right? You're just going to walk away from it? Walk away from the dream?"

Jonah nods. "That's the plan."

Dwight sneers at him. "You're just as insane as she is."

Of course, he's pointing at me. *Asswipe.*

"Leave Lia out of this, Dwight. This is between you and me."

"Of course she's behind this!" Dwight says. "From the very begin-ning, she put these thoughts into your head."

"You need to leave," Jonah says to Dwight, pointing at the door. "Now."

Dwight huffs and puffs out his frustration, then heads to the door. He jerks it open, then faces Jonah for one final volley. "Fine! Throw away a once-in-a-lifetime career. You'll come crawling back to me on your knees within a year – I guarantee it!"

Dwight slams the door on his way out. Jonah stares at the closed door, his chest heaving.

"Be right back," I say, and I follow Dwight out into the hallway, closing the door behind me. "Hey, Peterson!"

He stops and turns back to me, scowling with contempt. "What do you want?"

"Just this." I grab him by the shirt front and slam him into the wall. My hand slides to his throat and I tighten my grip, not hard enough to completely block his airway, but enough to get his undi-vided attention. "Look, asshole, I've put up with your shit because my brother asked me to play nicely. But if you give Jonah any more grief, I will put you on the floor. Do I make myself clear?"

Dwight nods vigorously. His eyes are wide as saucers, and it takes all my restraint not to laugh in his face.

I release him, then turn and walk away, not bothering to look back. When I return to the apartment, I find Jonah right where I left him.

"What'd you do?" he says, looking only slightly worried.

"Nothing. Just took care of some business, that's all."

He looks skeptical, but he doesn't press me for more information. Instead, he pulls me into his arms and kisses the top of my head. "I think we'd better go clear our stuff out of the rental house before Dwight does something stupid with it," he says.

* * *

"Once I clear my stuff out of the rental house, I won't have anywhere to go," Jonah says. He looks at me hesitantly. "Can I stay with you, at least for tonight? Or longer? Until I find another place?"

As we drive to the rental house, my stomach drops. There are big changes coming, and I don't know what they are exactly. I realize we're *together*, but we've never really talked about it. We haven't defined the nature of our relationship. Are we having a fling? Is he interested in something more serious, something long term? Is he going back to LA? I have no idea what's going on, and I have no experience to go by. I've never done anything more than a one-night stand since high school.

I don't want him to leave, and I can't imagine not seeing him every day. How in the hell did he become so important to me in such a short time?

"You're welcome to stay with me," I say. "As long as you want." I swallow hard. "Are you going back to LA?"

"No, I'm not going back. I like Chicago. Everything I want is right here."

Everything he wants? What the hell does that mean? I shoot him a look as my pulse speeds up.

He's watching me closely. "I'd love to stay with you," he says. "As long as you're okay with it. I can continue working in the rented studio. I guess since I'm staying, I'll have to un-fire you. Looks like you're stuck with me."

My pulse is racing, but I keep my eyes on the road.

It takes us nearly an hour to get all of our stuff out of the rental house and into my Jeep. Jonah says goodbye to the guys, promising to transfer money into each of their bank accounts to tide them over until they find new work. He also promises to make some calls for them to see if he can find jobs for them. They're all young and very talented, and he's sure they'll all find something soon. Jonah makes the same offer to Ruben and Esperanza.

* * *

That night, after taking a joint shower, we order in Chinese food and crash on the sofa to watch *Deadpool*, my all-time favorite movie. Jonah has never seen it, and I have fun watching him choke on his beer every time Ryan Reynolds says something outrageous, which is pretty much all the time. After the credits end, Jonah turns off the television.

My stomach drops when he turns to me, suddenly all seriousness.

"What?" I know I sound defensive, but I can't help it. He's making me nervous.

"We need to talk, Lia."

"No, we don't."

I get up and start collecting our empty food cartons, anything to avoid whatever it is that's about to come out of his mouth, but he grabs my wrist and pulls me back down beside him.

"That can wait," he says. "Right now, we need to talk. About us."

"What about us?" I'm so nervous, I'm going to be sick. "There's nothing to talk about, Jonah."

Jonah smiles at me as he laces the fingers of his good hand with mine. "We need to discuss the future, my prickly one."

I pull my hand back. "I'm not prickly!"

He valiantly tries to suppress a smile. "Look, I know everything's happened very quickly, and we haven't known each other that long, but the truth is I'm crazy about you. From the moment I first saw you, back in Shane's office, you're all I've been able to think about."

I frown.

"And the longer I've known you, the stronger I feel. You are fierce and beautiful and so strong. I mean it when I say I'm in awe of you." He brings the back of my hand to his mouth for a kiss. "I want you in my life, Lia, and I think you might possibly want me in yours, too."

The back of my hand tingles where he pressed his lips to it. "That's pretty presumptuous, don't you think?" I say, desperate for anything to slow this train down. I'm not ready for this. I'm not ready for a relationship.

He shakes his head. "No. I think it's a fact."

"And you know this, how?"

"When have you ever in your life given a guy more than ten minutes of your time? When have you ever spent an evening at home, eating take-out and watching a movie with a guy? When have you ever had a guy in your apartment?"

Never, never, and never. "So? That doesn't mean anything." *Yes, it does.*

He lays his palm over my heart, and I'm sure he can feel it thrashing around, like a wild animal trying to escape a trap. "I know you're scared, Lia. You've been in self-preservation mode for so long, it's hard for you to open up to someone. To take a chance, to risk getting hurt again. But I'm a good risk, Lia. I want you, in my life and in my bed. I want everything with you."

"What are you saying? You want us to *date?*"

He chuckles. "Try not to sound so horrified by the idea."

"I'm not."

"Yeah," he says, nodding. "I want us to date. Are you good with that?"

I know he's right about me being in self-preservation mode. I've spent the past six years shielding myself from pain, and that meant pushing guys away and sticking to my rules. I obliterated those rules to be with Jonah, and I've never done that before – not for anyone. I do know that I love having him here with me in my apartment. It feels good. It feels right. And I love sleeping with him – and I don't just mean the sex, although I have to admit that's phenomenal. No, I mean all the cuddling and the spooning too. I could get used to that. And he makes me laugh, which is a definite plus.

Jonah cups his hand behind my head and leans forward to kiss me. It's a soft, gentle, unhurried kiss, not sexual, but tender. *Oh, my*

God, he's stealing my heart. My lips tremble as I kiss him back.

He eventually pulls back to look me in the eyes. "So, how about it? Are you okay with us dating? Can we make it official? Boyfriend, girlfriend?"

Alarm bells start going off in my head, drowning out all rational thought. I think he can tell.

He smiles. "How about a trial run? Just until you get tired of me."

I'll never get tired of you. "You're crazy."

"Is that a *yes?*"

I shrug. "I guess so."

He chuckles. "Good enough. I'll take what I can get."

Two Weeks Later

After spending the morning at the recording studio so Jonah could start laying down some tracks on his new song, *I'll Catch You* – my song, as we've started calling it – we head downtown. The plan is to kidnap Beth and Sam and Erin for lunch. But first, I have some important business to take care of at McIntyre Security. Apparently, if you want something done right, you have to do it yourself. This is definitely one of those times.

Jonah and I are standing in front of Diane's desk, holding hands like a pair of goofballs. Diane's struggling to play it cool and not smile at us. Everyone else we crossed paths with in the building gawked at us – at Jonah, because he's so hot, and at me because they've never seen me with someone before.

"Hey, Diane," I say. "Is Shane available?"

"He's in his office," she says, picking up her phone. "Let me check." She punches in Shane's number. "Lia and Mr. Locke are here. Do you have time to see them?"

She hangs up her phone. "Go right on in, sweetie."

"Thanks."

Shane looks up from his computer monitor as we walk in. He eyes our clasped hands, but wisely says nothing. I'm still working on getting used to this myself.

"To what do I owe the pleasure?" he says, leaning back in his leather chair.

I let go of Jonah's hand, and he goes off to the credenza to pour us some coffee while I plop myself down on the corner of Shane's huge desk. "We need to talk," I say.

He lifts an eyebrow. "About?"

"Beth."

Suddenly I have his undivided attention. "What about Beth?"

"In case you haven't noticed, your girlfriend is heading straight for panic-ville."

He frowns, and his gaze flickers momentarily to Jonah.

"Oh, don't worry about Jonah," I say. "He knows everything."

Shane crosses his arms over his chest. "I've noticed she seems a little preoccupied lately. She's obviously worried about something, but when I try to get her to talk about it, she shrugs it off and says it's nothing."

"I know. That's why I'm here, to cut through all the drama and get you up to speed before the poor girl has a heart attack."

"What's wrong?" Shane's expression falls. "Is this about our engagement? Is she having second thoughts?"

"Don't be such a drama queen. It's nothing that serious."

"Then what is it?"

I lean toward my brother. "She's freaking out about the guest list."

He looks dumbfounded. "What? Why?"

I shrug. "Don't judge. The list is up to three hundred people now, with all your work associates and hers, all the family, and the friends. You have to admit we have a huge-ass extended family, Shane. Anyway, she's freaking out about standing up in front of over *three hundred people*. She wants to elope, but she's afraid to tell you. She has this crazy notion that having a big, fancy wedding is important to you, and she doesn't want to disappoint you."

Shane relaxes in his chair. "I don't care how we get married," he says. "We can get married on a street corner for all I care. I just want to be married to her."

"That's what I told her! Seriously! I said almost the exact same thing."

Jonah sits down in one of the chairs in front of Shane's desk. He'd carried over two paper coffee cups with little sleeve wraps and lids. It took him two trips since his hand is still in a cast. He hands me one of the cups. "Here you go. Black, no sugar, sugar."

"Ha, that's funny. Thank you," I say. Then I turn back to Shane. "So, elope."

Shane looks skeptical. "Are you sure she's not got *her* hopes set on a big wedding, with the gown and the bridal party, and all the decorations and hoopla? I thought that was something all females fantasize about."

I scowl at him. *As if!* "Yes, I'm sure. This is *Beth* we're talking about. Take her somewhere – anywhere, as long as it's quiet and private – and put a ring on her finger. You'll be doing her a favor, trust me."

Shane looks pensive as he processes the information. "You're sure about this?"

"Absolutely."

He nods. "All right. I'll do it."

I smile. "Excellent!" Then I hop down from his desk. "Good talk. Thanks for the coffee."

Jonah follows me out of Shane's office, and we shut the door behind us.

"Is everything okay, dear?" Diane asks.

"Yes. I just did your boss a huge favor."

She smiles, her soft blue eyes crinkling heavily at the corners. "Oh, well that's good," she says, even though she has no idea what I'm talking about.

Jonah and I head for the elevator and wait for an available car. Once we're inside – alone – Jonah backs me into a corner and leans in for a kiss.

"Careful, the coffee!" I gasp, as he bumps my cup. Thank goodness the cups have lids on them or we'd both be wearing their contents.

"Sorry." But that doesn't deter him. He leans in for another kiss, this one deeper and hungrier than the first. His lips feel heavenly against mine, warm and searching. I'm definitely getting used to this dating thing.

"I'm thinking of keeping you," I murmur against his lips.

He grins. "Really?"

"Yeah. You definitely have your uses."

"Just wait until I get my cast off. I'll be even more useful then. You should see what I can do with two hands."

"Don't push your luck, tiger."

The End...

Although it's just the beginning for Lia and Jonah

Thank you!

Dearest readers, I hope you enjoyed reading Lia's and Jonah's story as much I enjoyed writing it. I would be very grateful if you'd take a moment to leave a brief review on Amazon. You don't have to write anything long or involved. Just a sentence or two telling other readers what you thought about the book is all that's needed. I would be eternally grateful to you if you did. Thank you so much, from the bottom of my heart. :)

Stay Tuned for More!

Stay tuned for more books in the McIntyre Security, Inc. series! I have several exciting new books planned for 2017!

To keep up-to-date on upcoming releases, follow me on Facebook: authoraprilwilson

Or, subscribe to my newsletter for up-to-date information on the schedule for new releases: www.aprilwilsonwrites.com

.

Made in United States
Orlando, FL
17 March 2022

15897417R10221